Kay Kavanagh.
Sept. 98.

IRISH CHRISTMAS STORIES

IRISH CHRISTMAS STORIES

Edited by

David Marcus

BLOOMSBURY

First published 1995

Bloomsbury Publishing PLC, 2 Soho Square, London W1V 6HB

A CIP catalogue record for this book is available from the British Library

ISBN 0 7475 2302 9

10 9 8 7 6 5 4 3 2 1

Typeset by Hewer Text Composition Services, Edinburgh
Printed in Great Britain by Clays Ltd, St Ives Plc

Contents

CONTENTS

Introduction

The noted American essayist, E.B. White, wrote that 'To perceive Christmas through its wrapping becomes more difficult with each year.' Commercialisation has all but completely engulfed Christmas wherever the celebration has a place in the national calendar. It was a takeover imposed by the assiduous conversion into a salesfest of what started out as a religious observance, in which the sere and ochreously romantic overspill of autumn was driven from lantern-lit city streets while Santa and tinsel commandeered even October's shop windows. 'How many observe Christ's birthday! How few His precepts! O! 'tis easier to keep holidays than commandments,' Benjamin Franklin remarked two-and-a-half centuries ago, and with Christmas gradually homogenised into a brochured break it was inevitable that its religious significance would become cribbed, its spirituality dissipated. The more 'Peace on earth and goodwill towards all' is the vaunted message of the present Christmas, the less it tends to be part of the Christmas present.

Has all, or nearly all, been lost? How, nearing the end of the second millennium, may the ghostly shades of Christmas past as well as the fleshly shapes of Christmas today be perceived through its wrapping?

'Words alone are certain good,' W.B. Yeats declared in the first poem of his first collection. Despite the blandishments of screens large and small, the word still has both more redolence and more resonance than the image, and writers continue to be inspired by the unique spell of Christmas. Across their snow-bleached pages Santa's sleigh is forever drawn, stockings are filled and emptied, homecomings celebrated, Christmas spirit purveyed and poured, friends recalled. Recorded, too, are exilic angsts, financial strains, the rending of dreams and fantasies, the reluctant realisation that perhaps Santa does not really exist – for so many life's first great betrayal – and the withering of age-old Christmas responses under a technological tyranny that makes the real unreal and the unreal real. We cannot know what Christmas will be like in the coming century, but what it was and is like in the present century has been memorialised in these pages by Ireland's short-story writers.

It may be objected that this anthology is itself part of the Christmas wrapping deplored by E.B. White. But *this* wrapping does not obscure. It reveals, preserves, delights. It is the writers' gift, their Christmas present to all readers.

David Marcus

VINCENT BANVILLE

Christmas 1939

A place . . .

Merely a village, nailed to a crossroads. Twelve houses leaning on one another, for comfort, for companionship, for shelter. Officially there is no weather, for the presence of an unseen enemy has decreed that there be no weather forecasts. So we, the inhabitants of these twelve houses, resolutely set our faces against the wind that buffets us in this December month and, as it sings through the trees and moans round chimneypots, we sieve it into all the other sights and sounds of the dying year.

For this year is truly dying, not alone in our small village, but in all the villages, in all the countries, all over the world. Strains of great events have filtered through to us, although there is only one wireless set, a small voice amid crackles, quietly mentioning wars, and rumours of wars.

Taking our village from east to west, which is the manner in which travellers mainly approach it anyway, there is the two-storeyed, slate roofed house of the Pennys. He fought in the Great War and by all accounts was a fine figure of a man in his olive green uniform. She was Gertie Brooks from Temple East, a schoolteacher's daughter and a great beauty. Now they spend their time stamping about their draughty old house, eternally arguing.

Next there are the three cottages with the date 1882 cut into the stone above the door of each of them. In the first lives John Jackson, who was once a blacksmith. Sometimes, on nights when loneliness overcomes his faltering mind, he gets out his anvil and sends tattoos of shivering sound all the length and breadth of the place.

The remaining two cottages are inhabited by the Grosse family, or families, for no one, possibly themselves as well, is sure how many different permutations of relationship exist among them. One issue of one of the many entanglements is Miss Emily Grosse, a quiet, dark and shy girl, whose ripening presence sings in my blossoming, young man's consciousness during that month, and for many months afterwards.

After the cottages our commercial empire begins. There is Benson's Cycle Shop, Miss Mordaunt's Cake and Confectionery Shop, the Pierce's Hardware Emporium, and our own Grocery and Public House. My father, preferring to regard himself as a man of rectitude, albeit a capitalist one, wears a stiff wing collar and a hard hat. We live above the shop, in a rambling cornucopia of high-ceilinged rooms, my father, my mother and myself. There is no one else living there, although there is space enough for many. Most of my memories spring from these creaking, empty rooms, with their solid mahogany furniture, softly gleaming brass lamp fittings and yellowed lace antimacassars. I have bent and twisted those large areas of dusty space to my will, shaping castles and fortresses, jungles and flat, rolling prairies, ships in rolling seas, out of the familiar and the ordinary, until now, in my fourteenth year, a certain roughness has been diluted out of my imaginings, and a soft sigh of longing, for something indefinable, floats in my consciousness, cobweb-like.

Christmas 1939

My room, my things, myself . . .

But my childhood has been quite happy. For as long as I can remember I have had my own room. There is my high bed, my washstand with the sunken bowl, my desk with the pulldown top. My Hornby train set is laid out on the floor. I have my books, my stamp collection, my clothes. The room is me, and I am the room. Once, from a softly opened door, I saw my mother dreamily caress some of my things: a rumpled shirt, an open book, the pillow on my bed, and a well of feeling bled through my mind, shiveringly.

I am a solitary child – I have heard people proclaim it. My mother and father are counselled by my aunts to get me to go out more and mix with other children. But there are no other children, only the Grosses, and they are deemed to be unsuitable.

I go out and wander the hills, with Job, my dog, by my side. The air is thin and cold and there is snow on the mountains. Next year I will go away to school, and I am undecided whether I like the idea or not. Up to now I have gone to school in Temple East, where it nestles in the narrow neck of a valley across these hills that I am now tramping. The school is one large room with a wooden partition across the middle of it. There is a wood-burning stove which we have to take turns to keep lighting. The schoolmaster and his wife are not from these parts, and they have never settled into our part of the country. He is a tall man with an inbuilt stoop; she is small and plump and usually wears her hair coiled round and round her head, but when she releases it, it quivers down her back, a waterfall of blondeness.

I am at peace with myself, today. It is the week before Christmas and I fancy that I can already smell the odours of baking wafting up to me from Miss Mordaunt's shop. My mother is a very good cook, but she still buys all her cakes and puddings and mince pies from Miss Mordaunt. It is a question of free enterprise, I have often heard my father say: Miss Mordaunt buys the makings from him, he buys the completed articles from her. It is difficult for my mother, though, for she enjoys baking, and she often stands wistfully in our kitchen not seeming to know what to do with her hands.

I have reached the summit of the first hill, and I pause to look back. The land is not good land, and it has been chopped up into many small farms. The people scratch at the earth to sustain themselves and their families, and there is no rich person around for miles. No one goes hungry, however, and my father, although a self-professed hard-headed businessman, keeps accounts dating back many years in his well-thumbed ledgers.

As I look back down at our clump of houses, the light is beginning to fail. The wind is getting up once more, and it has in it the bite of coldness. Perhaps we will have snow for Christmas. Across to my left, silhouetted against the sullenness of the sky, I see a straggle of figures. Job sees them too and growls, deep in his throat. They are the Grosse children, probably on their way to bring in the holly.

I quieten Job and begin to move in a direction that will cut across their path. All of the boys are younger than me, but I still fear them. There is a sly knowingness about them that is disconcerting, as though they possess some information about everyone that would not be to their credit. But the image of their sister Emily haunts me in a way that I find intriguing and yet painful all at once.

In the shading darkness they file past me, but there is no sign of recognition from me to them, or from them to me. We are merely strangers on that windy hill, grey shapes moving across the dead land. And it is no different across the sea, where war is being waged so seriously, although, as Mr Penny has told me, in one of his moments of lucidity, in the Great War the soldiers fraternised with one another at Christmas, smiling and nodding, staring long stares out of sad, red-rimmed eyes, pulling their poor feet through frostbound slush: We, who are about to die, salute you!

But now, in the gathering darkness, with the wind blowing up all round me, I am alone with my unease. A short time before, I was happy. Or at least if I was not happy, I was content. There has been no transition period. Now I try to bring back that former feeling by thinking of my relations and friends, by thinking of my mother and father, by visualising them peering out into the gathering storm, full of fear on my behalf. The sky is very black. There are no stars. And the wind is very cold. I know that if I stay out here much longer I will freeze to death, and yet I am loth to go in. Perhaps, so young, I am, like the poet, half in love with easeful death.

The lights of our twelve houses slowly gleam into life, and they beckon me. They are the cornerstone of my existence. They are familiar to me. They will give me shelter and light and warmth. Gratefully I descend this wind-tossed hill, while across the world the people of Finland are being drowned in their own blood, and Captain Langsdorff of the *Graf Spee* is taking the Roman way out.

Our shop . . .

The shelves in our shop are always full, no matter how much is sold. In the dead of night my father fills those shelves, working away in the dimness of a shaded nightlight. He is not a tall man, but there is a solidity to him that can be intimidating. Sometimes he gets strange notions, about life, and business, and about how to bring up a growing son. I can never remember him being young. He came into my life wearing his wing collar and his hard hat. At first he had a moustache and beard, but when they began to turn grey he shaved them off.

At all times he endeavours to look fierce, but his eyes let him down. To me he is unfailingly kind, and it comes as a surprise to me to learn that there are people who are afraid of him.

In the week before Christmas the shelf filling goes on nightly. Without being asked, I stand beside him and hand him the various packets and tins. I am lost in the wonder of the names. The shelves groan beneath the weight of so many remedies, tonics, cure-alls and condition powders. There is Aspro which does not harm the heart; there are Bile Beans to improve the figure, the health and the vitality. I gaze at a tonic called Phosferine, a deodorant called Odo-Ro-No, an ointment called Zam Buk. Into my father's patient hands I place packets of Yeast Vite, tins of Beecham's Pills, bottles of Angier's Emulsion, and bars of Sunlight soap. Onto their allotted places go containers of Fry's Cocoa, Science Shoe Polish, Chef Sauce, Morgan's Pomade, Irel coffee essence, Bob Martin's condition powder, Brylcreem, Northlight Blades and Sloan's Liniment. Cartons of Sweet Afton and Kerry Blue cigarettes are balanced on top of one another, and I visualise all the coupons they contain falling into my hands for my own use.

When the shelves are full my father sits back on his heels and then stiffly gets to his feet. He does not thank me, but I know that he is pleased that I came to help him. He is a close man, close with his thoughts, close with his emotions. With his hard hat set squarely on his head, he looks a very serious person, and it is true that I have not often seen him smile. Whereas my mother is inclined to fuss, he never loses his composure. When Christmas Day comes he will sit at the head of our table, presiding over a raggle-taggle bunch of elderly aunts and uncles. Each Christmas they appear, as though out of the ground. They will pat me on the head, bring me little presents. I will be showered with hand-made toys, dolls, tortoise shell combs, boats in bottles, more boats carved out of bog oak, holy medals, rubber balls, brightly coloured paper fans . . . It is apparent to me that they forget, from year to year, whether I am a boy or a girl, but I take all the presents and thank them solemnly.

It is a time of great pleasure for me, that Christmas dinner. When it is over they will sit back, loosen various articles of clothing and begin to reminisce about old times, old places and whether so and so is alive or dead. In the lamplight their faces will glow, will soften with remembrance of other days when they were young. There will be snatches of song – 'The Old House', 'Among My Souvenirs' – and my shy mother will be prevailed on to recite her party piece, Pearse's 'The Wayfarer'. Furtively, then, I shall watch my father, how those hopeless, traitor eyes of his will let him down once more, as they fill with tears of love, for her, for me, for all of us on this day of days.

A person . . .

In the ninth house of our village, still moving in an east to west direction, there dwells William Holcomb Davis. It is a brick house, ivy covered, with rambling rose growing round the deep porched doorway. Old and weathered, like William himself, the house has withstood the ravages of time and tempest, new fashions and old. William, a sprightly nonagenarian, has been round the world more times than a caraway cake has seeds, and no one is quite sure if, this time, he is home to stay for good. It has always been his custom to spend Christmas in his own place, dreamily, in his memento-loaded sitting room.

I have been there, and it is a place come alive from the

technicoloured eye of childhood. One has only to turn one's head to be transported from an eskimo's igloo to a maharajah's palace to an African savage's grass hut. Out of niches stare ebony heads, hanging brass screens tremble, only waiting to be gonged, bamboo curtains click, raffia ones rustle, the skeleton of some lizard-like creature glares balefully from above the mantelpiece, inlaid boxes adorn tables and sideboards, chairs are carved in the shape of elephants' feet . . . And in the midst of it all crouches William, giving animate expression to all the exotica that he has accumulated over a long life.

For a man of ninety his eyes are jewels, being lit from within like coloured Chinese lanterns. His body is stick-like, yet his old bones do not break. His only difficulty, he tells me, is keeping warm, and I can see that there must be very little blood coursing through his fragile veins. Talking gives him solidity. He warms the winter air with his words, the strength of his life-force colouring the empty spaces round him. I breathe in his enthusiasm, for people, for places, for ideas yet to be acted upon, perceiving in this richness of expectation the secret of his continuance. For to William, the past and present are his future, his life is not then or now, nor is he confined by time or space. When he sniffs the wind or tastes the distant icy breath of snow on the mountains or gazes up at high places, he is full of delight, for all of these things are part of him. He has been there, and by being has absorbed them. Nothing is new to William, and yet everything is new. And when he strides into our sitting room on Christmas morning, where my mother plays host to all the village, attired in his flowing black cloak, the mad pacing of Mr Penny slows, John Jackson's faded eyes flicker with a kind of life, and even the Grosse brothers grin shyly at one another and then at everyone else. For it is a great thing to have such a worldly-wise and rakish traveller home amongst us, once again.

Christmas 1939

Family . . .

In the light of the gaslamp my father sits reading. My mother is threading together pieces of coloured paper, humming to herself as she works. I am making a fire engine from the Meccano set that my Uncle Isaak has sent me all the way from Dublin.

Our kitchen is the only one of our rooms that is on ground level. It is a spacious room, with a flagged floor, a large steel range and an open dresser with delft arranged neatly on its shelves, row by row. We spend most of our time here, the parlour upstairs only being opened on special occasions. It is the night before Christmas Eve, as the sprigs of holly behind the pictures and the puddings hanging in muslin sacks proclaim. It is the year 1939, and I am almost fourteen years old.

My father makes harrumphing noises as he reads, and it is apparent that what he reads distresses him. My mother glances at him from time to time, the empathy of her gentle disposition striving to bridge the gap between her and her impervious spouse. But the peaceful atmosphere of our kitchen continues to be interrupted by the small explosions of sound as he shuffles the paper and shifts about in his chair.

After a time, as is his fashion, he begins to talk about what he has just read in the paper. Roddy the Rover is discussing Christmas customs in other countries. Douglas Fairbanks Senr., a great favourite of my father's when he used to venture over to Temple East to the picture show, has died. Irish people intending to travel home for the holidays have to obtain exit permits from Britain. The Russian Bear is gobbling up more and more of Finland. On the Western Front the war is almost at stalemate.

As he talks the words take on colours, just like the coloured paper that my mother is twisting into various shapes. There are drifts of yellows and browns, spasms and pulse beats of greens and blues, but mostly there is the red of Finnish blood staining the whiteness of Finnish snow. It seems an abomination to me that such a fairytale, Christmassy country should be carrying the brunt of this far-off war. Especially at this time of year. Instead of tanks and gun carriers there should be the festive tinkle of bells and the swish-swish of sleigh runners whooshing through the powdered snow. In my mind's eye I picture the white shrouded figures of soldiers moving ghost-like through a silent landscape. Then those same soldiers lying motionless on the ice of a frozen-over lake.

Yet, really, I cannot visualise death. The idea is too big for me. Perhaps in those far off places, yes. I can come to terms with an ending, of sorts: the sudden hot stammer of guns, contorted bodies falling, falling . . . and the depth of silence when the remaining foes have gone elsewhere. But here at home, in the bosom of my family, death is unthinkable. My father is too much alive, his mouth opening, the words falling out in crystals of sound. I can see the blush of his heat-reddened face, can sense the beads of perspiration along his upper lip. He is vital, like some force of nature. And my mother too, in her quiet way, is as real and tangible to me as the cool metal under my fingers. They are my stanchions, they provide me with my grip on knowing, and being, and moving about. They are the instigators of my sense of wonder, the perpetrators of my individuality. I have bloomed in their love. I have sailed along it as though it were a river, and have come now to this place, from which I have never been away.

And my father talks on. He has opinions on everything, while my mother has none. Or at least none that she voices. I have never seen her angry, nor have I ever seen her weep. She often gets flustered, but one senses that it is only on the surface. Always with my father I have to put my feelings into words, but my mother's understanding needs no visible urgings. As now, when she smiles across at me, a tiny smile, almost to herself. But I know that her mind is behind it, and that she is as content as I am, here in our house, at Christmas time.

Three more houses, and the people in them . . .

There are no women in the last three houses in our village. Beside us, in a neat and well whitewashed cottage, lives Michael Strange. He is eighty-three years old, and is as neat in appearance as his cottage. He has false teeth and they sparkle in his mouth like stars. When he walks he swings his arms stiffly by his side, and he places his feet very carefully on the ground as if he were walking on glass. It is rumoured that he was once a great athlete, but he shows no signs of it now.

In the twelfth house, also a cottage, but as decrepit and rundown as ever a cottage can be, lives Michael's brother, Simon. He is seventy-nine, but looks much older. When he stops at the side of the road, as he often does, he appears like a gnarled old tree that has been struck by lightning. He never washes, nor does he trim his hair or beard. When he enters our public bar, he can be smelled in the furthest room of the house.

The brothers have not spoken to one another in living memory. Each evening they sit in opposite corners of the bar, on high stools. The silence between them is palpable, like smoke. They never look in one another's direction, yet one senses that they are watchful. One summer when Michael fell ill with a fainting sickness, Simon came, night after night, and stood in the ditch opposite his door, but he never ventured in. The Grosse children and myself would approach him from different directions and stare at him, but he paid us no heed. More than ever he looked like an old tree, planted in the ground.

Standing between the cottages of the Strange brothers is the brick bungalow of the Catholic priest, Fr John Carpenter. He is a big, red-faced man with a bluff manner and a great shock of coarse greying hair. He is the curate for the area, and his church stands in the fold of a hill exactly halfway between our village and the village of Temple East. He laughs and jokes a lot, but deep down there is an uneasiness in him that makes people equally uneasy in his company. He rides everywhere, on a huge grey horse. Sometimes, at night, looking out of my upstairs window, I have seen him, silhouetted against the sky. There is a harsh roughness about man and horse, as they gallop ponderously across the side of the hill. They do not wobble in the air, as people spied at a distance sometimes do. And I fancy that I can hear the thud of the horse's hooves reverberating deep in the earth beneath our house. Are they, man and horse, galloping perhaps to Jerusalem?

Midnight Mass . . .

It is to be a great treat for us this year: Mass at twelve o'clock on Christmas Eve night. It has not been heard of before in these parts, and the parish priest has frowned on the idea. But Fr John Carpenter is adamant, and the Mass will be celebrated.

My mother has insisted that I sleep for the early part of the night, but I am too excited, and I lie awake, snug in my cocoon of blankets and eiderdown, listening to the wind whistling through the rafters of the house. The room is dark except for a nightlight guttering in its saucer of grease. Shadows heave and sway across the ceiling, and I am happy to be by myself in my bed, which is a ship. It is carrying me onwards and outwards, away from our leaning row of houses, across the hills and towards the sea that is aflame with an almost swallowed sun. I have always half believed that a time will come when I must retreat from my valley, before the valley retreats from me. For I have learned early that contentment is a flicker in the wind, and that true happiness is inside oneself. Many of my dreams, then, are full of movement: I am flying, running, walking; I am a traveller travelling across great stretches of mountain, sea and forest; I am bounding away from hearth and home, with never a backward glance. Season follows season. The leaves bloom green, then they curl at the edges. One falls, then another, and soon they have all drifted away in the wind. The trees are bare, stark against the sky. And I am in my wintering, composing myself for yet another round of journeying, setting my mind against loss, so that when it comes I shall be ready for it. As if one ever is.

But now, on Christmas Eve night 1939, it is all before me, where I lie awake in the heavy, breathing darkness of my room. Soon my mother, her shadow monstrous on the stairs, will come with lamp held high to wake me safely from my reverie. And we will all pile into our almost new Vauxhall 10 h.p. De Luxe Saloon and, with my father uncomfortably at the wheel, we will pass along the lighted ribbon of road to church. In the company of all the others, my ancestors, yours and theirs, since the first Christmas, and before that too, in a never-ending line.

Christmas morning . . .

While we were all asleep, it has snowed. Everywhere has taken on an aspect of sameness, the snow covering all. There are no hills, no fields, no dividing hedges. Everything is smooth and white. There is no sign of life, no footprints even. If anyone has come to these houses bearing gifts then he must have come before the snow fell.

My breath is visible on the air as I bend my head towards the frozen pane of glass. It is Christmas morning, and a reckoning is due. I must share my happiness. I must share it with the Finns who, in a similar pristine landscape, are enduring the final death throes of their tortured country. I must share it with John Jackson whose frenzied anvil pounding only hours before guided us home. And I must share it with crazy Mr Penny where he dreams amid the poppies of Flanders' fields.

And as I stare out into that awful flat and featureless land, it is suddenly split apart by the slow meandering of a solitary figure. I incline closer to the window, and my breath fogs up the glass. Feverishly I rub it clear, fearing that by doing so I will rub away Miss Emily Grosse also. But she is still there, almost abreast of my house. Her hair is flowing free, and I can see that she is smiling as she walks. What thoughts are in her head as she wanders through that white immensity? And will she see me? Oh, she must, she must . . .

And then she does, raising her eyes so tantalisingly until they are gazing into mine, from where she stands below me in the snow. What passes between us then, silently, I cannot remember over the intervening years, but I surmise that she is mouthing the age old greeting, and I, in dumb show, mouth it back. Happy Christmas, Miss Emily Grosse, and Happy Christmas to all the rest of you too, where you lie, at home, in the recesses of my heart.

PATRICK McCABE

Apaches

The snow came and then the Apaches, sitting there in the hollow, a thin snake of purple smoke unwinding from a fire of blackened stones, the old squaw sucking a small pipe through teeth the colour of wood. A prairie dog tore at a bone, the snowflakes melting into its oily coat. The Chief cursed under a van, then emerged rubbing his hands. He had a battered black stovepipe hat on his head and a face of scored leather. The children pushed a gig with uneven wheels and shouted in their singsong language. A baby squealed as the radio blared 'I shot a man in Reno just to watch him die'. They were there to stay, their territory marked by tar barrels.

In the nights I dreamed about them. The Chief scaled a grey crag with a blade between his teeth, scuttled like a lizard beneath the burning sun. Below in the canyon was the town, Lavery's Grocery, the broken pump and James Potter Victualler. Small dustclouds gathered in the streets, tumbleweed clutched the wheels of covered wagons. The Chief bared his teeth in a grin, slipped the blade into his pouch and was gone. The prairie dog strained at the leash as he approached across the plains, the heat shimmered in the cacti.

I stared open-mouthed at the hypnotic glow of the screen. There was nothing Audie Murphy could do. A gap-toothed renegade looped a rope across a branch and sneered, 'It's a good day for a hanging, lawman.' Audie stood frozen as bleached bones stared up at him. 'If we hadn't gotten ya, them 'paches would have anyhow,' said the renegade.

Somewhere behind the canyon ridge they lurked, moving on padded feet.

'Give me down the sugar,' said Ma.

When I looked again, the renegade and his partners were on the ground staring out of dead eyes, Audie was galloping off on horseback with his hands tied behind his back and the Apaches were swarming like ants, the Chief standing above the dead men with an axe in his crossed hands.

'He steal from Apache, white man,' he said, 'you lie, white-eyes.'

The renegade stared at the sky as a drum boomed.

The moon hung in a corner of the bedroom window as I heard Da and Jimmy the stonecutter stumbling on the gravel. Da coughed harshly and swore.

'Goodnight, Jimmy,' I heard him say, 'I'll see you in The Vintage Christmas Eve.'

'Aye,' Jimmy said.

I heard the door close and the sound of the holy picture falling in the hallway. Crockery rattled as she fixed his meal. Clouds trickled across the moon's face, a cat passed in the darkness.

'You never were any different,' I heard him say, 'whining from the day you were born.'

I saw her face in the ensuing silence, taut white skin, wounded eyes.

'Should have left you in that hole of a butcher shop. All you were good for.'

It went on far into the night. I heard the bedroom door close as the window glass paled and P.J. Masterson stared down the lane on his way to work.

'Sonofabitch,' said Desie as we spied on them from the hill, 'they haven't moved for an hour. She just sits there – like a stone.'

The black-faced children crawled in and out of a drainpipe. We sat there until evening and then Desie spat onto the grass and said: 'Move 'em out, pard.'

We rode back into town on makebelieve colts.

We sat in the parlour listening to carols on the radio, its bead of light twinging in the half-darkness. Ma's needles clicked in time with the movement of the fireshadows. Da's lips moved in and out, he came out of a dream and said:

'Pete McDonald's not good. They say he won't see the Christmas.'

Ma shook her head and said nothing. He recalled a trip to Bundoran with Pete, hours spent climbing the cliffs in the hot sun.

'Nothing Pete didn't know about birds. A rare character. Wasn't a bird in the book he didn't know.'

Then he slipped away again, his fingers making tiny movements on the arm of the chair. A bird trotted along the garden wall. All you could hear was the sound of Ma's breathing.

'You travel long way?' said Desie as the Apache lad looked up at him with hunted eyes.

Desie pointed to himself.

'We,' he said, accentuating his words, 'we – friends.'

The lad started back a little, watching our hands.

'We-live-in-town. You – Apache brave. You hear the spirit voices of dead warriors.'

The lad's face contorted. He stumbled, then ran off without looking back. Desie looked after him.

'He doesn't understand.'

The teepee was rigid, the ponies shuffled closer to the ditch for warmth. The squaw struggled through the snow with an enamel bucket to the frozen river. The radio played *Silver bells, silver bells, it's Christmas time in the city*.

There was a party in the house. A car pulled up outside and they came in singing, pulling off snowspeckled overcoats and heavy scarves. Jody Lennon and Charlie Keenan sang *South of the Border*. Glasses clinked and cigarette smoke filled the kitchen. Someone put on a 78 and they began to dance to the muted trumpets of the Inkspots.

'Will you ever forget them, Benny?' said Charlie to Da.

'Who do you know in heaven that made you the angel you are?' smiled Da, the whiskey tipping over the side of his glass.

After the dancing they sat for a long time around the fire talking about the old days and past Christmases.

'This time last year, Harry was with us,' said Jody Lennon, 'poor Harry.'

'Who'd have thought it?' said Mrs McGirr, tapping her glass with thoughtful fingers.

'The time passes.'

'It does surely,' they all agreed, 'it passes like that.'

The car engines revved up suddenly in the white night. Voices huddled together in the doorway as they gathered up gloves and hats.

'Please God we'll all be here this time next year.'

'I think she'll freeze.'

'Well a happy Christmas to one and all.'

'And many of them.'

They left then and all there was was the stark carpet of snow and the flakes in mad clusters around the amber streetlight.

Lying there in the darkness, I heard them talking. Ma was upset over something.

'I have my self-respect too,' she said.

There were long silences. Then he said:

'You and your half-wit brother . . .'

'Why didn't you say that to his face? Why Benny?'

Their voices got louder. He shouted her down, then he cursed and I could hear her climbing out of bed. He called her back but she went downstairs. I could hear him dragging on the cigarette and the sound of the clock ticking as she sat by the fire downstairs. It was morning when her soft footsteps came hesitantly back up the stairs.

They were hardy because of all the winters they'd seen.

'He's like Crazy Horse,' said Desie, 'nothing would ever break him.'

We drew pictures of him, an imposing shadow before the sun, feathered spear poised as he drew a bead on a rattler. The prairie stretched away like a sky. The squaw and him did not fight or argue. They had their own ways and they followed their code in silence. The longknives came to the Apache village. Rory Calhoun played The Chief. He bartered with the General, laid out rugs and wood carvings in the centre of the village. They shook hands. Rory bowed. But in the night, the longknives crept into the village like cats. They burnt the teepees to the ground and rounded up all the braves. They tied Calhoun to a tree and tortured him. They humiliated him in front of his squaw and the whole village. Then his head fell on his bloodstained chest, his black pigtails dangling. The General slapped his wrist with his white gloves and gestured to his men. They rode off and left the squaws to pick their way through the blackened ash of the burnt village.

'The bastards,' cried Desie, 'the dirty bastards.'

We painted equals signs and arrows on our faces, sat parleying on orange boxes in the dimness of the deserted railway office. Desie pulled a rug around him and looked at me with wise, burrowing eyes as I explained why I had come to the village. He put on a deep voice and said:

'You come to the village of He-Who-Walks-The-World. We make you our brother.'

We mingled the blood of our wrists and then we smoked the pipe of peace. When it was finished, Desie looked out across the embankment and said:

'There's nothing else I want to be. I want to be one of them. They're free.'

'Yes,' I said, thinking of them on a wide open trail, winding towards blue mountain valleys, 'Free.'

One day I came home and found Ma crying over the sink. She just kept picking at the dishes with the tears coming down her face. I went white, I did not know what to do. I stood there not knowing whether to touch her or run out. She half-looked at me and struggled for words:

'I don't know why it happens, son . . . he was never bitter . . . some day I'll tell you . . . you wouldn't understand yet . . .'

She kept talking in muddled sentences about other times – a boarding house in Bundoran, a day at the Giant's Causeway, all about a time I knew nothing about. I stood there in silence, the hard frosted sun slanting in through the window, trying to make sense of what she said. It seemed like years passed as we stood there, a chainsaw drilling in the distance.

At night the orange camp fire flickered, its tarry smoke filling the air. Odd times Apaches came from camps far away, crept in like ghosts and sat around in a circle. Their hair was thick and black, ropes around their waists. You could see their tough, creased faces moving in and out of the light. Dead rabbits hung from a branch. The prairie dog's vigilant snout sat on its paws. Sometimes they sang in low voices, a deep penetrating hum that spread outwards like a fanning claw.

'They're calling to the spirits of the happy hunting grounds,' said Desie.

'The Manitou,' I said, 'they're praying to The Manitou.'

'Jesus,' said Desie, as we slipped back behind the hill into the darkness, 'The Manitou.'

Christmas Day the place was a ghost town. Beer trails from the night before froze on the sidewalk outside the bars, the grocery sign creaked relentlessly. In the evening Desie and me went tracking in The Hairy Mountains, trudging over crusted hoof-holes in search of badgers' imprints with our staffs in hand. When I got home the doors were locked. There was no answer, it seemed the house was deserted. I managed to prise the scullery window open with my penknife. In the kitchen embers glowed in the fire. I got the feeling of being in a strange world. In the half-light their picture looked down at me. She was wearing a wide-brimmed hat with a flower, her white handbag hanging from her arm. Behind them a poster *King's Hall Belfast – Gracie Fields – Jan.* 10 1953. The fire glinted in the brass ornaments on the mantelpiece, behind the clock memoriam cards and bound letters going back a long time, a photograph of uncle Joe in a summer hayfield. I stood there without moving, I did not know what to say about these things. Then I heard a sort of moan. I tensed and whispered 'Who is it?' but no answer came. For no reason I thought of a stalking hunter in a wolfskin. I crept slowly up the stairs then I heard it again. It was coming from their room. I bent and through the keyhole the image meant nothing to me at first, it was an optical puzzle that came slowly into focus. It was his back, marked with the startling whiteness of age. It moved up and down rhythmically. He groaned. I heard Ma, she seemed to be in pain. She kept saying 'Please, please'. For a long time they were like this. Then Da eased downward. There was silence. Then I could hear her sobs. Da turned away on his side.

'Why Benny?' she said. 'What happened Benny? Please . . . tell me . . .'

He did not answer. The silence seemed to swell up and fill up the room like a balloon.

The sky slowly inked itself in. The snow began again, in the distance the lights went out in the town. I lit a fire in the deserted office and burnt old papers and files discarded from the days of the railway. There were still posters on the walls, left from the days Ma and Da had first come to the town to live. A couple in old-fashioned clothes stood smiling with their suitcases, behind them the fading outline of London's Tower Bridge. Outside the Hairy Mountains rose up like black tidal waves. When the fire died I sat there thinking but everything was twisted in my head. I saw her smiling in an olden days café with wooden booths and weak-coloured advertisements. I saw her turn away as his parchment-like body heaved above her, felt the taut silence of the kitchen as we sat there under the drowsy spell of the kitchen, the days it brought back melting almost as they came. I could not hold any of the thoughts long enough to make anything of them, they dissipated like smoke and then converged under a new image. I kicked over the ashes of the fire and went out. There was no sound as I walked, the snow took my steps and made silence of them. For a long time I strode, through the hunting grounds of winter, thinking how there would be dead buffalo in the mountains. I kept saying the name to myself, it was the only thing kept me going, He-Who-Walks-The-World. There was still a tiny coil of smoke coming from the fire when I got there. I could hear The Chief snoring in the teepee. The pony pawed the dirt. I crept past the prairie dog and he didn't stir. I clung to what was left of the fire but the frost edged into my whole body, I could not stop shivering. When I looked up The Chief was standing there with a blanket around him. His long black hair half-covered his craggy face.

'He-Who-Walks-The-World,' I said.

'Yes,' he said, his voice deep, commanding.

After that everything seemed to move slowly before my eyes, a rabbit turned slowly over the fire, the blackfaced children stared with their fingers in their mouths, the squaw held out bread to me without speaking. The Chief and I ate together. He sat with his legs crossed and I felt his eyes inside me. The smoke curled and the snow fell hypnotically. We seemed to sit there for hours until I felt myself drifting across a vast plain where the sun beat down relentlessly on the red powdery sand. There came sounds of movement, of faces without shape gathering bundles and sending smokeclouds up from a fire as animals were made ready to press south to the fertile valleys now that the white men had killed all the buffalo, Rory Calhoun taking a last look at the settlers' cabins that now dotted his terrain, before waving to his gathered people and setting off into the night. Then I fell away again, tumbling above the plain like dust.

When I came to, they were gone, it was as if they had never been there. In the distance I saw Desie and Da on the hill. I waited, watching the snow covering their tracks. Desie hung back uncertainly. Da was white, he did not know what to say.

'They're gone, Desie,' I said.

Da's eyes darted between us.

'Yes,' said Desie.

'They had to Desie,' I said. 'The Longknives.'

Da stood looking at me. 'You should have told us son,' he said, 'anything could have happened. You don't know those people.'

I nodded. I didn't feel anything about it now. We said nothing more, just stood there for a long time as the snow blew in clouds towards the town where Ma stood waiting by the window, oblivious of their soundless passage through the deserted streets, in the kitchen's shadows.

MICHAEL McLAVERTY

Father Christmas

'Will you do what I ask you?' his wife said again, wiping the crumbs off the newspaper which served as a tablecloth. 'Wear your hard hat and you'll get the job.'

He didn't answer her or raise his head. He was seated on the dilapidated sofa lacing his boots, and behind him tumbled two of his children, each chewing a crust of bread. His wife paused, a hand on her hip. She glanced at the sleety rain falling into the backyard, turned round, and threw the crumbs into the fire.

'You'll wear it, John – won't you?'

Again he didn't answer though his mind was already made up. He strode into the scullery and while he washed himself she took an overcoat from a nail behind the kitchen door, brushed it vigorously, gouging out the specks of dirt with the nose of the brush. She put it over the back of a chair and went upstairs for his hard hat.

'I'm a holy show in that article,' he said, when she was handing him the hat and helping him into the overcoat. 'I'll be a nice ornament among the other applicants! I wish you'd leave me alone!'

'You look respectable anyhow. I could take a fancy for you

all over again,' and she kissed him playfully on the side of the cheek.

'If I don't get the job you needn't blame me. I've done all you asked – every mortal thing.'

'You'll get it all right – never you fear. I know what I'm talking about.'

He hurried out of the street in case some of the neighbours would ask him if he were going to a funeral, and when he had taken his place in the line of young men who were all applying for the job of Father Christmas in the Big Store he was still conscious of the bowler hat perched on top of his head. He was a timid little man and he tried to crouch closer to the wall and make himself inconspicuous amongst that group of grey-capped men. The rain continued to fall as they waited for the door to open and he watched the drops clinging to the peaks of their caps, swelling and falling to the ground.

'If he had a beard we could all go home,' he heard someone say, and he felt his ears reddening, aware that the remark was cast at him. But later when he was following the Manager up the brass-lipped stairs, after he had got the job, he dwelt on the wisdom of his wife and knew that the hat had endowed him with an air of shabby respectability.

'Are you married?' the Manager had asked him, looking at the nervous way he turned the hat in his hand. 'And have you any children?' He had answered everything with a meek smile and the Manager told him to stand aside until he had interviewed, as a matter of form, the rest of the applicants.

And then the interviews were quickly over, and when the Manager and John were mounting the stairs he saw a piece of caramel paper sticking to the Manager's heel. Down a long aisle they passed with rows of counters at each side and shoppers gathered round them. And though it was daylight outside, the electric lights were lit, and through the glare there arose a buzz of talk, the rattle of money, and the warm smell of new clothes and perfume and confectionery – all of it entering John's mind in a confused and dreamy fashion for his eye was fastened on the caramel paper as he followed respectfully after the Manager. Presently they emerged on a short flight of stairs where a notice – PRIVATE – on trestles straddled across it. The Manager lifted it ostentatiously to the side, ushered John forward with a sweep of his arm, and replaced the notice with mechanical importance.

'Just a minute,' said John, and he plucked the caramel paper from the Manager's heel, crumpled it between his fingers, and put it in his pocket.

They entered the quiet seclusion of a small room that had a choking smell of dust and cardboard boxes. The Manager mounted a step-ladder, and taking a large box from the top shelf looked at something written on the side, slapped the dust off it against his knee, and broke the string.

'Here,' he said, throwing down the box. 'You'll get a red cloak in that and a white beard.' He sat on the top rung of the ladder and held a false face on the tip of his finger: 'Somehow I don't think you'll need this. You'll do as you are. Just put on the beard and whiskers.'

'Whatever you say,' smiled John, for he always tried to please people.

Another box fell at his feet: 'You'll get a pair of top boots in that!' The Manager folded the step-ladder, and daintily picking pieces of fluff from his sleeves he outlined John's duties for the day and emphasised that after closing-time he'd have to make up parcels for the following day's sale.

Left alone John breathed freely, took off his overcoat and hung it at the back of the door, and for some reason whenever he crossed the floor he did so on his tiptoes. He lifted the red cloak that was trimmed with fur, held it in his outstretched arms to admire it, and squeezed the life out of a moth that was struggling in one of the folds. Chips of tinsel glinted on the shoulders of the cloak and he was ready to flick them off when he decided it was more Christmassy-looking to let them remain on. He pulled on the cloak, crossed on tiptoes to a looking-glass on the wall and winked and grimaced at himself, sometimes putting up the collar of the cloak to enjoy the warm touch of the fur on the back of his neck. He attached the beard and the whiskers, spitting out one or two hairs that had strayed into his mouth.

'The very I-T,' he said, and caught the beard in his fist and waggled it at his reflection in the mirror. 'Hello, Santa!' he smiled, and thought of his children and how they would laugh to see him togged up in this regalia. 'I must tell her to bring them down some day,' and he gave a twirl on his toes, making a heap of paper rustle in the corner.

He took off his boots, looked reflectively at the broken sole of each and pressed his thumb into the wet leather: 'Pasteboard – nothing else!' he said in disgust, and threw them on the heap of brown paper. He reached for the top boots that were trimmed with fur. They looked a bit on the small side. With some difficulty he squeezed his feet into them. He walked across the floor, examining the boots at each step; they were very tight for him, but he wasn't one to complain, and, after all, the job was only for the Christmas season and they'd be sure to stretch with the wearing.

When he was fully dressed he made his way down the stairs, lifted his leg over the trestle with the name PRIVATE and presented himself on one of the busy floors. A shop-girl, hesitating before striking the cash-register, smiled over at him. His face burned. Then a little girl plucked her mother's skirt and called, 'Oh, Mammy, there's Daddy Christmas!' With his hands in his wide sleeves he stood in a state of nervous perplexity till the shop-girl, scratching her head with the tip of her pencil, shouted jauntily: 'First Floor, Santa Claus, right on down the stairs!' He stumbled on the stairs because of the tight boots and when he halted to regain his composure he felt the blood hammering in his temples and he wished now that he hadn't listened to his wife and worn his hard hat. She was always nagging at him, night, noon and morning, and he doing his damned best!

On the first floor the Manager beckoned him to a miniature house – a house painted in imitation brick, snow on the eaves, a door which he could enter by stooping low, and a chimney large enough to contain his head and shoulders, and inside the house stacks of boxes neatly piled, some in blue paper and others in pink.

The Manager produced a hand-bell. 'You stand here,' said the Manager, placing himself at the door of the house. 'Ring your bell a few times – like this. Then shout in a loud, commanding voice: "Roll up now! Blue for the Boys, and Pink for the Girls".' And he explained that when business was slack, he was to mount the ladder, descend the chimney, and bring up the parcels in that manner, but if there was a crowd he was just to open the door and shake hands with each child before presenting the boxes. They were all the same price – a shilling each.

For the first ten minutes or so John's voice was weak and self-conscious and the Manager, standing a short distance away, ordered him to raise his voice a little louder: 'You must attract attention – that's what you're paid for. Try it once again.'

'Blue for the Boys, and Pink for the Girls!' shouted John, and he imagined all the buyers at the neighbouring counters had paused to listen to him. 'Blue for the Boys, and Pink for the Girls!' he repeated, his eye on the Manager who was judging him from a distance. The Manager smiled his approval and then shook an imaginary bell in the air. John suddenly remembered about the bell in his hand and he shook it vigorously, but a shop-girl tightened up her face at him and he folded his fingers over the skirt of the bell in order to muffle the sound. He gained more confidence, but as his nervousness decreased he became aware of the tight boots imprisoning his feet, and occasionally he would disappear into his little house and catching the sole of each in turn he would stretch them across his knee.

But the children gave him no peace, and with his head held genially to the side, if the Manager were watching him, he would smile broadly and listen with affected interest to each child's demand.

'Please, Santa Claus, bring me a tricycle at Christmas and a doll's pram for Angela.'

'I'll do that! Everything you want,' said Father Christmas expansively, and he patted the little boy on the head with gentle dignity before handing him a blue parcel. But when he raised his eyes to the boy's mother she froze him with a look.

'I didn't think you would have any tricycles this year,' she said. 'I thought you were only making wooden trains.'

'Oh, yes! No, yes, not at all! Yes, of course, I'll get you a nice wooden train,' Father Christmas turned to the boy in his confusion. 'If you keep good I'll have a lovely train for you.'

'I don't want an oul train. I want a tricycle,' the boy whimpered, clutching his blue-papered parcel.

'I couldn't make any tricycles this year,' consoled Father Christmas. 'My reindeers were sick and three of them died on me.'

The boy's mother smiled and took him by the hand. 'Now, pet, didn't I tell you Santa had no tricycles? You better shout up the chimney for something else – a nice game or a wooden train.'

'I don't want an oul game – I want a tricycle,' he cried, and jigged his feet.

'You'll get a warm ear if you're not careful. Come on now and none of your nonsense. And Daddy Christmas after giving you a nice box, all for yourself.'

Forcibly she led the boy away and John, standing with his hands in his sleeves, felt the prickles of sweat on his forehead and resolved to promise nothing to the children until he had got the cue from the parents.

As the day progressed he climbed up the ladder and down the chimney, emerging again with his arms laden with parcels. His feet tortured him and when he glanced at the boots every wrinkle in the leather was smoothed away. He couldn't continue like this all day; it would drive him mad.

'Roll up!' he bawled. 'Roll up! Blue for the Pinks and Boys for the Girls! Roll up, I say. Blue for the Pinks and Boys for the Girls.' Then he stopped and repeated the same mistake before catching himself up. And once more he clanged the bell with subdued ferocity till its sound drowned the jingle of the cash-registers and the shop-girls had to shout to be heard.

At one o'clock he wearily climbed the stairs to the quiet room, where dinner was brought to him on a tray. He took off his boots and gazed sympathetically at his crushed toes. He massaged them tenderly, and when he had finished his dinner he pared his corns with a razor blade he had bought at one of the counters. He now squeezed his bare feet into the boots, walked across the room, and sat down again, his face twisted with despair. 'Why do I always give in to that woman,' he said aloud to himself. 'I've no strength – no power to stand up and shout in her face: "No, no, no! I'll go my own way in my own time!"' He'd let her know tonight the agony he suffered, and his poor feet gathered up all day like a rheumatic fist.

Calmed after this outburst, and reassuring himself that the job was only for three weeks, he gave a whistle of forced satisfaction, brushed the corn-parings off the chair, and went off to stand outside the little house with its imitation snow on the chimney.

The afternoon was the busiest time, and he was glad to be able to stand at the door like a human being and hand out the parcels, instead of ascending and descending the ladder like a trained monkey. When the children crowded too close to him he kept them at arm's length in case they'd trample on his feet. But he always managed to smile as he watched them shaking their boxes or tearing holes in the paper in an effort to guess what was inside. And the parents smiled too when they looked at him wagging his finger at the little girls and promising them dolls at Christmas if they would go to bed early, eat their porridge and stop biting their nails. But before closing time a woman was back holding an untidy parcel. 'That's supposed to be for a boy,' she said peevishly.

'There's a rubber doll in it and my wee boy has cried his eyes out ever since.'

'I'm just new to the job,' Father Christmas apologised. 'It'll never occur again.' And he tossed the parcel into the house and handed the woman a new one.

At the end of his day he had gathered from the floor a glove with a hole in one finger, three handkerchiefs, a necklace of blue beads, and a child's handbag containing a halfpenny and three tram-tickets. When he was handing them to the Manager he wondered if he should complain about the boots, but the tired look on the Manager's face and his reminder about staying behind to make up parcels discouraged him.

For the last time he climbed the stairs, took off his boots and flung them from him, and as he prepared the boxes he padded about the cool floor in his bare feet, and to ensure that he wouldn't make a mistake he arranged, at one side of the room, the contents for the girls' boxes: dolls, shops, pages of transfers, story books, and crayons; and at the opposite side of the room the toys for the boys: ludo, snakes and ladders, blow football, soldiers, cowboy outfits, and wooden whistles. And as he parcelled them neatly and made loops in the twine for the children's fingers he decided once again to tell his wife to bring his own kids along and he'd have special parcels prepared for them.

On his way out of the Store the floors were silent and deserted, the counters humped with canvas covers, and the little house looking strangely real now under a solitary light. A mouse nibbling at something on the floor scurried off between an alleyway in the counters, and on the ground floor two women were sweeping up the dust and gossiping loudly.

The caretaker let him out by a side door, and as he walked off in the rain through the lamp-lighted streets he put up the collar of his coat and avoided the puddles as best he could. A sullen resentment seized his heart and he began to drag from the corners of his mind the things that irritated him. He thought they should have given him his tea before he left, or even a bun and a glass of milk, and he thought of his home and maybe the fine tea his wife would have for him, and a good fire in the grate and the kids in bed. He walked more quickly. He passed boys eating chip potatoes out of a newspaper, and he stole a glance at Joe Raffo's chip-shop and the cloud of steam rolling through the open door into the cold air. The smell maddened him. He plunged his hands into his pockets and fiddled with a button, bits of hard crumbs, and a sticky bit of caramel paper. He took out the caramel paper and threw it on the wet street.

He felt cheated and discontented with everything; and the more he thought of the job the more he blamed his wife for all the agony he had suffered throughout the day. She couldn't leave him alone – not for one solitary minute could she let him have a thought of his own or come to a decision of his own. She must be for ever interfering, barging in, and poking into his business. He was a damned fool to listen to her and to don a ridiculous hard hat for such a miserable job. Father Christmas and his everlasting smile! He'd smile less if he had to wear a pair of boots three sizes too small for him. It was a young fella they wanted for the job – somebody accustomed to standing for hours at a street corner and measuring the length of his spits on the kerb. And then the ladder! That was the bloody limit! Up and down, down and up, like a squirrel in a cage, instead of giving you a stick and a chair where you could sit and really look like an old man. When he'd get home he'd let his wife know what she let him in for. It would lead to a row between them, and when that happened she'd go about for days flinging his meals on the table and belting the kids for sweet damn-all. He'd have to tell her – it was no use suffering devil's torture and saying nothing about it. But then, it's more likely than not she'd put on her hat and coat and go down to the Manager in the morning and complain about the boots, and then he might lose the job, bad and all as it was. Och, he'd say nothing – sure, bad temper never got you anywhere!

He stepped into a puddle to avoid a man's umbrella and when he felt the cold splash of water up the leg of his trousers his anger surged back again. He'd tell her all. He'd soon take the wind out of her sails and her self-praise about the hat! He'd tell her everything.

He hurried up the street and at the door of his house he let down the collar of his coat and shook the rain off his hat. He listened for a minute and heard the children shouting. He knocked, and the three of them pounded to the door to open it.

'It's Daddy,' they shouted, but he brushed past them without speaking.

His wife was washing the floor in the kitchen and as she wrung the cloth into the bucket and brushed back her hair with the back of her hand she looked at him with a bright smile.

'You got it all right?'

'Why aren't the children in bed?'

'I didn't expect you home so soon.'

'Did you think I was a bus conductor!'

She noticed the hard ring in his voice. She rubbed the soap on the scrubber and hurried to finish her work, making great whorls and sweeps with the cloth. She took off her dirty apron, and as she washed and dried her hands in the scullery she glanced in at him seated on the sofa, his head resting on his hands, the three children waiting for him to speak to them. 'It was the hat,' she said to herself. 'It was the hat did the trick.'

'Come on now and up to bed quickly,' and she clapped her hands at the children.

'But you have to wash our legs in the bucket.'

'You'll do all right for tonight. Your poor father's hungry after his hard day's work.' And as she pulled off a jersey she held it in her hand and gave the fire a poke under the kettle. John stared into the fire and when he raised his foot there was a damp imprint left on the tiles. She handed him a pair of warm socks from the line and a pair of old slippers that she had made for him out of pasteboard and a piece of velours.

'I've a nice bit of steak for your tea,' she said. 'I'll put on the pan when I get these ones into their beds.'

He rubbed his feet and pulled on the warm socks. It was good that she hadn't the steak fried and lying as dry as a stick in the oven. When all was said and done, she had some sense in her head.

The children began to shout up the chimney telling Santa Claus what they wanted for Christmas, and when they knelt to say their prayers they had to thank God for sending their Daddy a good job. John smiled for the first time since he came into the house and he took the youngest on his knee. 'You'll get a doll and a pram for Christmas,' he said, 'and Johnny will get a wooden train with real wheels and Pat – what will we get him?' And he remembered putting a cowboy's outfit into one of the boxes. 'A cowboy's outfit – hat and gun.'

His wife had put the pan on the fire and already the steak was frizzling. 'Don't let that pan burn till I come down again. I'll not be a minute.'

He heard her put the kids to bed, and in a few minutes she was down again, a fresh blouse on her and a clean apron.

She poured out his tea and after he had taken a few mouthfuls he began to tell her about the crowd of applicants and about the fellow who shouted: 'We'd better all go home,' when he had seen him in the hat.

'He was jealous – that's what was wrong with him!' she said. 'A good clout on the ear he needed.'

He told her about the Manager, the handbell, the blue and pink parcels, the little house, and the red cloak he had to wear. Then he paused, took a drink of tea, cut a piece of bread into three bits, and went on eating slowly.

'It's well you took my advice and wore the hat,' she said brightly. 'I knew what I was talking about. And you look so – so manly in it.' She remembered about the damp stain on the floor, and she lifted his boots off the fender and looked at the broken soles. 'They're done,' she said, 'that's the first call in your wages at the end of the week.'

He got up from the table and sat near the fire. She handed him his pipe filled with tobacco, and as she washed the dishes in the scullery she would listen to the little pouts he made while he smoked. Now and again she glanced in at him, at the contented look on his face and the steam arising from his boots on the fender.

She took off her apron, tidied her hair at the looking-glass, and powdered her face. She stole across the floor to him as he sat staring into the fire. Quietly she took the pipe from his lips and put it on the mantelpiece. She smiled at him and he smiled back, and as she stooped to kiss him he knew that he would say nothing to her now about the tight boots.

CLARE BOYLAN

The Spirit of the Tree

Three weeks before Christmas we began counting trees. Crouched in the back of father's car, forbidden to talk in case we disturbed his concentration as he approached traffic lights, we silently prodded the window, leaving marks that were veined like flies' wings. The flaring vee of light in darkened drawing rooms was like a landing strip for the extraordinary event that would descend among us. In that first week there would be only two or three trees, mostly in big houses. The second week there might be eleven or twelve and then on that last Sunday, days before Christmas, they were convened behind windows everywhere – majestic evergreens bedecked like emperors and little crooked shrubs nobbled with lights that were bright and sticky as boiled sweets – a silent community signalling light.

What were they for? Hardly anyone seemed to know. But I knew. The spirit of the tree spoke to Santa Claus, telling him which houses he should visit. The fairy lights were to guide his way. I can't remember where I heard that, probably in a story, but I knew it must be true because it made sense.

We did not know it then but the atmosphere in those weeks coming up to Christmas, the sense of an unstoppable miracle, was very close to the feeling of falling in love. A space was carved in the ordinary world, where we were knocked into shape for hard lives ahead, and we could sit into this capsule for a while and be angels or astronauts. We wore a shimmering garment of rapture. Nothing could touch us – not the sharp December air, smelling of fog and frost, not even the curious humpy mood that sat over our parents as we drove home from our grandparents' house. The strange thing was that the happy tension surrounding us children seemed to strike our parents at a different angle and one could not help noticing that as the fairy-lit forests ran riot in suburbia, they grew more and more withdrawn, more peculiar. They reacted to the approach of Christmas as to the onslaught of a war, mother grimly setting forth for the city to lay in supplies, muttering about the crowds and the price of things, father swearing as he tacked up the paper accordion decorations, which frequently broke and teasingly drifted, snakelike, through the sombre living room. The biggest ordeal was putting up the Christmas tree. The huge conifer was dragged into the house like a dead bear, then wrestled into an upright position and dumped in a barrel, weighted with bricks. Father would retreat from this engagement, thistled with tiny green needles and looking offended as the tree flooded the house with its pungent green scent.

The small surprise parcels from Santa contained, year after year, the same novelties, the chocolate coins wrapped in foil, an orange. Our parents gave us books, our grandparents biscuits, a tin of sweets and a box of mandarin oranges tricked out like pantomime fairies in tissue and silver paper. Aunt Josie faithfully produced a bottle of Gilbey's Odd-On cocktail for mother and warm underwear for us girls. Small gifts from far-flung relatives were dangled from the tree or stacked at its base – bath cubes and puzzles and assorted chocolate bars in presentation packs called Selection Boxes. Still, each year, the shock of anticipation was new and when the long (and predictable) day had ended, my last act was always to search the Christmas tree for one unredeemed gift that I might claim for myself and not know its source. As with love, the rapture was always threatened by some small but fatal flaw. Only two days to go to Christmas and we still hadn't got our own tree.

We never approached any topic directly with our parents. We would either select a crabwise avenue or else open the subject with one parent and allow them to digest it before offering it to the other in a suitable form. Confronted head-on, they reacted like a rabbit caught in a car's headlights. Years later we understood that this was because their responses to everything were so different that it was necessary to find a meeting point before they could offer a united response. Our stark inquisitions were a challenge to their private relationship, the one we would never understand.

'They are selling Christmas trees off in Camden Street,' Betty said.

'That's because they're afraid they won't sell them at all,' Mercy suggested in an offhand way, though you could see the front of her dress twitching over her heart. 'Nearly everyone has one already.'

'When are we getting ours?' I unwisely burst out.

Mother stood up and began clearing away the plates, although we were still toying with our macaroni cheese. Father held on to his plate and slowly finished eating the wormy-looking pile. He glanced out the window, where the early afternoon had already flung up steel grey shutters over the sky and then, as if making a comment on the weather, he mildly observed, 'There will be no Christmas tree.'

There was a brief, somersaulting pause and then Betty and Mercy began to laugh. Father often made jokes and he kept a very serious face when he did. I had not yet got the hang of humour. I started to cry. Mother raced in to rescue me and father slapped both hands down on the table. 'There will be no Christmas tree! No turkey, no presents, no nonsense!' He said this angrily but immediately he looked sorry and added in a gentler voice, 'We are in a bad way. We owe money. We must all pull together. It is only one another day in the year.'

We all sat perfectly still at the table until at last father got up and went out. '*We* don't owe money,' Betty said mutinously.

'He has to sell the car.' Mother sounded shaken. 'He's going to have to make do with a bicycle.' She didn't mention any privations that might have affected herself. Women didn't. She did not tell us – and it was many years before we found out – that he had lost his job six months previously and they had been trying to live in a normal way in the hope that something else would turn up, and nothing had, except bills. All she said was that there was a tin of pineapple in the press and she would make a pineapple cake for tea.

Mercy, at eight, was an elfin little girl with white-blonde hair that made her look unnaturally pale, but now she seemed completely drained of colour.

'They have cancelled Christmas,' she said when we were alone.

'They can't cancel Christmas,' Betty said. 'It's not up to them. Christmas happens anyway. Santa comes anyway.'

'But Santa only comes if you have a tree in your window.' My thin voice rose in dawning horror. 'That's how he knows which houses to visit.'

'We'd better go and say a prayer,' Betty said. 'We'll go to the church and light a candle.'

The senior saints with their long robes and long faces seemed to offer no hope. They were greedy for suffering and would tell us, if they could (as grown-ups tended to), that sacrifice was an opportunity to add jewels to our crown in heaven. Instead, we knelt in front of the crib. Surely children everywhere wanted the same things.

On the way home it was so dark the earth seemed to have gone out. Only the bright arrowheads of Christmas trees lit the world. Despairingly, we counted the trees. Everyone had one. Even our own prim street was ablaze with colour. Even the old Misses Parker had one. I had streaked ahead of the older girls and was reaching for their knocker before they had time to stop me. 'What are you doing?' they gasped. But the Misses Parker, who were Quakers and were famously charitable, had already opened their door. I told them our father could not afford a Christmas tree and that Santa would not come to our house if he did not see the fairy lights. At once they agreed that we should have their tree and even carried it down the road with its decorations tinkling and light flexes trailing. Mother was confused, but she accepted the tree with thanks and left it propped up in the hall. We spent the afternoon stroking the cold silver strands of tinsel which the Misses Parker had threaded through its branches and which felt like mermaids' hair.

A couple of hours later father was to be seen striding down the street, the stiffly bedecked tree clasped in his arms like a war missile. We ran behind him picking up small ornaments as they clopped off on to the frosty pavement, and trying furtively to get around him to retrieve those decorations that belonged to us. The Misses Parker eyed him with hateful sympathy as he told them we had no need of charity.

Mercy and I looked at Betty. She was the eldest so she had to do something and she had to do it before that first, fatal leaching of faith, after which Christmas would never seem the same again.

'It's all right,' she said. 'We don't need the grown-ups. We'll get our own Christmas tree.'

'Where, Betty?' 'When?' 'How?'

'I'll think of something,' she said.

She went out alone the following day. She was gone a long time. We waited for her, watching behind the drawing-room window. When she came home she looked small and cold. 'Have you got it?' we pestered her, although we could see nothing. She nodded slowly. 'Where is it?' She took her hand out of her pocket and showed a small, greenish pine cone.

'I found this,' she said. 'We'll plant this in the garden. We'll grow our own tree.'

'But that will take ages,' I complained.

'Then we'd better do it right away,' she said firmly.

There was one apple tree in the garden, a thin forsythia, and in spring a clump of wallflowers. There was a forgotten region which had become a compost heap of leaves and trimmings and pruned branches. Betty instructed us to clear away the rubbish so that we could dig a hole for the Christmas tree. Gingerly we dipped in our mittened hands and began to lift the bits of half-burnt refuse and piles of dead leaves and old potted plants, layered up over some more substantial hulk. Whatever this was, you could tell that its personality remained intact, like a man preserved in a bog for a thousand years. Desiccated fingers pointed up at the sky. We pulled away more rubbish to discover a beautiful shape, like the skeleton of a leaf.

It looked like some old fish that had been nibbled dry so that only its bare bones poked out and its scaly spine. It looked like the rusted hulk of a ship that had sunk many years ago and its barnacled frame endured. It did not look the least bit like – but definitely was – a Christmas tree. Triumphantly, we hauled it out. Some of its branches were broken, but it had been a good tree once, before it was cast out after festive service in some better year. And it was ours. We had found it.

'It's a bit brown,' Mercy said, reluctant to criticise.

'We'll make it green,' Betty said.

Betty had learnt a thing in school, how to make crêpe paper leaves for bare branches. We had sixpence between us and bought two packets of dark green paper. We cut it into long strips and wound them round the branches, sellotaping the ends, until the entire frame was bandaged in green. Then Mercy, who was the artistic one, made fringed strips and taped these along branches to look like needles. Bumping it forward in little steps we managed to get the tree into the house and leaned it inside the window. It looked magnificent.

There was an anxious moment when father came home and discovered our curious mummified horticultural corpse. He was frowning. He seemed to be thinking. When he spoke, his voice sounded strange, as if he was getting a cold.

'It's all right,' he said. He bent to stroke our hair in the cautious way that we had stroked the silver mermaids' hair on the Misses Parkers' tree. 'I think,' he said, 'it will all be all right.'

From then on, everything proceeded as normal. Two big boxes were brought down from the attic, one with lights and one with ornaments. Father plunged his arms into the entrails of frayed wiring and the fairy lights clinked in an insouciant way like china tea cups as he tried to unsnarl them. Then for hours he was up on a ladder, locked into some intimate contest, cajoling and cursing, beseeching and loathing, muttering strange, enticing sulphurous words so that mother had to drag us away, while the lights twittered and wavered and at last responded to his male authority. Tinsel ornaments simmered with magical depths. Carnival colours bumped off every sober surface in the room, and in the window the lights radiantly glowed.

I couldn't sleep that night and at dawn I crept out on to the landing to see if Santa had come. I was worried about the spirit of the tree. It might have grown faint in its old parcelled trunk. In the back of my mind too I had begun to wonder if any part of Christmas could survive now that our parents had no money, if in some way every single thing that came to us must not begin and end with them. Santa's parcels were there. I couldn't resist it and began tearing mine open right away, crying out with pleasure as the familiar objects came into view.

From his bedroom came father's voice, a weary growl: 'Get back to bed or I'll take the lot away from you.'

After a transfixed and tremulous pause, Betty called defiantly back, 'You can't! They are not your property!'

There was even a turkey. Father had won it in a raffle. It was a giant, dinosaur-like creature, its languidly naked form looking like something that ought to be clothed. While we composed a jigsaw puzzle at the base of our tree, we could hear mother's anguished voice from the kitchen: 'Get into the oven, you big bastard!'

My sisters have related this incident to their children and they think it is a sad story but for the three of us it remains our best Christmas ever. It was the year we made Christmas happen. Perhaps it would have happened anyway. Our grandparents and Auntie Jo came as usual, the monstrous bird was finally cooked and consumed and everyone fell asleep. As usual, last thing, I checked the tree, walking around its mysteriously rustling branches, examining its paper folds to see if anything had been left behind. Nestling in the elbow of a branch was a tiny package wrapped in red and tied with gold tinsel thread. I unlooped it and slowly peeled back the paper. Inside was a little enamel box with a black cat painted on its front, framed in blue flowers. I opened the box and it was filled with doll-sized fruit pastilles coated in sugar. As I slipped it into my pocket my heart dipped in that perfect curve that lovers experience when they know, against all odds, the rewards of reckless faith.

FRANK O'CONNOR

The *Adventuress*

My brother and sisters didn't really like Brenda at all but I did. She was a couple of years older than I was and I was devoted to her. She had a long, grave, bony face and a power of concealing her real feelings about everything, even about me. I knew she liked me but she wasn't exactly what you'd call demonstrative about it. In fact there were times you might even say she was vindictive.

That was part of her toughness. She was tough to the point of foolhardiness. She would do anything a boy would do and a lot of things that few boys would do. It was never safe to dare her to anything. Someone had only to say 'Brenda, you wouldn't go up and knock at that door' and if the fancy took her Brenda would do it and when the door was opened concoct some preposterous yarn about being up from the country for the day and having lost her way which sometimes even took in the people she called on. When someone once asked if she could ride a bicycle she replied that she could and almost proved her case by falling under a milk-van. She did the same thing with horses and when at last she managed to break her collar-bone she took it with the stoicism of a Red

Indian. She would chance her arm at anything and as a result she became not only daring but skilful. She developed into a really stylish horsewoman.

Of course to the others she was just a liar, a chancer and a notice-box and in return she proved a devil to them. But to me who was always prepared to concede how wonderful she was, she was the soul of generosity.

'Go on,' she would say sharply, handing me a bag of sweets or a fistful of coppers. 'Take the blooming lot, I don't want them.' I suspect now that all she really wanted was admiration, for she would give the shift off her back to anyone she liked. Like all natural aristocrats she found the rest of the world so far beneath her own standards that all were equal in her eyes and she associated with the most horrid children whose allegiance she bought with sweets or cigarettes – pinched off my brother Colum most of the time.

She got away with a lot because she was my father's favourite and knew it. The old man was tall, gaunt and temperamental. He might pass you for weeks without noticing your existence except when you happened to be doing something wrong. We were all in a conspiracy against him – even Mother, who rationalised it on the plea that we mustn't worry poor Dad. When eventually there were things to worry about (like Colum taking to the bottle or Brenda heaving herself at the commercial traveller's head) the suspicion of all the things we were concealing from him in order not to worry him, finally nearly drove the old man to an early grave.

The rest of us went in fear and trembling of him, but Brenda could cheek him to his face and get away with it and to give her her due she never allowed any of us to criticise him in front of her. Oedipus complex or something I suppose that was.

One year she took it into her head that we should give him a Christmas box as we gave Mother one.

'Why would we give him a Christmas box?' asked Colum suspiciously. 'He never does anything for us.'

'Well,' said Brenda, 'how can we expect him to be any different when we make distinctions between Mother and him? Anyway, only for him we wouldn't be here at all.'

'I don't see that that's any good reason for giving him a Christmas box,' said Colum who was at the age when he was rather inclined to look on it as a grievance. 'What would you give him?'

'We could give him a fountain pen,' said Brenda who had it all pat. 'The one he had he lost three years ago.'

'We could,' said Colum ironically. 'Or a new car.'

'You needn't be so blooming mean,' snapped Brenda. 'Rooney's have grand pens for ten a tanner. What is it, only two bob a man?'

There was some friction between Brenda and Maeve as to which of them should be Treasurer and Colum supported Maeve only because he knew she was a fanciful sort of girl who would get out a Grand National Appeal in imitation print and then bother her head no further about it; but Brenda realised that this was sabotage and made short work of it. The idea was hers and she was going to be President, Treasurer and Secretary – and God help anyone that got in the way.

Two bob a man was reasonable enough, even allowing for another present for Mother. Coming on to Christmas we all got anything up to ten bob a man from relatives up from the country for the Christmas shopping and Brenda watched us with an eye like a hawk so that before Christmas Eve came at all she had collected the subscriptions. I was allowed to go into town with her to make the purchase and seeing that I was her faithful vassal she blew three and six of her own money on an air-gun for me. That was the sort Brenda was.

We went into Rooney's which was a combined book and stationery shop and I was amazed at her self-possession.

'I want to have a look at a few fountain pens,' she said to a gawky-looking assistant called Coakley who lived up our road. He gaped at us across the counter. I could see he liked Brenda.

'Certainly, Miss,' he said and I nearly burst with reflected glory to hear her called 'Miss'. She took it calmly enough as though she had never been called anything else. 'What sort of pen would you like?'

'Show us a few,' she said with a queenly toss of the head.

'If you want something really first-class,' said Coakley, producing a couple of trays of pens from the glass-case, 'there's the best on the market. Of course, we have the cheaper ones as well but they're not the same at all.'

'How much is this one?' asked Brenda, looking at the one he had pointed out to us.

'Thirty bob,' said Coakley. 'That's a Walker. 'Tis a lot of money of course but 'tis worth it.'

'They all look much alike to me,' said Brenda, taking up one of the cheaper ones.

'Aha!' said Coakley with a guffaw. 'They're only got up like that to take in the mugs.'

Then he threw himself across the counter, took a fountain pen from his own breast pocket and removed the cap. 'See that pen?' he said. 'Guess how long I have that!'

'I couldn't,' said Brenda.

'Fifteen years!' said Coakley. 'Fifteen blooming years. I had it through the war, in gaol and everything. I did every blessed thing to that pen only stop a bullet with it. That's a Walker for you! There isn't another pen in the market you could say the same about.' He looked at it fondly, screwed back the cap and returned it to his pocket. You could see he was very fond of that pen.

'Give it to us for a quid!' said Brenda.

'A quid?' he exclaimed, taken aback by her coolness. 'You might as well ask me to give it to you for a present.'

'Don't be so blooming mean,' said Brenda sharply. 'What's ten bob one way or another to ye?'

'Tell me,' said Coakley, raising his hand to his mouth and speaking in a husky whisper. 'Do you know Mr Rooney?'

'No,' said Brenda. 'Why?'

'You ought to go and ask him that,' guffawed Coakley behind his hand. 'Cripes!' he exploded. 'I'd love to see his face.'

'Anyway,' said Brenda, seeing that this line was a complete washout, 'you can split the difference. I'd give you thirty bob but I'm after blowing three and six on an air-gun for the kid. I'll give you twenty-five bob.'

'And will you give me two pound ten a week after I'm sacked?' asked Coakley indignantly.

Even then I thought Brenda would take the dearer pen even if it meant throwing in my air-gun to make up the price. I could see how it hurt her pride to offer my father anything that wasn't of the very best.

'All right so,' she said, seeing no other way out. 'I'll take the one for ten and a tanner. It looks good enough anyway.'

'Ah, 'tis all right,' said Coakley, relenting and trying to put things in the best light. 'As a matter of fact, 'tis quite a decent little pen at the price. We're selling dozens of them.'

But Brenda wasn't consoled at all. The very way he said 'a decent little pen' in that patronising tone reduced it to mediocrity and pettiness in her eyes while the fact that others beside herself were buying it put the finishing touch to it. She stood on the wet pavement when we emerged with a brooding look in her eyes.

'I was a fool to go near Coakley,' she said at last.

'Why, Brenda?' I asked.

'He never took his eyes off us the whole time. Only for that I'd have fecked one of the decent pens.'

'But you wouldn't do that, Brenda?' I said aghast.

'Why wouldn't I?' she retorted roughly. 'Haven't they plenty of them? If I had the thirty bob I'd have bought it,' she added. 'But that gang is so mean they wouldn't even thank me for it. They think I'm going to offer Daddy a cheap old pen as if that was all we thought of him.'

'What are you going to do?' I asked.

'I'll do something,' she replied darkly.

That was one of the joys of being with Brenda. When I came to an obstacle I howled till someone showed me how to get round it, but Brenda saw three separate ways round it before she came to it at all. Coakley had given us a nice box for the pen. The price was pencilled on the box and when we got home Brenda rubbed it out and replaced it with a neat '30s'. She smiled at my look of awe.

'But won't he know, Brenda?' I asked.

'How would he know?' replied Brenda with a shrug. 'They all look exactly alike.'

That was the sort of thing which made life with her a continuous excitement. She didn't give the matter another thought, but I kept looking forward to Christmas morning, half in dread my father would find her out, half in expectation that Brenda would get away with it again.

In our house we didn't go in much for Christmas trees. At breakfast on Christmas morning Maeve gave mother a brooch and Brenda gave Daddy the little box containing the pen.

'Hallo!' he said in surprise. 'What's this?' Then he opened it and saw.

'Oh, that's very nice,' he said with real enthusiasm. 'That's the very thing I was wanting this long time. Which of ye thought of that?'

'Brenda did,' I said promptly, seeing that the others would be cut in pieces before they gave her the credit.

'That was very nice and thoughtful of you, Brenda,' said my

father, making, for him, a remarkably gracious speech. 'Very nice and thoughtful and I'm sure I'm grateful to ye all. How much did you pay for it?'

(That was more like Daddy!)

'I think the price is on the box,' said Brenda nonchalantly.

'Thirty bob!' said my father, impressed in spite of himself and I looked at the faces of Colum, Maeve and Brigid and saw that they were impressed too, in a different way. They were wondering what tricks Brenda was up to now. 'Where did you get it?' he went on.

'Rooney's,' replied Brenda.

'Rooney's?' repeated my father suspiciously as he unscrewed the cap and examined the nib. 'Ah, they saw you coming! Sure, Rooney's have Walker pens for thirty bob!'

'I know,' said Brenda hastily. 'We looked at them too but we didn't think much of them. The assistant didn't think much of them either. Isn't that right, Michael?'

'That's right,' I said loyally. 'Them were the best.'

'*They* were the best, dear,' said Mother.

'Ah,' said my father, growing more suspicious than ever. 'That assistant was only taking you out for a walk. Which of them was it? Coakley?'

'No,' said Brenda quickly before I could reply. 'A fellow I never saw there before.'

'Hah!' said my father darkly. 'I'd be surprised if Coakley did a thing like that. That's terrible blackguarding,' he added hotly to Mother. 'Willie Rooney trying to get rid of his trash on people that don't know better. I have a good mind to go in and tell him so. Jerry Taylor in the yard has a Walker pen that he bought ages ago and 'tis still good for a lifetime.'

'Ah, why would you worry yourself about it?' said Mother comfortably. She probably suspected that there was mischief behind, and in her usual way wanted to keep it from Father.

'Oh,' said my father querulously, 'I'd like to show Willie Rooney he can't treat me like that. I'll tell you what you'll do, Brenda,' he said, putting the pen back in the box and returning it to her. 'Put that away carefully till Thursday and then take it back to Rooney's. Have nothing to say to any of the other assistants but go straight to Coakley and tell him I sent you. Say you want a Walker in exchange for that and no palaver about it. He'll see you're not codded again.'

I will say for Brenda that her face never changed. She had a wonderful way of concealing her emotions. But the fury among the family afterwards was something terrible.

'Ah,' said Maeve indignantly, 'you're always the same, out for nothing only swank and grandeur.'

'I wouldn't mind the swank and grandeur only for the lies,' said Colum. 'One of these days you'll be getting yourself into serious trouble. I suppose you didn't know you could be had up for that. Changing the prices on boxes is the same thing as forgery. You could get the gaol for that.'

'All right,' said Brenda contemptuously. 'Let them give me the gaol. Now, I want to know what I'm to do to make up the extra quid.'

'Make it up yourself,' snapped Maeve. ''Twas your notion and you can pay for it.'

'I can't,' said Brenda with a shrug. 'I haven't it.'

'Then you can go and find it,' said Colum.

'I'll find it all right,' said Brenda, her eyes beginning to flash. 'Either ye give me the extra four bob a man or I'll go in and tell my old fellow that 'twas ye persuaded me to change the price.'

'Go on, you dirty cheat!' said Maeve.

'Oh, leave her do it,' said Colum. 'Leave her do it and see will he believe her.'

'Maybe you think I wouldn't?' asked Brenda with cold ferocity.

Colum had gone too far and he knew it. It was always in the highest degree unsafe to challenge Brenda to do anything, because there was nothing you could positively say Brenda would not do if the fancy took her, and if the fancy did take her there was nothing you could positively say my father wouldn't be prepared to believe. I knew she was doing wrong but still I couldn't help admiring her. She looked grand standing there with the light of battle in her eyes.

'Come on!' she snapped. 'Four bob I want and I'm jolly well going to get it. It's no use pretending ye haven't got it because I know ye have.'

There was a moment's pause. I could see they were afraid.

'Give it to her,' said Colum contemptuously. 'And don't talk to her again, any of ye. She's beneath ye.'

He took out some money, threw two two-shilling pieces on the table and walked out. After a moment Maeve and Bridget did the same in silence. Then I put my hand in my pocket and took out what money I had. It wasn't much.

'Are you going to walk out on me too?' Brenda asked with a mocking smile.

'You know I wouldn't do that,' I said in confusion.

'That's all right so,' she said with a shrug. 'Keep your old money. I had it all the time and I'd have paid it too if only that gang had the decency to stick by me when I was caught.' Her smile grew bitterer and for a second or two I thought she might cry. I had never seen her cry. 'The trouble about our family, Michael,' she went on, 'is that they all have small minds. You're the only one that hasn't. But you're only a baby, and I suppose you'll grow up just like the rest.'

I thought it was very cruel of her to say that and I after standing up for her and all. But Brenda was like that.

L.A.G. STRONG

Christmas Eve

Big Kate went out into the road, and looked along it to the bend.

'Do ye see him?' screamed Little Kate, from the cottage.

'I do not.'

Big Kate's voice was deep, more like a man's. She was as strong as a man, and stood five feet eleven. Screwing up her eyes, she peered down the road, as if concentration could call into sight the figure of the postman. But the road was empty.

Suddenly, as if doing its best to help her, the setting sun came clear of a cloud, and splashed a last wintry gleam upon bog, foothills, and mountain. The misty, higher slopes of the bog leaped up and came near, pushing the foothills back. The mountain flushed dull rose. For a few seconds his majestic bulk was reared in challenge above the swimming dusk. Then the gleam blurred and left him; visibly he aged and huddled into a sullen shapelessness. A chill came from the little coppice across the road, wet, feral, mingling with the heath of the bogland.

Big Kate shivered. From habit, she shaded her eyes with her hand. The road was still empty.

A shuffling footstep sounded, and Little Kate came out to join her.

'Bad cess to him,' she pronounced. 'He was never late this way before.'

'He was, then.' Big Kate was annoyed. She knew Little Kate had come out from want of trust, to see for herself. 'Many's the time.'

'Not o' Christmas Eve.'

'Aye, o' Christmas Eve. Do ye forget, woman, the calls he has to make between this and the post office –'

'I do not, then.' Little Kate's teeth began to click, a sure sign that she was angry. 'I know them as well as yourself. Seventeen private houses, the presbytery, and Mooney's the grocer's.'

'And every one o' them making him stay and drink a sup to bless the season and warm him on the road. Faith, it'll be a wonder if he's here at all.'

'There's only three places after this. And Joe Cassidy doesn't have e'er a letter, only his pension.' She cackled. 'There's no one'd go sendin' Christmas cards to the likes o' him.'

Big Kate shook herself.

'Come in out o' this,' she said gruffly. 'We're doin' no good gawkin' here in the road.'

Little Kate turned after her, reluctantly.

'Ta' care he wouldn't ride past and miss us.'

'Ride past, how are ye! It'll take him all his time to compass the twist in the road.'

After a moment's hesitation, Little Kate followed into Big Kate's side of the cottage. The two old women had the same Christian name and the commonest surname in the country – there were eleven families of Coffey's in the one postal district.

Local nicknames distinguished them. Big and Little Kate occupied each one half of a lonely cottage on a winding road that, after seven miles of tormented wandering over bog and foothills, came to a dead end at the foot of a long hill, amongst three or four scattered cottages a mile beyond.

The two Kates lived in a basic enmity, varied by truces. Truces there had to be, if they were to survive at all, but, except on special occasions, each kept fiercely to her own side of the cottage. Christmas Eve was judged to be a special occasion: and anxiety for the postman encouraged them to inaugurate it earlier than usual.

Once inside, Little Kate didn't know what to do. Big Kate went to her fire, and made a clatter with the two big iron pots that showed dully in the gloom. Little Kate stood, nervously picking at her dress.

'Ta' care,' she volunteered at last, 'he wouldn't have gone by an hour ago, and we not lookin' for him.'

'Talk sense, woman. Doesn't he always call?'

'It could be' – Little Kate's tongue flicked slyly at the corner of her mouth – 'there was no letters for us.'

For you, she meant. Little Kate had no relations: or, if she had, they ignored her.

Big Kate banged the pots.

'Doesn't me nephew always send me a parcel, and a letter with a card in it?'

'It could be,' said Little Kate, even more slyly, 'he forgot.'

'It could be yourself is jealous, the way you always are and always will be! It could be you grudge me me nephew and me parcels, though the good God knows why, and you always getting your share, little though ye deserve it. Answer me that, now!' She looked round, huge, redfaced, formidable. 'Do I not always give ye your share? Do I not, now?'

Little Kate backed away, babbling. 'Musha, what ails ye, Kate Coffey, what ails ye at all! Who's sayin' a word to ye!'

'Hold your whisht, so, and don't be sowin' doubt in a person's mind.'

Little Kate, now near the door, fell into an aggrieved muttering. It was hard to quarrel with her. She insinuated her side of the question, with oblique hints and sniffs, so that she was never in a position from which she could not speedily retreat. To argue with her was like sweeping water away with a broom. She seeped back, pertinaciously. Big Kate made a furious clatter at her pots. She knew it all too well.

Sure enough, Little Kate came slowly back from the door, rubbing a hand on her dress.

'Indeed it'd be the hard thing, Kate Coffey, you not to be getting your parcel on Christmas Eve. I'd be mortal sorry for ye. Mortal sorry, I'd be.'

'Ye'd have cause. There'd be no pickings for yourself.'

'It's not that I was thinkin' of –'

'Yerrah, who cares what ye're thinkin' of! Go back to your place, or keep quiet.'

'That's no friendly way to be talkin' to a person, o' Christmas Eve.'

'Who wants to be talkin'?'

Evidently, Little Kate did. She stood plucking at her dress and clicking her teeth. The series of small fidgeting noises maddened Big Kate. Just as she was on the point of exploding, Little Kate spoke.

'Is there anything I can do to be helpin' ye?'

'Yis. Go out and keep watch.'

Little Kate went, grumbling. In the doorway, she turned round.

'It's bitter cold,' she complained. Then, as Big Kate pretended not to hear, she pulled her shawl round her shoulders, and went out. Once clear, she gave a malevolent chuckle, and scuttled into her own doorway. Leaving it open, she went to the fire, and sat huddled there, stretching her hands to the warmth, chuckling and muttering to herself. She could hear Big Kate moving about, at the other side of the wall, and was ready to run to the door, should she hear her coming. Though why should she do Kate's orders? Or any person's orders? It was Kate's parcel the postman would be bringing. Let her watch for it, so.

She fell into a long meditation, brooding on her wrongs: a lifetime of them. An owl hooted in the coppice. Little Kate shivered and crossed herself. Her meditations took a deeper note of self-pity. It was a terrible thing to be alone in the world, condemned to be neighbour to a graceless woman, an uncouth, hard woman the like of Big Kate. Then, warned by her instinct, she was on her feet and outside the door, peering, before Big Kate could catch her.

'Do ye see him?'

Big Kate was not deceived. She knew the vigil had not been kept.

'I do not. The two eyes are achin' in me head. It's gettin' too dark to see, anyways.'

She was right. All distances were confused now. The road was a livid grey ribbon, reared up on end in the darkness. Big Kate looked, her head forward, like a bull wondering whether to charge.

'Something's happened him,' she decided. 'We'd best go and look.'

Before Little Kate could object, she had started off at such a pace that she was all but lost from sight, and Little Kate had to trot after her.

'A nice thing,' she complained, 'to be leaving our houses open, the way any robber –'

Then she stubbed her toe on a stone, and was jerked into silence.

The road ran straight for nearly a quarter of a mile, till it came to a rocky mound. Turning sharply, it curved between a tangle of gorse and brambles to a second sharp turn, after which it climbed a short hill.

When she reached the first curve, Big Kate called out.

'Peadar! Peadar! Where are ye?'

'He's no place,' panted Little Kate angrily. 'He's in one person's house or another, swillin' an' guzzlin' an' neglectin' his work.'

'Peadar!' Big Kate strode on. Little Kate once more lost sight of her, and shambled forward in terror.

'Kate! Kate! don't leave me!'

There was no answer to this, but another cry of 'Peadar,' from yards ahead. Little Kate cursed, the spittle running down her chin. She could see nothing in the dark. On the straight road, it was fairly easy; but here, with the mounds and the rocks and the thickets –

A kind of dim mooing reached her ears. Big Kate again called 'Peadar,' and a vague voice replied. Little Kate, scrambling blindly, tripped, saved herself, recognised the shape of a boulder, rounded it, and all but ran into Big Kate, who was bending forward, and peering into the bushes.

'Peadar! Is it yourself?'

'Who else would I be?' retorted a voice from the gloom.

'Where are yez at all?'

'Faix, I don't rightly know. By the feel of it, I'm in the brambles.'

Big Kate stepped towards the voice, and banged into something. Little Kate heard the indrawn hiss of her breath. She'd hurted herself! Serve her glad!

'Is that me old bike ye're fallin' over?' inquired the postman's voice.

'It is.'

'Ye'd want to be wary of me old bike. It's a great warrant to take the skin off o' ye. There's more sharp corners to me old bloody bike than the pinnacles in Saint Patrick's Cathedral. Lacerated, it has me, many's the day.'

Judging by the sounds, Big Kate had avoided the bike, and reached the brambles.

'Where are ye at all, man?'

'Strike a match,' said the voice.

'Do ye think I carry matches? Strike one yourself.'

Fumbling sounds followed, and a sigh.

'Wisha, the way I am, I can't come at meself. Use the light on the bike. It works from the back wheel, ye know.'

'Have decency, man. How would I be cockin' me leg over that yoke? And what way would I ride it, to light ye, and you where you are?'

'It's a terrible thing,' the postman said sadly, 'to be talkin' to a person who has no imagination. Hol' up the bike with the one hand, and turn the pedals with the other.'

'Here,' interposed Little Kate, 'I'll help ye.'

The idea that Big Kate was failing to cope with the situation had restored her good humour. Together the two women groped for the fallen bicycle. Their eyes were getting used to the darkness, but even so they could not see the postman. There was a difficulty about turning the pedals, because that meant lifting the back wheel clear of the ground, and their first efforts merely lit up the ground in front of their feet. Not till Big Kate lifted the bike clear of the ground, and Little Kate, bending forward, jerkily turned the pedals – for all the world as if she was mangling, as she afterwards said – were they able to direct a weak unsteady beam on the postman.

'Musha, man!'

He was sitting up, his legs wide apart, in the midst of a

blackberry bush. The brambles were twined around him: his forehead and hands were all over blood from scratches. His postbag had fallen off, and lay open, with a few letters and parcels scattered around.

'I came off,' he announced superfluously, 'at the twist in the road.'

Little Kate, bent double and turning the handle, uttered an indignant croak.

'Where's our letters! where's our letters, ye drunken blaggard ye!'

'Help yerself,' the postman said, with a gesture that almost overbalanced him.

Forgetting her duty, Little Kate made a dart towards the bag – and the darkness closed over them like black water.

'Wait,' Big Kate said gruffly. 'I have the way of it now.'

Somehow, she propped up the bike with one hand, and vigorously turned the pedals with the other. A much brighter light sprang out: but Little Kate was too intent upon the letters to resent it. She had to move aside, so that her shadow was off the bag.

'Is my parcel in it?'

Big Kate's words came stertorously. It was hard work, holding up the bike and turning the pedals.

'Wait now – O'Kelly – Brannigan – James Coffey, bad cess to him – Kate Coffey! it is! Safe and sound!'

'There now,' the postman said happily, from the far edge of the light. 'What did I tell ye?'

'Is there anything more?'

Little Kate was ferreting about.

'Put them back, when ye're done,' the postman enjoined her.

'A letter. A Christmas card. And – by the holies – one for me! A card for me!'

'How do you know it's for you?'

'How do I know! when it's from Mrs McCann, that was lodging above at Roskelly! Her as I cleaned for in the month o' September. How do I know it's for me!'

'Well,' Big Kate said, with grim good humour, 'if that's all that's in it, put the rest back, and close the bag, and give me a hand with this hero.'

Little Kate did as she was told.

'I can't close the bag. The strap's broke.'

'It's been broke this twelvemonth,' said the postman.

'Think shame!' Little Kate scolded him. Then, 'How will we see what we're doin', if the two of us raises him?'

'Take this, so.' Grumbling, Little Kate took it. 'Keep it steady. Now – can ye stand at all?'

'I can't say till I try,' the postman replied. 'Me left leg is trapped.'

'Show us a light, woman, can't ye?'

Little Kate, unequal to the job of holding the bike and turning the pedals, was sending weak and wobbly shafts all over the place.

'I'm doin' – the best – I can.'

'Hol' up!'

Big Kate grasped him under the arms, and pulled him to his feet. There was a tearing sound, a surprised hiccup, and he stood embracing her tightly.

'Leave go of me, ye big gomm.'

'And fall down, is it? Lead me out o' this, woman. Amn't I dependin' on ye?'

Somehow she got him out into the road.

'We'll bring him above to the cottage. Wheel the bike, you. Have ye his bag?'

'I have not.'

'Get it, so.'

As long as he kept upright, the postman could walk. He clung to Big Kate with what she felt to be an unnecessary fervour, but she steered him without difficulty to the cottage, Little Kate pushing the bicycle behind them, grumbling to herself with a small bubbling sound, like an indignant brook.

'Now let's have a look at ye, man.'

He was the worse for wear, bleeding from a dozen scratches, and with a six-inch tear in the left leg of his trousers, but he beamed complacently on the two women. Clicking her tongue, Big Kate dipped a rag in water and scrubbed the blood off him with a vigour that brought the first sound of protest from him.

'Will ye take a sup?' she invited him.

'And I with a cargo o' varied liquor would sink a barge. Don't ask me, for the love o' God, when I've me round to finish.'

'Talk sense, man. How will ye finish your round, and you the way ye are!'

'Bear me to the brow o' the hill,' he assured her, 'set me on me bike, give me a hoosh off, and th'ould bike'll carry me down the slope. Sure, the front wheel knows the road.'

'Ye'll be off again at the butt o' the hill.'

'What matter. They'll be waitin' on me.'

Together they led him up the road to the top of the long decline. They held the bike steady while he mounted. They gave him a shove.

'Hurroo!' shouted the postman: and in a moment all they could see was the light on the road in front of him. It wobbled wildly, then became steady, rushed away from them, and was lost. 'Hurroo!' came back faintly. Then the stillness flowed in, from all sides, with the cold wet breath of the night: and the two women turned back to their cottage.

Little Kate hobbled along, chattering. The Christmas card sent to her by the lady she had looked after in the summer had raised her spirits. She felt regal, warm, and gracious. There was not a spark of bitterness left in her; and when Big Kate bade her come in, and began to open the parcel, she was ready to receive her share without resentment, as one from a higher sphere, conferring a favour by accepting her neighbour's gift.

LEO CULLEN

Clouds over Suez

Aunt, his father, Barry who worked for his father, and himself. They were all cut off from the midnight Mass by a high brown partition. On his side there were only four pews and the people packed into them. He could hear chanting from the other side and he supposed this was the way churches were in monasteries.

Aunt rose and promptly fell to her knees again in the certainty that without her the congregation would not have known whether to sit, stand or kneel. Barry slept in a heap on the edge of a pew. He himself sat attentively, his ears peeled for the alleluia. 'The Christmas alleluia will inspire you,' Aunt had forewarned him. He denounced Barry, as would Aunt, but it was his kneeling father who caused him greatest concern.

His father knelt all the time. As he always did. On the Sundays, the weekdays, the confraternity Monday mornings on which he accompanied him to their local church. He did rise for hymns but then crumbled again on his knees, his face covered behind outstretched hands, lost to the world. He knew he had a lot to pray about; many tragedies had befallen him. He knew his focus was Jesus on the Cross. Even tonight, as the incense wafted with the rise and fall of the psalms into their part of the church – into the part, he decided, where the monks allowed ordinary people – even on this birthday night in Bethlehem, his father's vision was the outstretched figure on the Cross. He sensed that as his father's tragedies grew darker so too would the intensity of his devotion grow more severe.

His own trouble was that he could not create in himself the same devotion. Oh, he could pray for a minute or two. He could tell Jesus about his good daddy. He could ask Jesus to look after him. And look after his mama in heaven. And Aunt, well Aunt didn't need prayers. Oh, he could pray, deeply too, rightly or wrongly, for those things he wanted. Or at least for some of them. Of course he could not ask God if he might stop his father from teaching him to ride the pony. Learning to ride the pony was the most dreadful cross on his horizon. But he knew that God's designs and his father's were somehow the same. There were other things he wanted and could ask for. The hosanna rumbled over him. 'Dear God, please please, I want a rifle from Santa for Christmas.'

No, he could never pray like his father. He could not pray like him or ride a horse like him. He could not, when Communion time would arrive, walk round that partition and up to the marble altar rails with him. And find out what was going on. After a time, long before the offertory hymn and then the pause, the tinkle of bells, the awakening of communicants as they shuffled into the inner sanctum, like Barry, he was numbed into slumber.

The last rousing notes, pumped from the organ, came to rest among the high rafters. The last of the congregation were leaving the church. But he waited. He waited for his father and for Aunt; both of them were still praying. He wondered if the alleluia had been sung. He hadn't heard it. He felt bad about himself and wondered could he tell Aunt, if she asked him about it, that he had. She was not easily fooled. Then, seeing his father's posture, isolated at his bench from the rest of the world, he wondered what he could be feeling so bad about. A fleeting image of his father passed through his mind as he pondered: a whip in his hand, standing alongside the jump, coaxing the pony over it, while he himself clung terrified to its back. 'Dig in your heels, blast you!' the raucous roar. Now he wanted to put his arms round his slumped father. He was the best person in the world.

It was just as he smelled the extinguished candles. He heard a titter of laughter from the other side of the partition.

He walked from the church and into a night transformed by magic. 'Happy Christmas' – the greetings warmed the air. 'Happy Christmas, Lally,' someone called to him. The line of cars drove down the monastery drive, quickening once they turned into the road to town. The stars shone brighter now, stiller and deeper in space than ever, and below them the fields had become strangely shadowed.

'Great young lad for your age,' Barry said. 'I hope you said your prayers. And told that man above to keep an eye on Santy, whatever you want off him.'

He hoped Barry might ask him what he wanted. 'Oh, a rifle,' he would have said. 'Oh, the black rifle with the brown stock and the air sights, the one in Aunt's American catalogue.' Then his father and Aunt would be sure to remember; even if his recent suspicions regarding Santa held substance he would be safe. But Barry was already cocooned within a corner at the back of the car. His mind was already deaf to Aunt's rebuttal: 'Silly Paddy Barry, you don't ask Jesus for things like that.'

He woke. His father had stopped the car in the middle of the country and was pointing up through the windscreen and into the heavens. 'There he goes,' he said, 'between the stars. The reindeers, the sleigh: listen.'

'Where is he?' He looked through the windscreen; there was such a tremor in his father's voice.

'He drove over us, did you not hear?'

'Oh yes.' He heard distant music. He saw a light, it slid between stars, it was there an instant and then dropped out of the sky. 'But he's gone.'

'He's gone on his rounds.' His father turned to him, bestowed on him the most childlike smile he had ever seen.

'We better get quickly to bed then,' Aunt said drily.

'He has a long old journey.' Barry woke up and fell asleep again.

He thought deeply. 'What did he look like, Dada?'

'I couldn't see, but I heard him laughing.'

The years of growing doubt, the rumours, that disturbing titter he thought he had heard from behind the partition at the end of Mass, all fell away in that instant. The uncertainty of Santa and yet the promise, the distant echo of Santa's laugh, the light that moved through the sky, these became real, enwrapped in the psalm of the choir still vibrating in his ears.

First he heard the dog bark. Then, opening his eyes to bright light, he heard shrill voices. He jumped out of the bed he shared with his father and ran to the window. There, on the street, were the cowboys. The sun glinted from the roofs. In its light, the cowboys stood comparing guns, a dog yelping about their heels. Was he dreaming? He was weak with the sight. He rubbed his breath from the window.

He puzzled over the night before. Had he been awake or asleep? There had been noise from the bar-room below his bedroom. The usual noise: someone dredging a song, over and over again, 'The

Wild Colonial Boy'. He imagined at one stage there was someone else in the bedroom. It would not have been his father. He would still have been in the bar cleaning the glasses after the drinkers. He imagined someone had moved across the room, there was a pinpoint glow of light. Like the cigarette glow every night when his father came to bed. Does Santa smoke cigarettes?

Suddenly he was in the present. He was awake. It was Christmas morning and he was standing at the window. In the silence of Santa's departure. His eyes darted across the expanse of empty bed, to its foot, to where a mound of parcels lay.

He threw aside a lightweight, fishnet stocking. It would be Ludo and Snakes and Ladders and some sweets, he received it every year. He tore at the parcel which, he could already see, was the wrong shape. He glimpsed something black and shiny through the wrapping paper. 'If it's not the rifle it must be a revolver.' It felt hard but did not have a revolver's shape. He pulled at it. It was the same as something of his father's, only smaller: a pair of binoculars.

It fell to the bed, tumbled onto the carpet. He did not pick it up. 'Oh Aunt,' he moaned, 'I asked for a rifle from Santy.' He had spent all last week looking at guns in the shop windows. In the light of day and under the streetlamps by night. Guns, revolvers, rifles; the rifle in the American catalogue he had pointed out to Aunt. In her *Saturday Evening Post*. 'We'll see,' she had said, 'we'll see.'

Then the door opened. His younger brother stood there, a holster on either hip, a gun in either hand. 'Oh look what I got from Santy.' The guns were so heavy, the barrels so long, he could hardly hold them straight. He had never seen such cool, blue barrels. 'You're too small, those guns are mine. Santy made a mistake. You're only five and I'm eight. Here, this is yours.' He picked up the binoculars and pushed them towards his younger brother. 'No.' His brother, armed to the teeth as he was, beginning already to feel outmanoeuvred, backed from the room. 'No, he gave them to me, they're mine.' He raised his voice; if Aunt was about, she would come to his assistance.

'Here, take this.' He decided on an approach. 'You're better on ponies than I am. I don't like ponies. You and Dada do. This is for you to watch the races with.'

It was a costly admission he was making. His father, he had often heard it said, was a fine horseman. He had ridden point-to-points, was now a prominent huntsman. His father tried to make horsemen of both his brother and him. He so much wanted to be like him but he stiffened in dread whenever he was seated on a pony, whilst his brother already loved them. And last summer . . . last summer his father had schooled him over low fences. 'I can't, I can't,' he had pleaded, with such conviction that his first reaction to every future task would be 'I can't,' and he had fallen off even before reaching the fences. Last summer had been a painful business. 'Here, take these binoculars and you can go instead of me to the races. Santy made a mistake.'

But then Aunt was at the door. 'Oh my, my,' she said. He could tell her tone indicated disappointment. He knew she had witnessed everything that had taken place. 'Tears, and on such a happy morning.'

Then her eyes lit up. 'Oh Lally, show me what you got. My my, a pair of binoculars. Your father will be so pleased.' Her eyes passed over his face, over his misery. 'I want you both to come downstairs and show him what Santa Claus, good good Santa Claus, brought you.'

He knew then, even before he said it, that what he was about to say next was untrue. That Aunt knew otherwise. 'It's a mistake,' he said sullenly. 'The guns are mine. The binoculars are for him.'

'Why is it a mistake?' she asked calmly.

'I didn't ask for binoculars.'

'Oh poor Santa. Fancy Santa making a mistake. But you must remember Santa is having a very difficult time this year. You do know about the Suez blockade don't you?' She had a way of making him look at her, of raising his eyes to hers.

'Yes.'

She had shown him a picture in the newspaper: a line of enormous ships whose prows reared above the banks of a narrow cutting of water while far below on the ground stood a camel. 'Only the camel budges,' she had said. 'And camels I'll have you know, Lal, are not noted budgers!'

'Yes.'

'Well, Santa wrote to me some time ago and explained how, because of the Suez blockade, he could only bring certain toys this year. Do your best, I wrote back to him. If you can't carry guns across the canal, I added, knowing guns would be a particular problem, my eldest nephew would be delighted with binoculars. Then when he goes racing with his father he can show them off.'

'Did you tell all that to Santa?' The younger boy was impressed.

'I did tell all that to Santa, and told him too what a spoilsport old Anthony Eden is.' She giggled.

Aunt scrutinised the listening children, looking pleased with herself. Lally squinted up at her: her story sounded plausible, he wanted to believe it, but was she making it up? She told so many stories: about all the parts of the world she had visited. Stories about herself, involved in all sorts of adventures. While she worked in Boston, before she had come home to look after himself, his brother and sisters. Aunt had been housekeeper to a houseful of young Catholic priests. They had sounded great fun: 'my big pets', she still called them. 'And I was their high priestess.' She had been receptive to ideas in America. 'Children must be treated just like adults.' America had taught her that. 'Truthfully, openly.

But remember too that imaginations must not be neglected.' Right now he didn't feel like having his imagination cultivated. 'Why did he get guns then and I didn't?' he asked.

Aunt was becoming annoyed because the older boy refused to be sidetracked by her elaborations. But she remained calm.

'Come, come,' she shivered. 'It's cold. Have you forgotten your posh new clothes. Christmas Day and still in your bare feet and pyjamas, what will your father say?

'Lally, you won't disappoint him, will you? You know he is taking you racing tomorrow. Oh, I can picture you two tomorrow. You and your father in the parade ring, as sharply turned out as two buttons.' She made a bouquet of her hand and blew it an admiring kiss, 'My two handsome men. It will be his first day back since your mama . . .' The hand she lightly laid on his shoulder weighed down on him heavily.

'Now let's see what nice clothes we will put on you today.' She took the smaller boy to his room and when she returned she again laid her hand on the bigger boy's shoulder. She stooped to his level and looked into his eyes. He could see in hers the reflection of his long face and of the binoculars where she had hung them over his neck. He held her eyes a moment, surprised at their pale blueness. As he looked they diminished in size so that his own reflection became lost. 'It does one good not to get what one wants,' she said. The black points of her eyes flickered away from him and focused somewhere away in the distance. He fought not to understand what she was saying, and at the same time wondered what it was her eyes were looking for.

The hotel was quieter than on any other morning of the year. This morning the only two guests on the register were the two permanent ones, middle-aged Miss Carroll and old Miss Dwyer.

As the two boys, now fully clad, walked down the stairs that led from the family quarters, Miss Dwyer was also making her way down the wider hotel stairs. All were headed towards the dining room, where Aunt and the boys' father were already seated over breakfast. They met beneath the arch in the dark, Christmas-decorated foyer.

'And look who Santa has come to,' Miss Dwyer wheezed. 'Look at his big guns and his lovely new clothes.' She admired the bigger boy. 'And what did you get?' The smaller boy was holding a pair of binoculars.

'Look through this, Auntie Dwyer,' the smaller boy said, 'and see.' As soon as Aunt had left them to dress the bigger boy had allowed his younger brother to look through the binoculars at the straggle of cowboys who had reappeared at the far end of the street. But only on condition he held the guns. The little boy had become infatuated with what he could see.

'Dear me.' Miss Dwyer looked through the wrong ends. The balloons she beheld on the foyer wall were distant cherries. 'Dear, dear me.'

'Santa made a mistake, Auntie Dwyer,' the bigger boy was sticking to his story. 'It was the Suez Canal. It was old Anthony Eden's fault.'

He would stick to his story too when they presented themselves to his father. He could already picture him. He and Aunt would be the only ones in the long dining room. They would be seated at its far end, in the weak sunlight, beneath the paper globe that decorated it each Christmas and which each Christmas seemed a little smaller than it had the year before. His father, this one morning, would have no mail to go through, would be the essence of gaiety. Eager to appraise whatever it was Santa had brought his children.

Aunt would be furious, but she would say nothing.

His brother pushed open the dining room door. 'Look, Dada,

look what I got' – he waved his binoculars – 'Santa made a 'istake.'

Suddenly he knew who would be the horseman in his family. He knew who would be the apple of his father's eye. He was appalled. But it was too late.

He knew too that this Christmas, on which he had celebrated his first midnight Mass, was the Christmas of his last real Santa Claus.

Bitterly, he wondered how he could have clung for so long to such a foolish notion. And yet . . . He hung back at the doorway, hands frozen to the revolver handles, a gunfighter in stasis. And yet . . . What other notion could there have been . . .? The notion of the remote figure of his father, parcel-laden at the foot of his bed . . .? His father . . .? Oh no. Ever since its first dawning in his mind that notion had seemed the most far-fetched of all.

As he struggled with his revelation of a world without Santa another revelation, somehow connected but even more far-fetched than the first, rushed at him. It blinded him as it too fought for consideration. It came between him and the sight of his younger brother, standing in the middle of the dining room, peering at him through the binoculars. 'Dada look, Lally got guns.'

It was something that had struck him once before. Once, when he had asked Aunt something about God and she had told him about her nervous breakdown in America. 'There are pitiable people,' she had said, 'who don't believe in God. Faith in Christ lost.'

'There aren't, Aunt?'

'Yes there are! Like me. When I lost my faith. And had my terrible crisis. My terrible emptiness.' As she had said it she had looked across her shoulder and shuddered as if a cloud hung over her. 'But for my dear Boston boys. They nursed me through.'

And now Aunt believed in midnight Mass again . . . Did she? In midnight Mass. His father certainly did.

And he did.

Even though he had not got what he asked for. The guns, oh the guns, he tried to walk like a sheriff. But as he skirted between the empty tables to that table at the far end of the dining room the guns hanging at his waist weighed him down heavily.

ANNE DEVLIN

The Journey to Somewhere Else

The snowroad to the Alps runs south-east from Lyons to Chambéry, whereafter, leaving the autoroute behind, it takes up with a steep mountain road north to Mégève on the western slopes of Mont Blanc.

The resort café, several miles above the village, was full of seventeen-year-old French millionaires – or so it seemed to us – and large Italian families: the women wore fur hats with their ski-suits and too many rings for comfort; their men had paunches and smoked cigars at lunch; and the twelve-year-old Italian girls confirmed for all time that fourteen was the only age to marry and Capulet's daughter might never have been such a catch had she lived long enough to look like her mother. There were probably some large French families as well, but they were less inclined to sit together as a group. The resort on the borders with Switzerland and Italy was fairly cosmopolitan; confirming too that the rich, like their money, are not different but indifferent to frontiers. Whatever nation they came from, they had nannies for their children, who cut up the food at different tables and did not ski. On Christmas

Day opposite me a black woman peeled a small orange and fed it to a fat white child, piece by piece. The smell did it: satsumas!

Christmas Day in '59; they ran the buses in Belfast; the pungent smell of orange brought it back. My brother, the satsumas in green and red silver paper on the piano in the parlour, the fire dying in the grate and the adults asleep in their rooms. And that year, in '59 when I was eight, it had begun to snow. The grate-iron to rest the kettle on squeaked as I pushed it towards the coals with my foot.

'You'll burn your slipper soles,' Michael John said.

'I'm bored.'

'We could go out.'

'How?'

'The bus passes to the City Hall every fifteen minutes.'

'They'll not allow us. I've no money and – '

'Ah go on, Amee. I dare you,' he said. 'Run out, catch the next bus to the City Hall and come back up on it without paying.'

'But the conductor will put me off!'

'That's the dare. See how far you can get. The person who gets furthest wins!'

My brother was small and fair and mischievous; there was ten months difference in our ages.

'All right then, I'll go.'

Joe is dark and tall and mostly silent; there are ten years between us.

'Would you like me to get one for you?' Joe said, putting the lunch tray on the table in front of me. 'Amee, would you like one?'

'What?'

'The oranges you keep staring at,' he said, handing me a glass of cold red wine.

'I'm sorry. No. I don't really like them very much.'

'You're shivering.'

'The wind's so cold.'

'Grumble. Grumble.'

'I'm sorry.'

With the life in the room the windows in the café clouded over.

'It would help if you stopped breathing,' he joked, as the window next to us misted.

It was a doomed journey from the start. Like all our holidays together it was full of incidents, mishaps and narrow escapes. Once, in Crete, I nearly drowned. I fell off his mother's boyfriend's boat and swallowed too much water. I remember coming up for air and watching him staring at me from the deck; he had been a lifesaver on a beach one summer, but I swam to those rocks myself. Four years ago in Switzerland, where he was working at the time, I fell on a glacier mountain, the Jungfrau, and slid headlong towards the edge with my skis behind me. I screamed for several minutes before I realised that if I continued to panic I would probably break my neck. I stopped screaming and thought about saving myself. At which point everything slowed down and I turned my body round on the snow, put my skis between me and the icy ridge and came to a halt. When I had enough energy I climbed back up. I suppose what happened this time was inevitable. About an hour after we crossed the Channel he crashed the car in Béthune. He drove at speed into the back of the one in front. I saw the crash coming and held my breath. On the passenger side we ended up minus a head-lamp and with a very crumpled wing.

'Why didn't you shout if you saw it coming?' he objected later.

'It seemed a waste of energy,' I said. 'I couldn't have prevented it happening.'

We exchanged it for a French car at Arrais and after I travelled apprehensively towards the Alps.

'Why don't we ski separately?' I suggested, after the first week. 'I'd like some ski lessons. Anyway, you're a far more advanced skier. I only hold you back.'

On the second day of that week I came back from ski class at four thirty and waited for him in the café by the main telecabin. There were so few people inside now the glass was almost clear. A family group sat at one table and ski instructors at the bar drank cognac. I waited for half an hour before I noticed the time.

It was snowing heavily outside then as well, and even getting dark. The snow was turning blue in the light. I closed the heavy front door behind me lightly till the snib caught and ran across the road to wait at the stop. I could see him watching at the lace curtains in the sitting room. The Christmas-tree lights were on in the room, the curtain shifted. Soundlessly, the bus arrived. I got on, and just as quietly it moved off. The conductor was not on the platform, nor was he on the lower deck, so I went to the front and crouched low on the seat and hoped he wouldn't notice me when he did appear. There was no one else aboard but two old ladies in hats with shopping baskets and empty Lucozade bottles. Noisily, the conductor came downstairs. He stood on the platform clinking small change; I could see his reflection in the glass window of the driver's seat. If I was lucky he would not bother me, I was too far away from the platform. Suddenly, he started to walk up the bus. I looked steadfastly out of the window. He rapped the glass pane to the driver and said something. The driver nodded. He spoke again. I was in such terror of a confrontation that I didn't hear anything he said. For a moment he glanced in my direction, and he remained where he stood. We were nearing the cinemas at the end of the road. At this point I decided not to go all the way round the route to the City Hall. I got up quickly and walked down the bus away from him and stood uneasily on the platform. At the traffic lights before the proper stop, he moved along the bus towards me, my nerve failed and I leaped off.

'Hey!' he called out. 'You can't get off here.'

It was snowing more heavily. Wet snow. My feet were cold. I looked down and saw that I was still wearing my slippers; red felt slippers with a pink fur trim. How strange I must have looked in a duffel coat and slippers in the snow. The clock of the Presbyterian Assembly Buildings read five forty-five. It chimed on the quarter-hour, and behind me the lights of a closed-up confectioner's illuminated a man I had not noticed before. 'You'll get your nice slippers wet,' he said.

'I'll dry them when I get home,' I said.

'You'll get chilblains that way.'

'No I won't.'

I looked doubtfully at my slippers; the red at the toes was darker than the rest and my feet felt very uncomfortable.

'Have you far to walk when you get off the bus?' he asked.

'No. I live just up the road. The bus passes my house,' I said.

'You'd better stand in here. It's drier,' he said.

I didn't answer. At that moment a young woman came round the corner into view and began walking towards us from the town centre. She walked with difficulty through the snow in high shoes. Under her coat a black dress and white apron showed as she moved. The woman looked at me and then at the man and stopped. She drew a packet of cigarettes from her apron pocket and lit one. At first she waited at the stop with me, and then, shivering, moved back into the protective shelter of the shop by the man's side.

'That wind 'ud go clean through you so it would,' she said.

'Aye. It comes in off the Lough and goes straight up the Black Mountain,' he said, looking away up the road. The woman and I followed his gaze.

Beyond us, a block or two away, was the dolls' hospital, we had been there a few weeks before with my mother.

'Leave the aeroplanes alone, Michael John,' she scolded. 'Just wait and see what Santa brings you.'

I loved that shop with all its dolls, repaired, redressed. My own doll had started out from there as a crinoline lady in white net with hoops and red velvet bows. That year, when we left it at the shop minus a leg, it had been returned to me as a Spanish dancer in a petticoat of multicoloured layers. We only ever visited the town with my mother; during the day when it was busy and friendly, when the matinées at the cinema were going in and the traffic moved round the centre, the cinema confectioner's shop in front of which I stood was always open and sold rainbow drops and white chocolate mice – the latter turned up in my stocking – so were there too, I noticed for the first time, satsumas in that window.

The snow, and the quiet and the darkness had transformed the town. In the blue-grey light the charm of the life went out of it, it seemed unfamiliar, dead. I wanted to go home to the fire in the parlour; I began to shiver convulsively, and then the bus came.

'Ardoyne.' The woman looked out. 'That's my bus.'

I was so grateful I forgot about the dare.

'No good to you?' she said to the man.

He shook his head and pulled up the collar of his coat.

'Merry Christmas,' she called out as we got on.

I was sitting brazenly at the seat next to the platform when the conductor turned to me for the fare.

'I forgot my purse,' I said. 'But this bus passes my house, my Mammy'll pay for it when I get home.'

'Oh, your Mammy'll pay it when you get home!' he mimicked. 'Did you hear that now!'

The young woman, who had gone a little further up the bus, turned round. We had only moved a couple of streets beyond the stop, the toyshop was behind me. A wire cage encased its shop front.

'Please don't put me off now,' I said, beginning to cry.

'I'll pay her fare,' the young woman said.

'Does your Mammy know you're out at all?' he asked and, getting no answer, moved along to the woman. 'Where are you going to anyway?' he called back.

'The stop before the hospital stop,' I said weakly.

'The Royal,' he said to the woman. The ticket machine rolled once.

'And Ardoyne. The terminus,' she said.

The ticket machine rolled once more and they grumbled between them about having to work on Christmas Day.

'I'll be late getting my dinner tonight. Our ones'll all have finished when I get in.'

'Aye, sure I know. I'm not off till eight,' he said. 'It's hardly been worth it. The one day in the year.' He snapped the tickets off the roll and gave her change. 'And no overtime.'

Someone, a man, clambered downstairs to the platform. He had a metal tin under his arm. The conductor pulled the bell.

'No overtime? You're kiddin',' she said.

'That's the Corporation for you,' he said.

Before the hospital stop he pulled the bell again. I stepped down to the platform. I could see the Christmas-tree lights in the bay window of the parlour. I jumped off and ran towards the house, and wished I hadn't been too ashamed to thank her. But her head was down and she wasn't looking after me.

Michael John opened the door: 'You did it?' he said, half in awe. 'I saw you get off the bus. You did it!'

'Yes,' I gasped. My heart was pounding and my feet hurt.

'All the way to the City Hall?'

'Of course.'

He followed me into the parlour.

'But look at your slippers, Amee, they're ruined. You went out in your slippers. They'll know.'

'Not if I dry them. No one will ever know.'

I put my slippers on the fender and stood looking at the red dye on the toes of my white tights. I pulled off the stockings as well and saw that even my toes were stained.

'Look at that, Michael John! My toes are dyed!' I said. 'Michael John?'

The front door closed so quietly it was hardly audible.

'Michael John! Don't go!'

From the sitting-room window I could see him crossing the road.

'Oh, I only pretended,' I breathed. 'I didn't.'

But he was too far away. And then the bus came.

I waited at that window until my breathing clouded the glass. I rubbed it away with my fist. Every now and then I checked the slippers drying at the fender. Gradually the dark red faded, the toes curled up and only a thin white line remained. I went back to the window and listened for the bus returning. Several buses did come by, but Michael John did not. I got under the velvet drapes and the lace and stood watching at the glass where the cold is trapped and waited. I could tell him the truth when he came back. The overhead lights of the sitting room blazed on and my mother's voice called:

'Ameldia! What are you doing there?'

She looked crossly round the room.

'You've let the fire go out! Where is Michael John?'

'Excusez-moi? Madame Fitzgerald?' the waitress in the café asked.

My ski pass lay on the table, she glanced at it briefly; the photograph and the name reassured her.

'Telephone!' she said, indicating that I should follow.

The ski instructors at the bar turned their heads to watch as I passed by to the phone. They were the only group left in the café. I expected to hear Joe's voice, instead a woman at the other end of the line spoke rapid French.

'Please. Could you speak English?' I asked.

She repeated her message.

'Your friend is here at the clinic in the village. We have X-rayed him. He will now return to your hotel. Can you please make your own way back.'

'Yes. But what is wrong?'

'I'm sorry?'

'What is wrong with him?'

'An accident. Not serious.'

'Thank you,' I said, and hurried away from the phone.

Outside it was dark and still snowing. I knew two routes back to the village: there was the mountain route we had skied down on after class a few days before, half an hour earlier by the light; and there was the route by road which we had driven up on in the morning. I could also take the bus. It was five twenty. The lifts and telecabins closed nearly an hour before. The bus which met the end of ski class had long gone; so too had the skiers to the town. The only people left seemed to be resort staff and instructors, most of whom lived on the mountain. It took five minutes to ski down to the village on the mountain, and forty-five minutes to go by road – if a bus came. Without further hesitation I made the decision to take the shortest route back. It was too dark to ski, so I put my skis on my shoulder and started out to walk along the ski-track down the mountain.

I followed the path confidently at first, encouraged by the sight of three young men who were walking fairly swiftly ahead. Half-way down the hill through a farm, which even in deep snow smelt of farming, I passed a woman going in the opposite direction, who looked at me briefly and said:

'Bonsoir, madame.'

The surprise in her voice and the weight of the skis on my shoulder arrested me momentarily so I stopped: 'Bonsoir.'

I shifted my skis to my other shoulder and in so doing realised that I had lost sight of the other walkers ahead. I walked on to a turning point by a chalet and found there that the path forked two ways. There was no one ahead any more, and looking back uphill I found that the woman had disappeared. The lights of the village twinkled before me, directly below the treeline, luring me down the slope. The other path stretched more gradually down around the mountain. In the light it had been so easy. I stood for a moment staring at the mute grey wetness. Were there really two tracks? The longer I stood in the dark looking, the more confusing it became. If I don't move now it will be too late. I moved. I set off again rapidly downhill, but the weight of the skis on my shoulder and the slippery gradient propelled me onwards at a hair-raising speed towards the treeline. The hard plastic boots made it impossible to grip the snow. I slipped badly and then stopped suddenly against the slope. My legs shook. I was breathless. If I moved another inch I would probably break a leg. Lost. I'm lost as well. If I could only be sure that this was the right way. Perhaps the wider, more gradual path is the one. I set off to climb back to the fork again. A light in the chalet further up the slope reassured me. I could always ask there.

Breathless, I regained the beginning of the two paths. I did not approach the chalet, but set out confidently on the wider path. The route ran between the snowdrifts higher on the mountain side than on the valley, but I saw also that now I was leaving the lights of the village behind, and this path, although easier to follow, was leading directly into a wood of pines above me. I came to a small grotto on the valley side of the slope, and beyond, a little further up the mountain, I could see the white stone façade of a closed church. A mound of snow nestling uneasily on the steep roof of the grotto slid off quietly in slow motion into my path, seconds before I reached it. Perversely, I plundered on. This is the wrong way, I'm sure it is, I thought. More precious energy sapped by the extra effort of wading through the drift, I came once more to a halt. The wind blew relentlessly. I noticed it for the first time. There is something noxious about the innocence of snow in its insidious transformation of familiar routes. I must go back. I turned and hurried back between the church and grotto, and reached, with a great deal of effort, the turning point on the path yet again. If I meet someone now, will they be friend or foe? If I go to that chalet to ask, will I be welcome? If I could somehow find the energy to climb further. I suddenly understood more perfectly than at any other moment that Fate, like a love affair, is a matter of timing: the right person passing at the right time; a combination of moments from experience which keep coming round like a memory, recurring, inducing in us the same confusion. It was as though I had stood all my life in the same cold place between the curtain and the glass. How stupid I am. This whole journey is pointless, I said aloud to no one, I could have gone for the bus. I closed my eyes and breathed painfully.

* * *

'Where is Michael John, Ameldia? Why did you let him go? You're older, you should be more responsible! What bus? At what time?'

The conductor remembered him. He didn't have any money. No, he didn't put him off. On Christmas Day for thrupence? It wasn't worth it. He didn't remember when he got off. He hadn't seen him get off. There was a memorial service on the feast of the Purification; they waited and waited. There was no coffin, only flowers in the church, and my mother's tears all during the service. He went away so completely, he even went out of my dreams. Fair and small and mischievous.

When I opened my eyes a white mist was forming. I would have to hurry and get to the road before it enveloped me completely. Every step uphill was excruciatingly painful as again and again the skis bit into my shoulder. As I neared the top of the hill, passing through the farm smells, I heard voices. Two girls and a boy appeared, I went very slowly, passing them higher up the slope; I had climbed very high. They took the downward path, several feet of snow separated us. They did not glance in my direction and I had lost my curiosity about the route. We passed in silence. I got to the road again where I started out, exhausted. Did anyone pass him that night and not know?

Once on the highway I walked more easily where the traffic of the day had beaten down the snowtrack. My alarm had evaporated like the mist on the mountain. But I was hungry and tired and when I reached the car-park where the ski bus turned it was deserted, no one was waiting. I put the skis into a bank of snow and lay against them. My face burned, and my hair clung to my forehead from the effort and panic of climbing. A car passed. It was too dark to read my watch. If I walked on to the road towards the lights I would be able to read the time. I was too tired to move. My shoulders ached. I could not lift my arms above my head. My clothes clung. The backs of my knees were damp. My leather gloves looked swollen and bloated. Another car passed. It must be late; perhaps he will come out looking for me. If I go and stand on the road he might see me. I was too weary to move, so I stayed on. Then a familiar throaty rattle of an engine sounded, and a bus turned into the coach-park.

'Mégève?'

'Non. Sallandes.'

'Oh.' I must have looked disappointed.

'Dix minutes!' he assured me.

'Oh. Merci, monsieur!' I brightened.

He was back in half the time to pick me up. I dropped my skis into the cage at the back and in a few minutes we were hurtling down the mountain towards the village.

At seven thirty I got to the hotel. Joe was not there. The X-rays from the clinic were lying on the bed. Perhaps he was worried and has gone out looking for me, I thought. I was drying my wet clothes on the radiators when he came in.

'What on earth happened?' I asked at the sight of the sling.

'Oh, some idiot got out of control and jumped on my back this afternoon. Arrogant lout. He didn't even apologise. He said I shouldn't have stopped suddenly in front of him.'

'Why did you stop?'

'A girl in front of me fell down. I stopped to help her.'

'It's dangerous though, isn't it? You should have skied round her to safety and then stopped.'

'Well, anyway, I won't be able to ski again this holiday,' he said. 'The ligaments are torn.'

'Is it very painful?'

'It's a bit sore.'

'I'm sorry. Shall we go back tomorrow?'

'Well, we could go to Paris tomorrow instead of on Friday.'

'Let's do that, I'll drive,' I said.

'There's no need. I can manage. I have no trouble driving,' he said. 'How are you then, all right? Had a nice day?'

'Joe, I got lost on the mountain.'

'Did you?' he said. 'Oh, by the way, I've been downstairs talking to Madame. I told her that we were leaving earlier. She was very sympathetic when she saw the sling. She said she wouldn't charge us for the extra nights even though we've booked to stay till Friday.'

'I tried to walk down the path we skied on and then I couldn't find it.'

'That was silly,' he said. 'Why didn't you get the bus?'

'I don't know.'

It wasn't the first time in our ten-year relationship of living together and not living together that I found I had nothing to tell him. He never guessed the fury of my drama; and now he looked pale and tired.

'What's the matter?' he asked, catching me watching him.

'Nothing. Nothing's the matter.'

Even in Montmartre there was snow and coldness.

'There's a hotel! Stop now!' I said.

We had been driving all day, yet it seemed as though we never left the snowline.

'Stop! Please. That hotel looked nice. Joe, I'm not navigating a street further.'

'Ameldia, it's a five-star hotel!' he said, in a voice that reminded me of my mother. 'We are not staying in a five-star hotel!'

'It's on me,' I said extravagantly. 'Whatever this costs, it's on me!'

'But Amee, you don't have any money!'

'I'll argue with the bank manager about that, not with you,' I said. 'I have a little plastic card here which will settle everything. Now, will you get out of the car? Please, Joe. You look exhausted!'

We signed into a fourth-floor side room. Through the nylon curtains I could see the traffic of Paris and the lights of the Eiffel Tower. 'We can walk to the Sacré Coeur from here. I think I remember the way,' I said.

My last visit had been as a schoolgirl fifteen years before.

There were tangerines in the restaurant – I lifted my head to them as they passed on the fruit tray to the table next to us – and ice-cubes on the grapes. I shivered involuntarily. I don't remember satsumas any other year.

'I forgot to ring my mother on Christmas Day!' I said suddenly.

'From the French Alps? Why would you want to do that?' he said.

'You know what they're like about me being away for Christmas.'

'No, I'm afraid I don't, I've never met them,' he said firmly. 'And I'm afraid I don't see why you think they should still be so obsessed with you. You are thirty years of age now, Ameldia, and you do have other brothers and sisters!'

'Yes, I know. But I was the only one around when – '

'Forget it!' he said. 'I didn't spend all this money and bring you all this way for you to drag that up now!'

'Madame? Monsieur?' A waiter stood eyeing us, his pencil poised like a dagger ready to attack his notepad.

Later as we passed through the square in Montmartre, sad-eyed artists were putting their easels away. An African spread out ivory bangles and elephants on a cloth on the pavement and I stopped to admire. He spoke English: 'Are you English?'

'No. Irlande.'

'Ah. Irlande is good,' he said, putting an arm around me and drawing me towards his wares. I felt like a schoolgirl again, shy, drawing away, explaining I had no money to buy anything. Joe watched me from a distance and I said: 'Don't be so grumpy.'

'I'm not grumpy,' he said crossly.

'Wouldn't it be nice to go and have a glass of wine in one of those bars?' I said.

'Well, they look very crowded to me and I'm tired,' he said.

'Do you know why I love Montmartre?'

'No, but I'm sure you're going to tell me!' he said.

'Because whatever time you come here, it's always open, full of people.'

I wished I hadn't brought him to Montmartre. He seemed so uneasy amidst the haggle of trading in the streets. I had forgotten how he hated markets. He did not relax until we got back to the hotel.

I was not tired and didn't find that sleep came easily. My tossing and turning kept him awake.

'Where did you get that cough from?' he asked.

'I must have got a cold somewhere.'

I got up and went to the fridge for a glass of mineral water, and as I opened the door in the dark, I thought I smelt oranges.

'Did you spill the fruit juice?' I asked.

'No,' he said wearily. 'When will you go to sleep?'

I went to the shower room to drink the water so as not to disturb him, and when I returned to the bedroom I found it was very much colder than when I'd left it. The curtain shifting slightly caught my attention. The glass in the window was so clear it looked as if it wasn't there at all.

'Joe?' I called softly. 'Did you open the window?'

'No,' he said without stirring.

The room appeared to be filling with a white mist. It's like on the mountain, I thought. The white mist of the night outside seemed to grow in the room.

'That's funny.' The smell of oranges was very strong. 'Somebody is eating satsumas!' I said aloud.

Joe didn't answer. I got into bed and lay down trembling. The walls of the room were gradually slipping away to the mist. 'No. I will not watch,' I said firmly. 'I will not watch any more.' I closed my eyes tight against the dark and breathed softly.

Where the white rocks of the Antrim Plateau meet the mud banks of the Lough, three small boys netting crabs dislodged a large stone, when one of them reaching into the water after the escaping crab caught instead the cold hand of my brother. In May, a closed coffin filled the sitting room and the Children of Mary from the neighbourhood came to pray there and keep the vigil.

'I will not watch,' I said. 'I will not watch.'

An angel of Portland stone marked the grave and we sang: 'Blood of my Saviour wash me in thy tide'. 'He was bound for heaven,' my mother said often, and that seemed to console her. And every Sunday of the year we went to the cemetery, my mother and I; on Christmas Day ever after we left offerings of flowers and things until even the angelstone aged, became pockmarked and turned brown. It was the first Christmas I had not gone to that grave.

In the morning Joe drew back the curtains in the room and said: 'What a sight! I'm glad I didn't know that was there last night.'

'Didn't know what?' I said, moving to the window.

'Look!'

A huddle of stone crucifixes, headstones and vaults marked the graves which jostled for the space under our window against the side wall of the hotel.

'Montmartre cemetery!' he said.

There were no angels among the headstones.

'How creepy! Well, I'm glad we're going,' he said, with a last glance before dropping the curtain.

But I could still see.

'Last night,' I began to say, 'this room was very cold and I asked you if – '

'Oh, do come away from that window and hurry up and pack,' he said. 'We need to catch the lunch-time ferry.'

I wanted to tell him what I now knew, that the future was already a part of what I was becoming, and if I stopped this becoming there would be no future, only an endless repetition of moments from the past which I will be compelled to relive. 'It would help if you stopped breathing,' he had said. But it wouldn't; because there would always be the memory of existence – like a snare; a trapped moment, hungover in the wrong time. Unaccountable. And I wanted to tell him before it was too late that the difference is as fragile between the living and the dead as the absence of breath on a glass. But already he was rushing on a journey to somewhere else.

Bound for heaven, was it? Yes. Hand and foot.

PATRICK CAMPBELL

Leetle Chreesmus Weeemen

As we rolled out into the river from the shelter of the breakwater, bound for a night in the cold darkness of the Bay, Dooley put his head out of the afterhatch.

He was wearing, as usual, his revolting brown balaclava with the uniform cap perched, like a battered bird, on top of it. He surveyed the lights of the city, gleaming with the special radiance of Christmas Eve.

'Roll on the grave,' said Dooley. 'Roll on the grave.'

'Don't start,' I told him. I'd been cooped up with him for nearly a year. I knew what was coming.

'I shoulda gone sick,' Dooley announced. He tried a tentative cough. It sounded frightful, the result of a lifetime of fag-ends and the dregs of porter barrels. 'The courage of a lion,' said Dooley, inviting agreement.

I looked at him steadily without saying anything. Then the performance started. His eyes bulged, he clutched his heart through three exceptionally dirty jerseys, and he coughed. It lasted nearly a minute, interspersed with shuddering gasps of 'Aw Gawd – ' Then he fell back, manifestly exhausted. 'I'm done,' said Dooley. 'Yez'll have to put me ashore.'

'I'll put you in jail,' I said.

'Ah, shut up – ' said Dooley wearily, and vanished below. Above the thump of the ancient diesel engine I heard him settle down to a deafening denunciation of the unfortunate boy Pearce, who was occupied with the hopeless task of creating some kind of order out of the insoluble mess of rifles, rations, coal, sea-boots, and old newspapers that littered the small space in which we ate and slept.

I went up to the wheelhouse and squeezed in beside Leading-seaman Gooch. His hands were in his pockets. He steered with an inaccurate pressure of his stomach against the wheel.

'Oughta be takin' the missus to the panto tonight,' said Gooch. 'You've made a right lash-up of the lot of us.'

My conscience was a little tender. I had, in fact, been talked into the Christmas Eve watch, although it wasn't really our turn. 'Oh, stop groaning,' I told him. 'Someone's got to do the job, and it's – '

'What job?' said Gooch malevolently.

I decided not to go into it. Our task, in fact, was to search all incoming vessels, in the interests of preserving our neutral status. In the closing months of the war the business seemed, in considerable measure, to have lost its point. Our customers, in the main, consisted of small colliers on their cross-Channel run, the crews of which we'd got to know so well that even their home lives had become open, if somewhat unreadable, books.

Pearce rattled on the wheelhouse door. He looked like a ferret, wearing a muffler. 'Surr,' said Pearce, 'surr – himself's on the machine, creatin'. Somethin' about the *Pampona*.'

'Flynn!' I exclaimed. 'He ought to be in bed hours ago.' I ran down aft, a prey to a variety of anxieties. A radio message from headquarters always meant trouble.

Dooley was stretched out on the locker with three overcoats on top of him in spite of the appalling heat of the cabin. The stove was almost incandescent. Some nameless preparation smoked in the frying-pan.

I leant over Dooley and switched the radio telephone over to 'receive'. It was Flynn all right. 'Hey!' he roared. 'Hello! Can y'hear me? Hello? Come in! Over!'

I told him I was present and ready to receive. Something important must have happened.

'Hey!' roared Flynn – his customary form of address. 'Hey! Get out to the *Pampona*! She's . . .' The rest was drowned by a sudden blast of atmospherics. Flynn came back again, shouting something about 'unauthorised persons', and then the whole apparatus went dead. It had come back the previous day from a three week holiday on the repair benches of the Army Signal Corps.

I didn't like the sound of the message. The *Pampona* had been lying to at anchor in the bay for nearly a fortnight, a rusty old tramp with a dubious Panama registration. She had been boarded on arrival by one of the other watches, who reported variously that she was picking up refugee Japanese and/or waiting for a cargo of stewed steak for Belgian relief. We had been glad to leave the *Pampona* alone. Her situation was too complicated for the smooth running of the examination service.

I told my crew what we were in for. Each of them resisted the proposition with a specific complaint, topped by Flack, the garage-hand engineer, who announced bluntly that the engine was about to go on fire. Seeing that I was adamant the four of them retired to the cabin in search of tea.

I took the wheel, and about an hour later picked up the *Pampona*'s riding light. I circled her in the darkness, looking for signs of life.

Then I stopped in her lee and shouted '*Pampona* ahoy!' through the megaphone.

Suddenly a voice almost speechless with indignation bawled, 'Vot t'blotty hell you vant?' I could see a vague shadow near the stern.

'Examination Service!' I shouted. 'We're coming aboard!'

There was a long silence, then the voice was heard again. This time it was conciliatory, yet with undertones of irritation. 'Go avay, you boyss! Vee oll are zleepink here!' The figure vanished and all was silent again, save for the seas splashing against the freighter's rusty sides.

'Get the fenders out,' I told Dooley. 'We're going aboard.'

As we came in against her I realised this was going to be more difficult than I had thought. The *Pampona*, with no cargo, was riding uncomfortably high in the water.

Without warning someone let go a rope-ladder from above. It crashed on our deck, missing Dooley narrowly. I flashed up a torch to see who had provided this amenity, and saw, bathed in the yellow glow, the face of a coal-black negro, wearing a Panama hat.

'Jaysus!' said Dooley. 'A Liverpool man!' He backed away.

I slung my rifle round my neck – a weapon poorly suited to close combat at sea – and seized the swaying end of the ladder. 'Follow me,' I told Pearce and Dooley, wishing that either, or preferably both of them, were going first. I was half-way up when the ladder performed a trick high in the repertoire of all rope-ladders. It twisted itself round and slammed me against the side of the ship, with my rifle wedged between the rungs. I shouted instructions impartially to Dooley, Pearce, Gooch, and the Panama-hatted negro. It was probably this disturbance, and the crashing of my boots and rifle against the plates, that brought the small reception committee out on deck to welcome me, when I eventually reached the rail.

There were five of them, including the negro. It wasn't easy to see them clearly in the darkness, but pock marks, razor slashes, gold teeth and poor shaving stood out among their distinguishing features.

Dooley and Pearce joined me and together we shouted at them, 'Captain! Capitain! Skipper! Skeeper! Officer! Mate!'

They slunk back, and before I knew what had happened, they'd all disappeared into the fo'castle, slamming and locking the door.

I posted Dooley outside the fo'castle and Pearce down aft. I opened a door below the bridge and found myself in a narrow passage smelling of garlic and Turkish cigarettes. There was absolute silence, save for the creaking of the ship as she rolled.

I tried a couple of doors. They were all locked. I shouted 'Captain' several times, but there was no answer. I began to think of the *Marie Celeste*, so strongly, indeed, that I felt suddenly compelled to join Dooley on deck. The same idea had occurred to Pearce at the same time. The three of us huddled in the shelter of the funnel, as far removed from the family joys of Christmas as any of us had ever been.

When she appeared at the fo'castle door I knew she must be a ghost. Her hair was fantastically tangled, she wore a leather flying-jacket over what looked like the remnants of a boiler suit, and she was as pale as death. She flew past us like the wind, silently on bare feet, and vanished down the engine-room ladder.

'Holy fly!' breathed Dooley. 'That was Josie Noonan!' He clutched me by the arm. 'Josie Noonan – from Parnell Terrace!'

I was glad he knew her. It put the next move up to him. 'Go and ask your friend Josie Noonan,' I said, 'just what she's doing here.'

He looked at me doubtfully. I could see he was wondering if it was an order, or my usual faint request for assistance. 'That's an order,' I said, helping him.

'Aw Gawd – ' said Dooley. He unslung his rifle. With his finger on the trigger he advanced to the engine-room door.

He was gone for five whole minutes. I was certain the ghostly Josie Noonan had got him when he suddenly reappeared. He looked at me with what seemed to be acute embarrassment.

'Well?' I said.

Dooley gulped. 'She's spendin' – spendin' Christmas here,' he announced hoarsely. 'Came out three days ago in a motor-boat.'

'With this gang of cut-throats!' I said. 'She can't be! She's mad!'

Dooley shuffled his feet. He fiddled with the strap of his rifle. 'There's a few – a few friends with her,' he murmured. 'Spendin' Christmas – '

'How many?' I snapped.

Dooley raised his head. 'Twenty-seven,' he said, and there was envy in his voice, and wonder, at the scale of the enterprise. 'Twenty-seven, the word musta gone round.'

'My God,' I said. 'Twenty-seven women in this thing! And they've been here a week!'

The mouth of the barely adolescent Pearce dropped open.

'We've got to get them out,' I said. 'There's going to be hell to pay.'

'There *will* be hell to pay,' said Dooley mournfully, 'the minute you begin.'

He was right. We advanced, the three of us, into that dimly lit fo'castle, counting it in our own minds to be one of the major actions of the war. 'Come on, girls!' I shouted. 'That's enough now! All out on deck!' 'Home to your mothers, ye divils!' roared Dooley – 'before I give ye the flat of me hand!'

A moment later we were surrounded by the pirates and their lady friends. But the lady friends had had enough. Most of them were in tears. Perhaps the sight of our honest shaven faces reminded them of home. At all events they started to straggle out on deck.

Then an astonishing thing happened. The buccaneers themselves became lachrymose. The negro clutched me by the arm. 'Boss,' he begged, 'not tek away my leetle Chreesmus woooman – ' A Moor, with ear-rings, beat his breast and cried, 'Loff – loff!' in an agony of dismay. Heartened by these signs of weakness we shoved them about with the butts of our rifles, even the child Pearce joining in. It was the marines to the rescue all right.

One by one we sent the leetle Chreesmus weeemen down the rope-ladder, Gooch receiving them with the look of a man to whom anything could happen now. Our last act was to rescue Miss Noonan from the chief engineer and then we cast off from the *Pampona*, laden to the scuppers with ladies, and slowly rolled home.

When the engine died out it was clear to me that Flack thought he was being over-worked, and wished to share in the social life which was being so richly enjoyed by Dooley and Gooch in the cabin, but the wheelhouse was so tightly packed with Josies and Marys and Kathleens I couldn't get out to remonstrate with him.

We got back to our berth up the river shortly before dawn, and even at that early hour I was not surprised to see that the jetty was crowded with marine officers, police, several figures in clerical garb, and a whole battalion of mothers scarcely able to wait to get hold of their young.

Hours of confusion followed while names and addresses were taken, while I filed countless reports, and Flynn ramped about wanting to know what had kept us the whole blazing night at sea.

It was breakfast time, on Christmas morning, before Dooley and I came together again. He had a cup of cocoa in one hand, and an enormous slice of fried bread in the other.

'There ye are,' he cried, 'me lovely man!' He lowered half a pint of cocoa into himself. 'Do you know what I'm goin' to tell you?' he roared. He took a deep breath. There was a look of ineffable peace on his face.

'I never spent a better Christmas,' shouted Able-seaman Dooley, 'with a better lot of unauthorised persons in the whole of me natural life!'

JOHN McGAHERN

Christmas

As well as a railway ticket they gave me a letter before I left the Home to work for Moran. They warned me to give the letter unopened to Moran, which was why I opened it on the train; it informed Moran that since I was a ward of state if I caused trouble or ran away he was to contact the police at once. I tore it up, since it occurred to me that I might well cause trouble or run away, resolving to say I lost it if asked, but Moran did not ask for any letter.

Moran and his wife treated me well. The food was more solid than at the Home, a roast always on Sundays, and when the weather grew hard they took me to the town and bought me Wellingtons and an overcoat and a cap with flaps that came down over the ears. After the day's work when Moran had gone to the pub, I was free to sit at the fire, while Mrs Moran knitted, and listened to the wireless – what I enjoyed most were the plays – and Mrs Moran had told me she was knitting me a pullover for Christmas. Sometimes she asked me about life at the Home and when I'd tell her she'd sigh, 'You must be very glad to be with us instead,' and I would tell her, which was true, that I was. I mostly went to bed before Moran came from the pub as they often quarrelled then, and I considered I had no place in that part of their lives.

Moran made his living by buying cheap branches, or uncommercial timber the sawmills couldn't use, and cutting them up to sell as firewood. I delivered the timber with an old jennet Moran had bought from the tinkers; the jennet squealed, a very human squeal, any time a fire of branches was lit and ran, about the only time he did run, to stand in rigid contentment with his nostrils in the thick of the wood smoke. When Moran was in good humour it amused him greatly to light a fire specially to see the jennet's excitement at the prospect of smoke.

There was no reason this life shouldn't have gone on for long but for a stupid wish on my part, which set off an even more stupid wish in Mrs Grey, and what happened has struck me ever since as usual when people look to each other for their happiness or whatever it is called. Mrs Grey was Moran's best customer. She'd come from America and built the huge house on top of Mounteagle after her son had been killed in aerial combat over Italy.

The thaw overhead in the bare branches had stopped, the evening we filled that load for Mrs Grey; there was no longer the dripping on the dead leaves, the wood clamped in the silence of white frost except for the racket some bird made in the undergrowth. Moran carefully built the last logs above the crates of the cart and I threw him in the bag of hay that made the load look bigger than it was. 'Don't forget to call at Murphy's for her paraffin,' he said. 'No, I'll not forget.' 'She's bound to tip you well this Christmas. We could use money for the Christmas.' He'd use it to pour drink down his gullet. 'Must be time to be moving,' I said. 'It'll be night before you're there,' he answered.

The cart rocked over the roots between the trees, cold steel of the bridle ring in the hand close to the rough black lips, steam of the breath wasting on the air to either side. We went across the paddocks to the path round the lake, the wheels cutting two tracks on the white stiff grass, crush of the grass yielding to the iron. I had to open the wooden gate to the pass. The small shod hooves wavered between the two ridges of green inside the wheeltracks on the pass as the old body swayed to each drive of the shafts, as the wheels fell from rut to rut.

The lake was frozen over, a mirror fouled by white blotches of the springs, and rose streaks from the sun impaled on the firs of Oakport across the bay.

The chainsaw started up in the wood again, he'd saw while there was light. 'No joke to make a living, a drink or two for some relief, all this ballsing. May be better if we stayed in bed, conserve our energy, eat less,' but in spite of all he said he went on buying the branches cheap from McAnnish after the boats had taken the trunks down the river to the mill.

I tied the jennet to the chapel gate and crossed to Murphy's shop.

'I want Mrs Grey's paraffin.'

The shop was full of men, they sat on the counter or on wooden fruit boxes and upturned buckets along the walls. They used to trouble me at first: I supposed it little different from going into a shop in a strange country without its language, but they learned they couldn't take a rise out of me, that was their phrase. They used to lob tomatoes at the back of my head in the hope of some reaction, but they left me mostly alone when they saw none was forthcoming. If I felt anything for them it was a contempt tempered by fear: and I was here, and they were there.

'You want her paraffin, do you? I know the paraffin I'd give her if I got your chance,' Joe Murphy said from the centre of the counter where he presided, and a loyal guffaw rose from around the walls.

'Her proper paraffin,' someone shouted, and it drew even more applause, and when it died a voice asked, 'Before you get off the counter, Joe, throw us an orange?' They bought chocolate and fruit as token payment for their stay. Joe stretched to the shelf and threw the orange to the man who sat on a bag of Spanish onions. As he stretched forward to catch the fruit the red string bag collapsed and he came heavily down on the onions. 'You want to bruise those onions with your dirty awkward arse. Will you pay for them now, will you?' Joe shouted as he swung his thick legs down from the counter. 'Everybody's out for their onions these days,' the man tried to defend himself with a nervous laugh as he fixed the string bag upright and changed his seat to an orange box.

'You've had your onions: now pay for them.'

'Make him pay for his onions,' they shouted.

'You must give her her paraffin first.' Joe took the tin, and went to the barrel raised on flat blocks in the corner, and turned the copper tap.

'Now give her the proper paraffin. It's Christmas time,' Joe said again as he screwed the cap tight on the tin, the limp black hair falling across the bloated face.

'Her proper paraffin,' the approving cheer followed me out the door.

'He never moved a muscle, the little fucker. Those Homeboys are a bad piece of work,' I heard with much satisfaction as I stowed the tin of paraffin securely among the logs of the cart. Ice, over the potholes of the road, was catching the first stars. Lights of bicycles, it was a confession night, hesitantly approached out of the night. Though exposed in the full glare of their lamps I was unable to recognise the bicyclists as they pedalled past in dark shapes behind their lamps and this made raw the fear I'd felt but had held down in the shop. I took a stick and beat the reluctant jennet into pulling the load uphill as fast as he was able.

After I'd stacked the logs in the fuel shed I went and knocked on the back door to see where they wanted me to put the paraffin. Mrs Grey opened the door.

'It's the last load until after Christmas,' I said as I put the tin down.

'I haven't forgotten.' She smiled and held out a pound note.

'I'd rather not take it.' It was there the first mistake was made, playing for higher stakes.

'You must have something, besides the firewood you've brought us so many messages from the village that we don't know what we'd have done without you.'

'I don't want money.'

'Then what would you like me to give you for Christmas?'

'Whatever you'd prefer to give me.' I thought *prefer* was well put for a Homeboy.

'I'll have to give it some thought then,' she said as I led the jennet out of the yard delirious with stupid happiness.

'You got the paraffin and logs there without trouble?' Moran beamed when I came in to the smell of hot food. He'd changed into good clothes and was finishing his meal at the head of the big table in tired contentment.

'There was no trouble,' I answered.

'You've fed and put in the jennet?'

'I gave him crushed oats.'

'I bet you Mrs Grey was pleased.'

'She seemed pleased.'

He'd practically his hand out. 'You got something good out of it then?'

'No.'

'You mean to say she gave you nothing?'

'Not tonight but maybe she will before Christmas.'

'Maybe she will but she always gave a pound with the

last load before,' he said suspiciously. His early contentment was gone.

He took his cap and coat to go for a drink or two for some relief.

'If there's an international crisis in the next few hours you know where I'll be found,' he said to Mrs Moran as he left.

Mrs Grey came Christmas Eve with a large box. She smelled of scent and gin and wore a fur coat. She refused a chair saying she'd to rush, and asked me to untie the red twine and paper.

A toy airplane stood inside the box, it was painted white and blue and the tyres smelled of new rubber.

'Why don't you wind it up and see it go?'

I looked up at the idiotically smiling face, the tear-brimmed eyes.

'Wind it up for Mrs Grey,' I heard Moran's voice.

While the horrible hurt of the toy was changing to rage I was able to do nothing. Moran took the toy from my hand and wound it up. A light flashed on and off on the tail as it raced across the cement and the propellors turned.

'It was too much for you to bring,' Moran said in his politic voice.

'I thought it was rather nice when he refused the money. My own poor boy loved nothing nothing better than model airplanes for Christmas,' she was again on the verge of tears.

'We all still feel for that tragedy,' Moran said and insisted, 'Thank Mrs Grey for such a lovely present. It's far too good.'

'I think it's useless,' I could no longer hold back rage, and began to sob. I have only a vague memory afterwards except the voice of Moran accompanying her to the door with excuses and apologies.

'I should have known better than to trust a Homeboy,' Moran said when he came back. 'Not only did you do me out of the pound but you go and insult the woman and her dead son. You're going to make quick time back to where you came from, my tulip.'

Moran stirred the airplane with his boot as if he wished to kick it but dared not out of respect for the money it had cost.

'Well you'll have a good flight in it this Christmas.'

The two-hour bell went for Midnight Mass, and as Moran hurried for the pub to get drinks before Mass, Mrs Moran started to strip the windows of curtains and to set a single candle to burn in each window. Later, as we made our way to the church, candles burned in the windows of all the houses and the church was ablaze with light. I was ashamed of the small old woman, afraid they'd identify me with her, as we walked up between the crowded benches to where a steward directed us to a seat in the women's side-altar. In the smell of burning wax and flowers and damp stone, I got out the brown beads and the black prayerbook with the gold cross on the cover they'd given me in the Home and began to prepare for the hours of boredom Midnight Mass meant; but it did not turn out that way, it was to be a lucky Christmas. A drunken policeman, Guard Mullins, had slipped past the stewards on guard at the door and into the women's sidechapel. As Mass began he started to tell the school-teacher's wife how available her arse had been for handling while she'd worked in the bar before assuming the fur coat of respectability, 'And now, O lordy me a prize rose garden wouldn't get a luk in edgeways with its grandeur.' The stewards had a hurried consultation whether to eject him or not and decided it'd probably cause less scandal to leave him as he was. They seemed right for he quietened into a drunken stupor until the Monsignor climbed into the pulpit to begin his annual hour of the season of peace and glad tidings. As soon as he began, 'In the name of the Father and of the Son and of the Holy Ghost. This Christmas, my dearly beloved children in Christ, I wish . . .' Mullins woke to applaud with a hearty,

'Hear, hear. I couldn't approve more. You're a man after my own heart. Down with the hypocrites!' The Monsignor looked towards the policeman and then at the stewards, but as he was greeted by another, 'Hear, hear!' he closed his notes and in a voice of acid wished everybody a holy and happy Christmas, and angrily climbed from the pulpit to conclude the shortest Midnight Mass the church had ever known. It was not, though, the end of the entertainment. As the communicants came from the rails Mullins singled out the tax collector, who walked down the aisle with eyes closed, bowed head, and hands rigidly joined, to shout, 'There's the biggest hypocrite in the parish,' which delighted almost everybody.

I thought of Mullins as my friend as I went past the lighted candles in the window, and felt for the first time proud to be a ward of state. I avoided Moran and his wife and from the attic I listened with glee to them criticising Mullins. When the voices died I came quietly down to take a box of matches and the airplane and go to the jennet's stable. I gathered dry straw in a heap and as I lit it and the smoke rose he gave his human squeal until I untied him and he was able to put his nostrils in the thick of the smoke. By the light of the burning straw I put the blue and white toy against the wall and started to kick. Each kick I gave, it seemed a new sweetness was injected into my blood. For such a pretty toy it took few kicks to reduce it to shapelessness, and then in the last flames of the straw I jumped on it on the stable floor where the jennet was already nosing me to put more straw on the dying fire.

I was glad, as I quietened, that I'd torn up in the train the letter that I was supposed to give unopened to Moran. I felt a new life for me had already started to grow out of the ashes, out of the stupidity of human wishes.

VAL MULKERNS

Home for Christmas

The Christmas of that year stands out in my mind with a kind of finality. I was fourteen, and abruptly at the end of the holidays some soft, almost physical appendage of childhood seems to have fallen away, like the tail off a tadpole, and I would never be quite the same again.

My father came in a hired car to collect me from my aunt's house where I was boarded during the school term. He was ushered up in state to what they called 'the room' which was now several degrees below zero. My aunt took from his numbed hands the bright bundle of Christmas presents from Mother and fussed him into an armchair by the stark fireplace, black except for a paper fan made from newspapers which was presumably intended as a decoration. In a few freezing moments the small underpaid servant girl (recently acquired from the orphanage) came in carrying a lighted oil stove which was sometimes used in the bedrooms if anybody was sick. Those were the cold war-time years when only the poor, with tiny houses, could really keep warm. But no house I had ever known was as miserably cold as this handsome farmhouse a few miles from the marble city of Kilkenny.

'Thanks very much, Bernie,' said my father to the girl. 'And how are you this fine hearty morning?'

'Grand, sir, thanks.' When my aunt turned to get the whiskey he slipped Bernie a ten-shilling note, winking elaborately and motioning her to silence. She skipped away beaming, closing the door behind her.

'Are you sure now, Daniel, you wouldn't like the fire lit? 'Twouldn't be any trouble and indeed it would give that bone-lazy young one something to do.'

'I can't stay too long, so don't trouble yourself, Ellen.'

'Anyway,' said my aunt, 'sure the sun is so strong 'twould likely put the fire out.' She handed him his whiskey and I knew by the tight curl of his lip as he raised his glass to drink her health that he was trying to smother a laugh. Later he would tell my mother about this – Ellen's latest scientific discovery – and they would roar laughing together.

'Won't you join me, Ellen, and the festive season that's in it?'

'Sure maybe a taste of the sherry wine would be no harm and me with a cold,' my aunt agreed.

'Do you all the good in the world, Ellen,' said my father heartily, and though I could see his throat stretching for the bite of the whiskey, he waited until she had filled her glass. He was just about to give the wish when Ellen thought better of her self-indulgence and poured half of the sherry back into the bottle, spilling some in the process. She was no doubt remembering how near Christmas was, and how as many as six distant cousins might drop in over the season.

'Your good health, Ellen, and here's a happy Christmas to us all and many of them!'

'Amen to that,' said my aunt, taking a sip and then watching nervously as my father joyously swallowed half his drink in one go and smacked his lips genially after it.

'Good stuff, Ellen. The best. Warm the cockles of your heart!' and the practiced charm of his best professional smile brought a slight response even from Ellen though you could see that a smile of any sort hurt her, as the effort to walk hurts a rheumatic.

'Tell me,' said my aunt grudgingly, 'how was it Peg couldn't have come over with you and you with the car got and all?'

'Work, Ellen, work. Christmas party dresses for gay young things who have been saving their clothes coupons which ought to have been spent on good woollen stockings to keep the cold out. All sorts of refurbished finery for the old – overcoats "turned" and that sort of thing. She said she'd have to let some of her clients down if she took the whole day off to come here. Assured me you'd understand.'

'And so I do,' Ellen conceded. 'How is she keeping, tell me?'

'Splendid form, thank God. In fact, hopelessly elevated at the thought of seeing our young friend here after three long months. I must say, Ellen, he's looking a credit to your good care. A credit.'

Head down, I continued my perusal of the mouldering fox in the glasscase, an unfailing delight because in strong winter sunlight like this you could see that really the taxidermist hadn't done such a good job. If you watched one patch of fur closely until your eyes ached, you became aware that infinitesimal life was moving along each stiffened hair, minute flaky things like the inhabitants of old damp books. No wonder. You could see the unused furniture gently steaming in the slight combined warmth of sun and oil heater. The windows of this room were always kept hermetically sealed except in high summer.

'He's a sturdy lad enough,' my aunt agreed, 'and a great help to us at the harvest.' This was dangerous talk although she was too stupid to be aware of it. My father might easily enquire why I hadn't been at school then. But my aunt's tongue, loosened by the sherry, ran on. 'Your Danny reminds me something wonderful of Martin, you know. Come over here till you look at him the year before he left the priests' college when we still thought he was going on for a priest.'

My father went at her bidding to the far wall, blotched with damp, whose mud-coloured wallpaper fell in loose folds around the smiling face of my disreputable uncle. The photographer seemed to have caught the moment before a wink. His clerical collar looked like fancy dress and if the family had looked honestly at him they'd have known themselves that he had his own future planned despite them.

'Look at the chin now,' said my aunt, 'and the cock of the head and the way the hair grows over the forehead. The dead spit of Dan. Look up at us now, Danny boy.' I did, and instantly lowered my head again as my father nodded.

'You have a point there, Ellen, no doubt about it.' He had not allowed himself to be separated from his drink, and now swallowed the remainder with relish, maybe for consolation.

'I don't suppose you'd take another drop, Daniel?' said my aunt in the tone of voice that made lady visitors refuse another slice of madeira cake.

'Do you know, I think I will, Ellen – a mere tincture, mind, one for the road. We must be off in a minute or two if we're to be home before dark.'

My aunt poured another half-glass of whiskey and even I could detect the portentous gloom in her voice when she spoke again. 'We're after getting a Christmas card below from Nellie – would you credit it after all these years?'

'And how is she?' said my father lightly.

'Don't you know well how she is though she never says a word?

There was a man from here went working to Boston not long ago – one of the Clearys, I don't know if you remember them? Well, he caught sight of Nellie, not so much changed as you'd think, he said, but the worse for drink in the company of two men outside a public house. Drink is the curse of the world, Daniel, and sure poor Martin himself only for it wouldn't have any wife at all to live on after him and hold his name and ours up to ridicule.'

'As I remember the somewhat distressing story, Ellen, it was *after* Martin had been shipped away by his family that he sought the consolations of alcohol – and later of matrimony.'

'All that's as may be,' said my aunt briskly. 'The fact is the same Nellie is a disgrace to us all and shouldn't use his name at all at all if she had any shame.'

'The name nevertheless *is* hers,' said my father with finality. 'Thank you, Ellen, for the kind drop but we must be off now.'

'You're in a great hurry,' said my aunt slyly. 'You wouldn't let me fill your glass again to keep the cold out, Daniel?'

'I wouldn't, Nellie. My insulation is completed now.' As I went to him he bent to examine the dusty artificial roses in the bowl on the table, into which little sprigs of lurid green celluloid holly had been stuck. 'There's a touch of the artist about you, Ellen,' he said, and I could have cheered at the wickedness of him. 'Before I go won't you allow me to wish a happy Christmas to my niece and nephew, Ellen? Where have you hidden them?'

'Ann and Matthew is below stairs with the young one,' my aunt said, somewhat put out. 'They have a cold on them and we didn't bother cleaning them up today.'

'Nevertheless.' His smile was really quite charming as well as indomitable, and my aunt Ellen reluctantly led the way downstairs. The fact is, he really *liked* children. In the kitchen, glowing with warmth from the unguarded fire, we found Ann wiping her nose on a dirty pinafore and Matthew throwing small pieces of torn-up paper into the fire and watching them roar up the chimney. Bernie made at once for the yard as my aunt appeared.

'I shouldn't do that, Matthew,' my father said, lifting the small boy up in one arm and Ann in the other. 'Little boys who do that have a habit of not growing up.' He smiled at both children and they beamed back with delighted grubby faces. Born long after aunt Ellen was judged to be past the age for childbearing, they were usually ignored in that house or left to the overworked Bernie to look after. During term-time they were kept clean enough for school but in the holidays nobody bothered with them. My father however worked hard at making them laugh, and ended up being a bear for them on the stone-flagged kitchen floor. Just before we left he produced, to my utter astonishment, two brown paper parcels from his pocket and I knew he must have stopped on the way to buy them himself: Mother's presents would have been with the big brightly-wrapped bundle upstairs.

We left Matthew racing a toy car around the kitchen and Ann with a small curly-haired black doll snug in her pinafore pocket. Colds and all, they rushed out into the icy farmyard to wave goodbye and I had never seen them so animated. I knew that if toys were given to them for birthdays or Christmas which were judged to be 'too good', they were often taken away by my aunt to be donated elsewhere after the children had forgotten them.

'Curious,' my father mused as we drove away, 'a study for an anthropologist, that family.' Suddenly he braked, got out of the car when we were half way down the lane, and ran back towards my waving aunt. 'Compliments of the season to P.J.' he shouted, and my aunt called genially, 'I'll tell him, Daniel. He's away out with a sick cow.' Impatiently I waited until my father returned and urged him to drive as fast as he could until that loathsome place was out of sight.

At home everything was beautiful. Even the brasses on the green hall door glittered as I'd never noticed before and a huge mass of red-berried holly was arranged in a brass pot-stand before the fresh white lace curtains. In the dark little hall there was more holly and ivy and then suddenly there was my mother rushing from her sewing-machine to scoop me up like a small boy into her arms. She smelled of *eau de cologne* and her brown hair newly-washed was breaking loose from its pins and she had apple cheeks. Not handsome, not young, but unlike her sister Ellen, wholesome and reassuring and – suddenly I saw it – happy.

And then the house. Never before I went to stay in the house that Ellen made had I noticed the touches that made ours different from the other houses in our modest terrace and a veritable palace in comparison with the O'Boyles' house. At the foot of the little staircase that glittered with old brass stair-rods was the grandfather clock of carved mahogany which my father had never been able to bring himself to sell. Its brass face shone, and its chime was as mellow as the polished wood. Gradually he had pushed it into the background of his secondhand furniture shop until finally it had arrived here and would stay, as he told my mother, until somebody offered him what it was worth. Our equivalent of the O'Boyles' 'Room', which was used by us always on Sundays and whenever anybody dropped in, had a red Turkish carpet that my father also claimed nobody had ever offered him a proper price for; it had a lot of old brasses too, and oddments of antique furniture kept in gleaming order by my mother who pretended to believe the fiction that any piece might at any time be sold for a fortune. She would have kept it gleaming anyway. Always in the centre of the round mahogany table was a bowl of flowers, or berries, or autumn leaves, always something fresh. Today there was more holly, and beside the hanging Chippendale wall-cabinet a little Christmas tree, the first we ever had. They were only beginning to be popular in Ireland when I was a child and naturally only the wealthy could afford them. As I exclaimed over the pretty thing, my mother bent down to put in the plug and the tree came alive with fairy lights and shimmering baubles.

Father attempted to heap more coal on the blazing fire, pausing to say over his shoulder to my mother: 'Are you sure now, Peg, you didn't let the sun at this fire earlier in the day? – it looks a bit dawny to me!'

And then all the news of Gurteenbeg came out, my mother laughing as she was expected to do over Ellen's theory about the sun's destructive rays. Wandering restlessly around the cosy room, I wanted to tell her about the full horrors of the place I had left, but I found it difficult.

She and my father regarded the O'Boyle marriage as something to be amused at and, certainly, to be grateful for since they couldn't afford to send me to St John's College as a boarder. There was something slightly affectionate in their jeering which disturbed me. They didn't *know*.

Off and on during Christmas I tried to tell them. It was hopeless. I tried to tell them – especially my mother – how I hated Gurteenbeg and everybody in it except Bernie. I tried to tell her about the hunger and the cold that were part of accepted daily life there, about the gloom that settled over my head like a cloud as I approached the house from school every evening, about evil-smelling P.J. and the crimping meanness of Ellen. My mother turned the talk so neatly whenever I approached danger points that quite suddenly I realised she didn't want to know. She didn't want to know because boarding with the O'Boyles for the moderate sum agreed on was my only chance of a 'suitable' education, the sort neither she nor my father had been given, that would in due course lead to the University in Dublin and all they desired for me. My acceptance of the O'Boyle footbridge for what it was, they took for granted, and as Christmas ebbed away I began to grow desperate.

Once I even thought of describing to her what I had seen P.J. do to Bernie when he waylaid her one night on her way back from milking the cows, but I had no words for that extraordinary sight only an obscure but positive feeling that my mother would refuse to understand even that. Especially that, because it would have been considered something I had no right to know if I had been minding my books and my own business.

And so came the day when we put away the Christmas baubles in cardboard boxes, as we did every year, and the fire was noisy with dry crackling holly. That was the day I made my last appeal.

'Don't send me back and I'll do anything for you.'

'Such as?' grinned my father.

'Such as studying night and day at home for my exam even if it kills me,' I said recklessly.

'In which case you wouldn't pass it,' said my father. 'Look, Dan, you know you *have* to go to school.'

'Can't you let me go back to the Christian Brothers, then?'

'Why not?' said my father happily, always less fiercely ambitious than my mother. 'Why not, Peg?'

But this was apparently too much. Dropping a box that had once held Christmas crackers and would now house the glass baubles which she had protected with tissue paper over the years, my mother flung herself into an armchair and wept noisily as my father and I swept the shattered spun glass off the carpet. Then I helped him wrap up again in their coloured tissues those baubles which had escaped the holocaust.

We put them away on the highest shelf of the china cupboard and I knew with a shrivelling of the soul that Christmas was over and that Gurteenbeg with its multiple miseries must be faced, as my father advised, like a man. And indeed in the clear cold challenge of January I knew too that I would never under any circumstances think like a child again.

AUBREY FLEGG

Timpani

Timpani, the kitten, was woken by a spluttering flare from the fire as a handful of holly leaves blazed up. He blinked in the brightness, stretched and yawned. It had been a disturbing day and he had been hunted from one end of the house to the other by restless people. At last he had discovered the fire in the sitting-room, and had found a place in the shade of the brass fender, where the heat from the logs rippled over his back while his nose lay in the little draught of fresh air being drawn in towards the blaze. Mrs Drumm had come in earlier, all of a bustle, and had lifted him away, tut-tutting about roasted cats, but it was hotter out on the mat where she had put him, so he had crept back to his old place when she had gone. Now he rolled over onto his side and looked at his tail. It was lying on the rug quite quietly. Until recently it had stuck straight up like a small Christmas tree but now that it had grown it seemed to have a will of its own and was inclined to wiggle when he did not expect it to. He was just about to pounce on it when he became aware of a pair of stockinged feet on the hearth-rug beside him.

Mr Drumm had had the day off. He did not usually get home on Christmas Eve but as it fell on a Saturday, he was at home and had just spent an hour putting holly over the pictures. He was glad to have it done now. Whenever he had got one sprig in place he would upset it trying to put up another. He was in his socks because he had been standing on a chair, and Mrs Drumm was particular about the chairs. Now, warming himself in front of the fire, he wiggled his toes as he surveyed his handiwork. The Christmas tree stood in the corner of the room, the glass ornaments reflecting the flickering light from the fire. The children were in bed, tucked up with their Christmas stockings at their feet. Mr Drumm yawned and stretched, and, as he stretched, his two big toes cocked up. Timpani rolled over into a crouch, his orange fur sleek and flat; his gaze was fixed upon Mr Drumm's toes. But Mr Drumm did not even know that he was there; he was thinking about Father Christmas. Despite the fact that Mr Drumm was actually a very serious sort of man, he had always believed in Father Christmas. He flatly refused to believe that such a nice and sensible idea could not be true. He had argued with Mrs Drumm about it, but she had just laughed, and now she teased him about it whenever the subject came up. The children stuck up for him of course, but still he had a sneaking suspicion that, when he was not looking, Mrs Drumm crept into the children's room and filled their stockings without his knowing. He worked his toes into the soft pile of the carpet. He had finished the holly, so he was not going to worry about anything now.

While Mr Drumm had been thinking about Father Christmas, Timpani had been crouching lower and lower. The very tip of his tail moved gently back and forth. Mr Drumm's legs disappeared above him like forest trees, his feet were like great roots in the thick carpet. From time to time there was a movement down at the toe end, a gentle unsuspecting movement, like a mouse in the grass; it stopped. Then, there it was again, an irresistibly tantalising wiggle. With claws extended and little white teeth sharp as thorns, Timpani landed on Mr Drumm's toes.

Mrs Drumm threw down her dish cloth and ran towards the sitting room as Mr Drumm's bellow rang through the house. As she opened the sitting-room door something orange shot between her legs, tripping her up as she jumped to avoid it. Mr Drumm was capering around in his socks, holding one foot in both hands. 'Where's that cat, I've been attacked, ouch! my foot, I'm sure it's bleeding.' Mrs Drumm picked herself up from the floor by the door feeling rather cross. She had been sure that Mr Drumm had broken a leg at least and here he was hopping around because of a mere scratch from the kitten. He had taken off his sock now and was anxiously inspecting his foot for signs of blood. She put her hands on her hips and looked at him with her long-suffering look. At that moment there was a crash from the region of the kitchen. Mrs Drumm rose into the air with a little shriek. 'The turkey!' she cried, and was gone.

Timpani was not quite sure what had gone wrong. His pounce had been perfect, a curving flight of vengeance bent solely on that provoking toe. But then, it was as if the forest about him had torn up its roots and gone for a dance. He had held on grimly while he could but, in a second or two, he had been flung clear, and Mr Drumm's bellow had almost flattened him to the ground where he had landed. Escape was clearly indicated but there seemed to be no line of escape that he could see. Then, as if he had said 'open sesame', the door opened. Weaving and dodging between Mrs Drumm's legs, he made for the kitchen. There seemed to be a commotion behind him. The moon, a great orb of silver light, shone through the misted panes of the kitchen window. Timpani sat looking at it, drawn towards it. The curtain moved slightly; the window was open. It was a long jump up onto the draining board below the window, and Timpani had slipped more than once trying to jump up onto the stainless steel. The turkey lay, ready for the oven, on a plate at the edge of the board, it seemed to offer some purchase for his claws. He leapt and dug his claws in deeply. It was most satisfactory. He heaved himself up, but the bird began to roll, and in a panic he scrambled over it and kicked himself off in a spring for the window-sill. The turkey rolled off the edge followed by its plate. Timpani licked his paws thoughtfully but footsteps were approaching so he slipped behind the curtain and out into the cold night air.

The turkey had been rescued and peace once more reigned over the Drumm household. Mr Drumm limped slightly as he brought Mrs Drumm a cup of coffee after dinner. He found she was watching him and looked a little sheepish. They cleared away and then arranged their presents about the bottom of the Christmas tree before sitting down in front of the fire. A log shifted and collapsed into the grate. The place which Timpani had found on the mat was empty. The Drumms talked quietly to each other as the fire died down lower and lower. It was close to midnight when Mr Drumm looked around and asked 'Where is the kitten?'

While Mrs Drumm had been rescuing the turkey from the kitchen floor, Timpani had ben sitting on the window-sill oblivious of her lamentations. He was just a little bit frightened, he had never been outside in the dark before and, despite the bright moon, everything looked different. He licked his paws to see if he could get again the taste of turkey. The garden was bounded by a high curving wall against which old fruit trees had been trained. A pond formed the centre-piece of the garden, separated from the bed below the wall by a path of paving stones. Timpani gazed down at the reflection of the moon in the pond. He remembered the fish which had risen so tantalisingly below him when he had sat at the edge of the pond in the sun. Keeping both eyes on the reflection of the moon, he slid his front paws over the sill of the window and walked them down the wall until he nearly overbalanced. Then he sprang lightly down onto the path below and scuttered, in a series of little sideways hops, to the edge of the pond. The reflection of the moon had come across the pond to meet him. It did not move again, so Timpani gave a little skip and a twist and jumped up as if to catch an imaginary bird. But the moon remained unimpressed, so Timpani forgot about it and made his way round the pond and into the flowerbed beneath the wall.

He found himself at the root of an old gnarled pear tree which reached to the top of the wall. His claws gripped the rough bark and he began to climb. After each short ascent he stopped to survey his progress. He would look down, but it was dark below and the shapes of the branches were confusing, so he would adjust himself and look up. Above him the sky was bright and the branches clear and well defined; it was easy to go on up. He found that he could hear small noises in the night about him; small rejoicings. He felt he must continue to climb or he would be missing something. But the branches were getting thinner and after each move he took it took him longer and longer to pluck up his courage to move again. At about the time when his absence was first noticed by Mr Drumm, inside the house, Timpani was about a cat's length below the top of the wall and was clinging with all four paws to a slender branch which swung away from the wall alarmingly whenever he moved. He stretched out one paw gingerly, trying not to overbalance. The branch swung out and out and then slowly back. His claws caught on the rough stone, with a sudden scramble he plastered himself to the wall, scrabbled at it and was up. Again the air seemed to be full of tiny cheering voices and bells. Timpani shook his head. Above him the full moon shone down and Timpani felt that it had been calling him – well, he had come. He sat down and licked the mortar and cobwebs from his paws and chest.

Mr Drumm was feeling that perhaps he had made just a little bit too much of a fuss about the attack on his toes and so was disposed to be kind and forgiving. Mrs Drumm was not feeling forgiving at all. The assault on her turkey was, she felt, a much more serious crime than anything the kitten could do to her husband. It was getting late and she was worried that Mr Drumm might not get around to filling the children's stockings. He was so silly about it, always pretending that it wasn't he who did it. She could hear him now going through the house, saying: 'Puss wuss wuss.' By the time he had come back into the drawing room and was backing about the room on hands and knees, still going, 'Puss wuss wuss,' Mrs Drumm felt that she ought to lend a hand. After all, the turkey was all right and the plate had not been a good one.

They met in the hall ten minutes later, at a loss as to where to look next. Mr Drumm had even crept into the children's room to see if one of them had taken Timpani in. They were fast asleep, the only sign of activity being that one of them had obviously crawled down to examine a still empty stocking. Mr Drumm felt nervous. He did not want to be caught in there by Father Christmas, or Mrs Drumm for that matter; he closed the door silently. It was when Mrs Drumm went into the kitchen to collect the milk bottles that she realised that the window was open. She drew back the curtains. The rim of the moon gazed up at her over the edge of the pond. She gave a little gasp. Could the kitten have fallen in? She collected Mr Drumm and they both ran out and searched the water anxiously for any sign of a poor drowned cat.

Timpani watched with interest from the top of the wall. He did not want to come down now. The night was full of a sort of magic which he had never felt before. He could feel it tingling in his fur. He wished they would stop blundering about in the dark below. At that moment Mrs Drumm looked up and spotted him.

'Puss wuss wuss,' she called.

'Where, where?' asked Mr Drumm anxiously, still peering into the pond.

'Up on the wall, silly,' said Mrs Drumm. 'Puss wuss wuss.'

'Don't, he might jump,' said Mr Drumm, 'I'll get the ladder.'

Mr Drumm trotted off in the direction of the house. Mrs Drumm looked up anxiously at Timpani, who now sat looking down at her. He had coiled his tail across his toes and did not look as if he was going to move for anyone, let alone jump. The wall was very high and curved round the garden until it ran up against the wall of the house. There was no way down except where some steps, leading up to the loft, came up beside the wall. Mrs Drumm devised a plan of action. At this moment Mr Drumm appeared around the corner of the house carrying a heavy extension ladder, straight up in the air; he looked like someone about to toss the caber. When the ladder tilted in the direction in which he wanted to go, he would run with short rapid steps, but when it decided to go some other way, he would resist it manfully and bring it back on course with a few sideways hops. He got round the pond without mishap, and prepared to lean the ladder up against the wall, having extended it as far as he could. The top end of the ladder came to rest among the upper branches of the pear tree not far from Timpani. The lower end rested on the mossy paving about three feet from the edge of the pond. Having instructed Mrs Drumm on how to hold the bottom of the ladder Mr Drumm began to ascend. The ladder settled in amongst the branches against the wall and the foot slipped just a little on the stone slab. 'Careful, my dear,' said Mrs Drumm.

Timpani had watched the preparations for his rescue with apprehension. He was very fond of Mr Drumm but he wished now that they would stop thrashing about and listen. They seemed to be oblivious of the music which filled the air for him. Even the stones of the wall seemed to be quietly humming deep notes.

A crashing in the pear tree and heavy breathing heralded the approach of Mr Drumm. His anxious face appeared out of the shadow below. Timpani started towards him. 'Puss wuss wuss,' said Mr Drumm. Timpani stopped. Mr Drumm leaned over to try to catch the kitten. Timpani promptly turned and ran along the top of the wall towards the house and the steps.

Watching from below Mrs Drumm had guessed that Timpani would do just this. Abandoning the foot of the ladder, she ran towards the steps. Mr Drumm recovered himself with difficulty after his lunge and steadied himself. Gradually he felt the ladder beginning to slip from underneath him. 'Hold it, my love,' he cried, but all he heard was Mrs Drumm calling 'Puss wuss wuss' from the other end of the garden. He tried to grab the top of the wall but then realised he would be left hanging there if the ladder went from under him. Rapidly he began to descend, but as fast as he climbed down, the ladder slipped faster. He was within a few feet of safety when the foot of the ladder reached the edge of the pond and he found himself shooting out over the dark pool. There was a crash and a splash and there he was sitting up to his waist in water.

Time seemed to stop. Mrs Drumm gazed aghast from the steps of the loft at Mr Drumm sitting among the lilies in the pond. But Mr Drumm seemed to be oblivious of his fate, for he was gazing at the roof of the house, a look of delight on his face. Timpani also stood gazing. At last it had happened; despite the noise of those ridiculous humans, the reason for his joy and excitement had come. From the sky in the north-east a wave of light had rolled, great hooves reaching out and trampling at its crest. Horns swung and harness jingled as runners slipped crisply over a crust of stars. The great sleigh halted above the house; a figure detached itself from the back of it and seemed to melt through the roof. A timeless second passed before he was there again, a bearded figure shaking the reins and leaping on to the runners of the sleigh as it started off and was gone.

Mr Drumm slowly stood up from among the lilies. Mrs Drumm rushed to help him. Timpani made his way to the end of the wall, jumped down onto the loft steps, and proceeded into the house. Some time later Mrs Drumm came into the sitting room with a steaming cup, to where Mr Drumm sat wrapped in a blanket in front of the fire. He put his arm around her. She was feeling very apologetic about the ladder but he *had* looked very funny sitting in the pond.

Mr Drumm's mind was elsewhere. On his way down from the bathroom he had peeped into the children's room. At the end of each bed was a stocking, full and inviting. He chuckled to himself. Mrs Drumm thought what a funny old dear he was, and began to laugh.

In his place below the fender, Timpani was woken from a deep sleep by Mr and Mrs Drumm rocking backwards and forwards on the sofa, laughing till the tears ran down their cheeks.

DAVID PARK

Angel

The too-brittle toast fragmented beneath the butter knife and splintered on the plate like a jagged jigsaw puzzle. Uneaten crusts curled toothless smiles at him across the empty table, strewn with the remains of family breakfast, while the radio roared out a babble of voices, and a discordant beat hammered in his head. He buttered the pieces of toast and ate them one by one, crunching them noisily, and sipped the coffee that had lost its first heat. His head felt heavy and dull, as if he hadn't fully woken up, and each sip of coffee tasted more bitter than the last. Although he was already late, he could not bring himself to rush. He would blame the traffic. His tongue felt furred and thick, and he knew only one thing would clear it, but that was still a long way off. Staring at the cornflakes that floated in the bowl opposite him, he wondered why she never quite managed to finish anything. As his daughter grew older, it seemed that the house was constantly filled with the sound of music. Pop blared from morning to night – but he supposed it was harmless enough. There were parents with worse problems to worry about than that. She was growing up so quickly – he didn't know where the years had gone. One moment she was a child, her bedroom wall decorated with Walt Disney characters, and the next almost a teenager, her bedroom plastered with pictures of pop stars he had never heard of. Next year she would start secondary school, and some part of him regretted it very much, as if it marked the end of a childhood period that he was unwilling fully to let go. Already she was growing in complexity and self-reliance, and it hurt him a little to find her less dependent on him, pushed aside in favour of other centres in her life. He wondered where she was now – probably searching for some misplaced book or pen. She had inherited his carelessness. The coffee was bitter to the taste and he put it down, the cup and saucer clinking a note of sour finality.

'Is there anything else you want, Tom? I'm taking Paula to school now.'

He shook his head and stood up from the table as if he, too, was on the point of leaving.

'You'll not forget, now.' She lowered her voice to a whisper. 'Call at Johnstone's and say the bike has to be delivered tomorrow afternoon – it's the only time we can get it into the garage without her being around to see it. And Tom, please don't forget about tonight – you know it's important to her.'

'Give me a break, Claire. Of course I won't forget!'

He saw that his wife was about to respond, but she let it pass, and he knew that she had been about to cast up past failures. He felt aggrieved by the eternal unremitting sharpness of her memory, but had neither the energy nor the desire to start a slanging match. Taking his cup to the sink and rinsing it, he plumped for reassurance.

'I promise I won't forget. When my girl steps up to sing, I'll be standing in the front row. And I won't forget about the bike either. Santa Claus never forgets.'

His attempt at humour evoked a silence, broken only by their daughter clattering into the room. She was buckling her school-bag and trailed a woollen scarf behind her like the tail of a kite. She took up where her mother had left off.

'You'll definitely be there, won't you, Dad? You know what time it starts – after the fireworks, right in front of the City Hall. Right beside the Christmas tree.'

He took the trailing scarf and wrapped it snugly around her neck.

'Don't you worry about it, Angel. Your dad'll be there all right to hear you sing – wild horses couldn't keep me away. Do you know your words all right?'

'Of course I do – have you not heard me singing it all week? I only have to sing one verse by myself.'

'Don't be nervous, pet – just step right up and do your best.'

But he could see she wasn't listening to his advice, and he rummaged in the pockets of his suit to find some money to give her, but found only some keys and a book of ballot tickets. Her mother called her from the hall and she paused just long enough to give him a perfunctory peck on the cheek and tell him that she would look out for him, and when she said it he knew that it was her final reminder. With a slight flinch he realised that she was treating him as if he was the child, but he did not let it show, and, waving her goodbye, he shouted after the disappearing figure.

'Don't you worry about a thing, Angel. Your old man'll be there to see you break their hearts.'

The front door slammed shut. Immediately, he switched off the radio and soaked softly in the silence. He felt vaguely hurt. A glance at his watch told him that he was already late, but he could not bring himself to hurry. He had reached a period in life when timekeeping no longer seemed important – there was no one to impress any more, and he felt safe in the knowledge that the wheels would turn reliably without his presence. He would blame the traffic, or, better still, he would say he had stopped off to view some property. What did it matter? The house seemed strangely quiet, as if the sound had been switched off, and in the silence he searched for some interest or enthusiasm to spark the hours that lay ahead. But he found nothing, only a dreary list of petty duties and formalities that froze the day ahead with a deadening predictability and left him scrambling for some escape from its icy clutches. With growing self-pity, he imagined how crowded the city centre would be, and the difficulty involved in finding a parking space. Perhaps he could phone Johnstone's from the office – no, you could never trust some anonymous jobster at the end of a phone to do anything he promised. It would need a personal visit to evoke a cast-iron guarantee of delivery at the correct time, and even then he wouldn't believe it until he saw the damned thing safely secreted in the garage. He supposed it would be worth it when he saw the look of pleasure on her face, and watched her wobble off down the driveway on her first spin. He remembered the Christmas when he, too, had woken to find a bicycle sitting in the hall – it hadn't been brand new but his father's paint job had left it sparkling and virginally fresh. When he had opened the little packages that sat under the tree, he discovered the loudest bell in the world, a black stream-lined pump, and a narrow leather pouch that clipped on to the back of the saddle and contained an assortment of spanners and bicycle tools. The memory carried him into the past on a current of unaccustomed nostalgia, and he drifted pleasurably back to a tiny box room with a sloping ceiling, awash with selection boxes, *Topical Times* football books, torches, model planes, knitted gloves and scarves. The memories ignited a little spark of warmth in him, and he tried desperately to fan them into some kind of sustaining flame before they slipped once again into the oblivion of the past.

Perhaps Christmas wouldn't be so bad, after all it was really for the children and Paula was already bubbling with excited anticipation. That was his pleasure now – sharing in his child's excitement and reliving, through her, the sense of wonder that the moment brought. He would go to Johnstone's first thing and get everything sorted out. But his resolution weakened as his mind returned to his wife's admonitions, and his feeling of annoyance burgeoned and blotted out all other thoughts. He grasped hold of nothing except the cold reality of it all. Christmas. What did it really mean? Families locked together with no avenues of escape, bound tightly by the hoops of some false festivity until they grew irritable and discordant; exuberant and extravagant expense that hung round the neck of the New Year; betting on the blind in the weekly poker school; kissing the young tease of a typist you'd lusted after during the previous twelve months. Drinking too much. That was something he needed no excuse for, but at least it was a chance to really push the boat out. There was no harm in it. It kept him sane, stopped him cracking under the pressure of competitive business, and, for a while at least, made him feel good inside. A few drinks, that was all, just enough to light the slow fire that made him feel warm and relaxed; a few drinks to free him from the daily burden of responsibility that grew loathsome and unending. Better, too, than anything else, it came closest to recapturing that feeling a young man has when it's the weekend, and he's a few quid in his pocket to burn, and the lads are rarin' to hit the town. It opened up the stultifying prison of the present, freed it from the restrictions of duty and routine, and invested the moment with a glow of mellow optimism. Claire didn't understand – she never had, always seeing it as some kind of personal rival that she had to battle and defeat, instead of something that held him together, keeping him there for her.

He let his gaze wander round the expensive kitchen and into

the hall and felt angered by her apparent lack of gratitude for the material benefits his career had brought them. She was a typical woman – nagged for things until she got them, proceeded to take them for granted, and then in a remarkably short period of time, wanted something else. She was quick enough to criticise him and harp on about things as if he was the worst in the world, but she wasn't so quick to appreciate the hard graft that had gone into getting them where they were today. As if he would forget! Who did she think he was? Didn't he dote on his daughter? Didn't he worship the very ground she walked on? She'd no right to snipe at him like that when she knew he would cut his hand off before he'd hurt the child.

His anger galvanised him into energy, and, gathering up his coat and briefcase, he hurried out to the car. He turned on the radio to catch the news. A man shot dead in front of his wife and child . . . a litany of internecine political squabbles . . . industrial initiatives . . . snow falling on the Glenshane Pass. It washed over him without registering and he switched it off again. The roads were slow and congested, and he noted the number of traffic police about. He would have to be careful – the days were long gone when a nod in the right quarter would smooth over a charge.

The office was busy and he sought to cloak his lateness with a purposeful display of unloading a sheaf of paperwork from his briefcase. His secretary informed him that there had been no calls, and no one had been looking for him. He opened his post while watching a junior typist balance precariously on a desk as she tried to put up Christmas decorations, joking with her about falling and possible insurance claims, and offering to hold her ankles, until the girl coloured and climbed down with the job unfinished. Slowly and with some difficulty, he clambered on to the desk and fastened the line of tinsel. The sudden movement had reminded him that he wasn't feeling good, and as he sat down, the incessant thunder of typewriters rattled his brain.

The morning dragged by and he continued the pretence of being busy without actually ever completing anything of importance. He shuffled papers round his desk and made some phone calls, but nothing could distract him from the knowledge that he needed a drink. He tried to postpone it as long as possible and had another coffee, but it didn't help. The clock seemed to have stopped. Eventually, as lunch approached, his impatience and restlessness overcame him, and collecting some keys from the office safe, he told his secretary that he was going to value some commercial properties. When she asked him where he could be reached, he replied that he would be on the move and would phone back at intervals, then he put on his coat and set off into the city streets. He pulled the collar of the coat up round his neck and dug his hands deep into his pockets. It was cold enough for snow. A bloody white Christmas – that was the last thing he needed; all right for the front of Christmas cards, but misery for everyone else. His dismal thoughts were interrupted by a slap on his back.

'Sell us a house, mister. Any oul hovel'll do.'

It was George Monroe, a fellow traveller of old, an accomplice in crime. They were glad they had found each other – company made each feel less swamped by the overwhelming mass of anonymous faces that flowed about them.

'In search of a little respite, Tom? Do you want a companion? I owe it to your wife to keep an eye on you!'

Their journey to Mooney's was lengthened by the density of the crowd, and at times it was easier to flow temporarily with it into divergent channels than attempt to fight against its powerful tide. Every other person seemed about to collapse under a burden of parcels, and the polythene bags they carried, emblazoned with trade names, flapped like flags in the sharp-toothed wind. A

Salvation Army band played in the pedestrian precinct, and his eye caught a glimpse of young girls in dark uniforms and bonnets, quivering the air with a parabola of ribboned tambourines. Queues were forming to enter the big stores and in each doorway collecting tins were rattled for silver. Buskers competed with piped carols, and an old man without a coat sold rolls of cheap wrapping paper. A troupe of orange-robed Hari Krishnas wove their tinkling, chanting way through the crowds, while an old man, armoured in a breastplate of scripture, distributed tracts. A few yards further on, they fluttered to the pavement and mingled underfoot with bills advertising seasonal offers in the wine store. A mother cut across their path, trailing behind her a screaming child, and at every step the crowd seemed deeper and more desperate.

'Hell, Tom, the whole world's gone crazy!'

'If we get to Mooney's we'll deserve a medal as well as a drink.'

They pushed on, steering each other in the best direction by little tugs and pulls of their coats, pausing at intervals to ponder the best route, until eventually they reached the entrance to the bar. A squeal of young girls breezed out through the doors, clutching at collars and coats in anticipation of the biting cold, and giving a second's preview of the crowded inside, long enough to show that they had found no refuge of tranquillity or seclusion. As they shouldered their way through the mêlée inside, his companion turned and grimaced.

'There's no room in the inn – it's standing room only.'

'Let's go to Henry's, George – this'd put your head away. There's not room to raise your elbow.'

Reluctantly, both men turned and edged their way back out on to the street, then trudged somewhat miserably round the corner to the less fashionable Henry's. At a corner table, they found spare seats and, squeezing into them, opened their coats with simultaneous sighs of relief. A round of drinks was set up and favoured. For him, the first was always the sweetest and the only one he ever really tasted. It felt good, and he settled back into the chair.

'Thank God, George, Christmas only comes once a year. You'd need to go into training to survive it. It's getting worse every year.'

'It'd be all right, Tom, if it didn't end up costing you an arm and a leg. Marion writes cheques like there's no tomorrow, buys expensive presents for half the world – excluding me, of course – but what really kills me is what she spends on that witch of a mother, and what I get in return. The old bat's loaded up to the eyeballs, and when she gives you a present it's something like a set of coathangers, or some plastic knick-knack that she bought in the 50p shop.'

'I can't complain about Claire – she's not bad really, keeps things within reason. It still costs, mind you – I suppose there's no way round it. Listen, McClenaghan told me this joke about mothers-in-law. "My mother-in-law visits us every Christmas. Next year we're going to let her in."'

The two men leaned forward over the table and chuckled expansively. Monroe took out two cigars from an inside pocket and they lit up.

'Sometimes, George, I think it'd be really good to go away over Christmas. Go to the sun, or even skiing. Don't suppose, though, Claire'd ever agree – she's a bit of a traditionalist.'

'Now you're talking. I've always fancied the idea myself. I bumped into Perry Foster last week, and he's off to some Austrian ski resort.'

'Perry Foster? I can't imagine him on skis, shooting down some mountain.'

'Neither can he, Tom. Never puts his feet anywhere other than under the bar. Après-ski all day long. And, I'll tell you better still – he doesn't go alone. Takes a bit of fluff with him.'

'The old dog,' laughed Tom. 'How does he get away with it?'

'The wife goes her own way. No questions asked, no lies told. Perfect relationship.'

The two men supped their drinks, and blew smoke while they reflected on the escapee and their minds conjured up images of snow-covered chalets, blazing log fires, and easy company.

'Good luck to him, George, and all, but there has to be something said for a family Christmas and carving the old turkey.'

'True enough, true enough.'

There was a pause in the conversation as both men tried to convince themselves that they didn't envy Foster's bid for freedom.

'A bad business that, last night, Tom. You'd think they'd give it a break for a couple of weeks – call a truce or something, out of respect for the time of year.'

'Those boys have respect for nothing.'

'That's the truth. Did it right in front of his wife and child. Some Christmas that kid's going to have – now and for the rest of her life.'

'Paula's class is doing the carols tonight at the City Hall. She's singing a verse on her own. I'm going to hear her. You should come, George – hear a real performer.'

'Like to, Tom, but it's my night on duty at the golf club. Anyway, between late night shopping and fireworks, the town'll be hell. There'll not be breathing space.'

Their conversation was temporarily halted by the approach of a mutual friend.

'You two boys are starting early today. Am I the only one working?'

The newcomer smiled down at the two drinkers and placed a hand on each of their shoulders.

'Sit down, Ross, and take the weight off your feet. And you're not doing much work yourself, standing in here. Has the Law Society started allowing you boys to go out touting for clients? Tom and I are just having a wee jar while we sort out the world's problems. What can I get you?'

'A hot whiskey'd go down well – it's freezing out there. But just one, now – I can't stay.'

As George manoeuvred his way to the bar, the two men smiled at each other, knowingly.

'He's a desperate case. You're keeping bad company, Tom. Have you run out of houses to sell?'

'Plenty of houses, Ross, too many bloody houses. The whole world's putting their house up for sale and buying someone else's. It's like one big property roundabout that never stops.'

'If you're so busy, Tom, how can you find time to sit in here?'

'Delegation, Ross, delegation – the first skill of management. And sure isn't it boys like me keeping the likes of you in work. The only difference is that you charge them almost double for half the work.'

'True enough, but you get to work with a better class of customer. You wouldn't want to meet some of the trash I'm rubbing shoulders with every day. Some days you feel you should disinfect yourself before you go home. Money wouldn't pay you.'

'Money never comes easily, Ross – we all have to grub in the dirt sometimes, and the richer the man, the more dirt he's grubbed in. You can bet on it. But, tell me this – what do you think of this new tax? Is it not going to hit your pocket as much as ours?'

'There's ways and means. A bit of artistic accountancy goes a long, long way. Our accountant's the most creative man I know. But here we go.'

The drinks arrived, and they settled back into the mellow depths of the afternoon, rounds of drinks and conversation easing them through the hours. They went out for food and returned, then, for a change of scenery, made the short journey to Mooney's. Familiar faces came and went and the hours passed, gliding along on well-oiled rails, journeying through business talk, gossip, reminiscences, solemn bouts of setting the world right, and always the clink of glasses and the palliative company of old friends. He felt safe and sheltered from the madness outside, and gradually the day lost its boundaries of time.

The coldness of the air made him flinch, and for a moment he felt tempted to return to the warm security behind him, rather than embark on the hazardous and uncertain journey that duty told him stretched ahead, but the warm glow inside him mingled with the memory of his promise to his daughter and compelled him into the undiminished flux. He felt strangely at one with the anonymous faces that flowed around him, and he nodded and smiled, as if to old friends. He bumped into someone and apologised with a bestowal of the season's greetings and an elaborate bow. His step took on the jaunty spring of a man cresting the waves and, for the first time, he began to feel finely festive in mood. He found himself singing along with a carol that blared from an outside speaker, and his right hand conducted imaginary choirs. Confronted by a collecting tin, he searched in the depths of his pockets before chinking a stream of coins into it, then sported the badge on the breast of his coat like a medal of honour.

The Christmas lights were on now, and the city centre crystallised in a white brightness as lights and neon tinsel stretched across the main streets like fluorescent icing on a cake. For a second, the noise and lights confused and disorientated him – he had drunk too much too quickly – but he laughed at himself and, with a little skip in his step, headed onward. As he passed a jewellery shop, he remembered that he had not yet found a Christmas present for his wife. He edged himself into a space at the window and viewed the contents, not quite managing to focus his attention exclusively on any one object. The display was a meaningless and undifferentiated grotto of trinkets and baubles that gave him no guide or inspiration. Still, finding something would remove the need for a return shopping trip and at that moment his spirit of well-being encompassed even his wife. A neck chain or bracelet would probably fit the bill, might even buy some short-lived credit. It was a good idea.

The shop was not as crowded as he had expected, and in a few moments a girl came to serve him. She wore a black suit, and a white blouse that seemed to have lost none of its crispness, and only the tiny beads of damp on her top lip spoke of a long, hard day. She smiled at him and he smiled back, his eyes drinking in her youthful freshness, and everything about her gratified his senses. She greeted him as if he was the most important customer of the day. Her glossy black hair was cut in a bob and flowed with the movement of her head, accentuating the whiteness of her skin and the soft red mouth. He wondered what she would be like. He looked at her, slowly savouring each part of her as he had savoured that first drink. She was young, but she wasn't a child. Looking over her shoulder he caught his reflection in a mirror – he wasn't over the hill yet, there were still plenty of good years left. He wondered if he could still cut it. Leave aside a couple of meaningless indiscretions along the way, and, by and large, he had been a faithful husband, and what was his reward? A dried-up husk of a relationship that functioned in a mechanical way, stuttering along with predictable, timetabled pretences of passion. His eyes rested on her neck as she leaned across the counter to show him a series of gold chains. He wanted to touch her. If he no longer had youth, he did possess the maturity money brought, and he had read that some girls found that an attractive feature. He teased her gently, and when she mentioned prices, he dismissed the subject with a 'sure it's only money'. She smiled at his jokes, but he couldn't detect any personal edge to her professional charm. He bought a gold neck chain and was vaguely aware of spending more money than he had intended. She wrapped it carefully, making a decorative package topped with a pink bow, and for a second he thought of saying that the present was for her, but it wasn't like buying a barmaid a drink, and as he watched the manicured fingernails tie the bow, a little seed of doubt was sown in his optimism. She probably had a trail of followers after her . . . she wouldn't be interested in the likes of him . . . he was old enough to be her father. But, a decade earlier, then it would have been a different story. He consoled himself with this belief as he left the shop. A gold necklace and a bottle of her favourite perfume – that would do the job. There couldn't be any complaints about that, no unspoken suggestions of negligence. In the outside window, his eyes fixed on a digital clock and with some shock it struck him that he had lost track of the time. He would have to hurry if he was to get a good position for the carols. He wondered if Paula was nervous before her big moment, but he knew with pride that she would be able to carry it off. She had always been like that – a real trouper – and he was proud of her.

As he stepped out into the street, there was a sudden explosion, and the night air shattered with splinters of light. Involuntarily, he stepped back into the shelter of the shop doorway, startled and a little frightened, and then, as a garland of light twisted in the sky, he realised with a feeling of foolishness that the firework display had already begun. He would have to hurry. Following the momentary frieze of frozen stars, he walked as quickly as his co-ordination would let him, and threaded his way uneasily through the milling crowds. Fiery rockets screeched into the night sky above him and fragmented into a fall of luminous petals, while fluorescent reds and yellows ignited the dark pockets of the night and cascaded into nothingness. Spangled rosettes of blossom burst into transient life and were greeted by applause and gasps of pleasure. He hurried on. The bicycle – he had forgotten the bloody bicycle. He stopped and looked at his watch, but knew he would never make it in time. First thing in the morning he would phone; better still, he would go round himself and sort the whole thing out. A bright tracery of light laced the sky ahead, and as he set off again, a final crescendo and eruption of colours showering over the green domes of the City Hall signalled the end of the display.

He çould see the covered stage at the side of the giant Christmas tree and he could hear the children's voices rising up in song. His tired eyes fixed on the bright star, and he left the pavement for the greater freedom of the road. The sound of 'O little town of Bethlehem' called him on, and he knew nothing could prevent him from reaching his destination. He was a good father – no one could deny him that, and he knew Paula would be looking for him, wanting him to be there. He would never let her down. He felt warm inside, benevolent to all men and at peace with the world. It was a special time – he couldn't deny the emotions and feelings bubbling up inside him. All the cynicism and world-weariness washed away, and he opened his heart to the holiness of the hour. He thought of all the mothers who, at that moment, were wrapping presents for their children and sealing them with love; of fathers working overtime to gather up the means of providing their families with the festive feast; of the children with every sense alive and tingling. In his imagination, he saw the great snow plough clearing the Glenshane Pass, throwing the fresh, white snow to the sides of the road, its yellow lights splitting the dark and lighting the way for travellers. He caught some of the words of the carol, and he thought, too, of the city he loved, tinselled and shimmering in the safety of the fire that burned so brightly and fended off the wolves, who waited and watched in the darkness of the woods.

He was almost there now. He was conscious of bumping into people, and aware that people were looking at him, but nothing mattered, he had to be there to hear his Angel. Shouldering his way through the spectators, he reached a position against the crash barriers in front of the nativity scene. He could see her now, and his hands gripped the cold metal bar. She was dressed in white, with a silver tinfoil halo hovering above her head and cardboard wings fluttering precariously in the breeze. Yellow light bathed the crib and lit the children's intense faces as they grouped round the manger and the holy infant. He wanted to call out to her, let her know he was there, but the terrible sanctity of the scene bound him in silence. He wanted to kneel, but the press behind him prevented any change in his position. The voices of the children rose on fragile wings through the cold night air, heralding the miraculous birth. He too wanted to worship, bring his gifts, and as their music faded into the darkness, tears of remorse started to his eyes.

MARY MORRISSY

Rosa

From his palace in Rome the Pope had ordered a holy year. Everyone in our small city was touched. Even Penbridges, the big department store where I work, had pushed Santa Claus to one side. Usually he holds the centre stage in the large foyer on the first floor, sitting beneath a great, needle-dropping tree, its branches laden down with silvered, snowy baubles. This year he was huddled in one corner while in the centre was a huge crib with life-size figures. The management had even considered having real animals, a donkey and an ox, nuzzling close to the child, but they couldn't risk the possibility of steaming turds on the carpet so they settled for plaster-cast models of the animals instead. But the *pièce-de-résistance* was the baby, a black baby. It was a stroke of genius. We rarely see a dark face in these parts and so it seemed Penbridges had absolved all our prejudices with one bold gesture.

It was Rosa who pointed this out to me. Rosa is my sister, younger than me by five years although it has never seemed that way. I live on the edges of her dark, livid world until it seems that without her I would barely exist, that I would be a mere spectre, passing in and out unseen through the sullen doorways of her life. Even her name, Rosa, is a sort of concoction. At home we used to call her Rosie – a dark, freckled child squatting in patches of mud or clumps of grass, burrowing with her tiny, dimpled hands. When she came to the city she became Rosa, conjuring up an image of deep, sultry eyes and a small, fluid body. And in time she became that, as if, chameleon-like, her wish was enough to create.

In the last months of her confinement she visited Penbridges' crib daily. Then, I dismissed these trips as just another vagary of pregnancy like the early cravings for pineapple and raw meat. And I thought perhaps this, the ultimate picture of maternity, was actually taking hold of her. It was, at least, warm and safer there than the crowded, wet streets which she tramped constantly. She would come back to our rooms barefoot, soaked through, her hair wringing, her sodden shoes in her hand, their dye leaving faint red patches in the hollows beneath her ankle bones. But in Penbridges she made quite a pious picture, a heavily pregnant girl kneeling before the crib, tinselled angels hanging above her, little scrolls emanating from their trumpets with Gothic-red messages emblazoned on them. Oh, they had got everything right – the melting snow on the roof, the obsequious hunch of the shepherds, the stained wooden slats of the manger, even the acrid smell of the stable. But to me it reeked of artifice; all this elaborate effort to create an imitation.

'Look,' Rosa said to me when we went there together. 'Look at Joseph and Mary, how pale they are. They don't seem a bit put out that the baby is a different colour.' She cackled. 'That's religion for you . . .'

He was like a cat, fleeting in moonlight. I heard them thrashing in the night, then the sudden, shocked stillness of their union. Did I imagine a coldness in their pleasure? Perhaps. But, like the crib, it was a fine imitation. I watched them as one might trace with a finger the gentle lashing of fish against the glass of an aquarium. When he was gone she would sit with her back to me, her lips suppressed with a kind of excitement. I would stand behind her, one hand in hers, the other settled in the sad curve of her neck parting the tiny strands of hair with my thumb until I had laid bare her forlorn nape and her bridled fervour had melted away into a sated melancholy. I knew, of course, that he would abandon her, and I simply waited. And, sure enough, one evening I heard him fleeing, down the stone flights and through the landings below, the clatter of his footsteps fading like the tinny jubilance of an empty vessel hurled into the depths of a well.

We were left to count the days. The pale squares of the calendar seemed to grow hollow-eyed from our attention. Every morning I sought tell-tale signs on her white underwear but it yielded up only the indolent smell of sex which clung to her long after he was gone. Rosa grew strangely listless. When we went to the clinic she held my hand, placing herself trustingly in my care. We sat silent as a haggard woman with skin like suede and a soothered child on her lap addressed the waiting-room.

'Never had any trouble with the other three, but this one has my heart broke. Always sick, always cranky . . .'

The child sat, stoppered and somehow accusing. I winked and smiled at her, believing that such clownish behaviour was expected, but she stared back, unblinking, solemn.

As we went home, Rosa glanced at her newly confirmed shape in shop windows. Serpentine mannequins, their fingers arched mockingly like Balinese dancers, their heads tilted quizzically, smiled back at her. She stopped once, staring through them at her own reflection.

'It's not really there,' she said, flattening her stomach.

'Rosa, Rosa . . .'

'It's like a balloon . . . I could easily burst it.'

'Rosa, we are not murderers.'

And, even if we were, who would have helped us in a year when vigils were held at grottoes and rosaries were broadcast in railway stations?

'We must tell Father,' I said.

The thought of going home filled us both with dread, not for what we had to tell him, but for the mastery of his dismal existence over us. He has been alone for years, ever since Mother died in childbirth with our stillborn brother. Now he shuffles around our dark little cottage, swamped by moss-coloured clothes. Crumbs of cigarette ash settle on the sheeny crotch of his pants as he sits by the dim glow in the grate. He runs a crinkled hand through his thick, grey strands which are as coarse as horse hair, and sighs. It is not great unhappiness. No, it is as if he expected this grim ebb-tide in his life and is mesmerised by its seething undertow.

It was I, in the end, who told him while Rosa sat in the overgrown garden, idly plaiting her hair. He shifted once in his chair but said nothing. I knew then that nothing we did or said could ripple the hypnotic stillness of his own gloom. But, as we were leaving, he caught me roughly by the arm and said with a sagging smile, 'She has won you over, our little Rosa.' Was it then I passed over into Rosa's world? No, even then, there were corners of it into which she retreated that I could only guess at. Once I found a half-empty bottle of gin in the bathroom and a rim of grime around the tub where she had lain for hours. Another time she tried to prick the surface of her belly with a safety pin as if to tear it open, until I prised the pin from her hand.

I used to bring her gifts from the outside world – small, strawberry-filled chocolates, a pink velvet ribbon for her hair, a bright crimson dress. I brought her books, manuals of motherhood full of tranquil passages and soft photographs of swollen women, but she only pointed to the protective male hands on each of their bellies as if I were trying to taunt her. I remember the rolling gait of two, her arms encompassing the bump in a gesture of aborted protection. When we passed blooming, bulbous girls on the street she would point after them. 'Dromedaries, one-humped camels, beasts of burden, that's all we are.' And yet, she had never looked healthier. Abandonment had given her a luring, almost sexual glow.

But sometimes, late at night, I would hear her softly whimpering in her sleep. Once she woke in terror crying, 'How will it come out?' as mind overtook body in the nine-month race. The thumping being beat in her like a drum, she said, resenting its confinement, the distended part so ugly now, displacing all her innards, leeching energy, dictating. I had no answers, but held her head in my lap until she went back to sleep. In time, her body answered for her, flexing its muscles, preparing regardless, tightening, clenching around its prize, her skin stretched to translucence. Full-blown, circumferenced, we awaited the eruption.

I could not be with her for the birth. The week before Christmas is Penbridges' busiest time and I had to report for work as usual. I was on Cold Cuts in the food hall, sawing through flaky breasts of chickens or using the slicer on sweating joints of ham. While Rosa lay somewhere else on a cold slab, the midwife in a butcher's apron, the nurses gathered around like spectators at a bullfight, their urgent cries mixing with hers of pain. As I passed cold, wet bags of giblets across the counter, there might be a great tearing of skin . . . The doctor would hold the balloon up, a small, shrivelled thing. It would hang there for a moment, then he would pass it to her. And Rosa would catch it up by its slim neck and put it to her lips. At first it might make no move – then it would leap, salmon-like, into life. Or would she just gently let it go, releasing her fingers from its slender neck, and watch it shudder and recede . . . I longed to be with her.

The store did not close until nine. I walked home through the soiled, littered streets thinking only of her. On my way I bought flowers. Not roses because she said they reminded her of death, but speckled orange tiger lilies. She was standing on the doorstep when I arrived, the baby muffled in her arms.

'Rosa, what's happened?'

She put her finger to her lips and motioned for us to go in. We made our way up the stairways, slowly, because her stitches were still raw and broke her tread. Beneath her coat I could see a hospital shift. Her feet were in slippers and her hair at the back was clotted with sweat. No one passed us. When we got to our rooms, we pulled out a drawer from the dresser, lined it with a soft blanket and placed the child in it. I lit a fire (the room was icy) and made some broth. We sat for hours saying nothing, until I could bear the imposition of her silence no longer.

'You want to get rid of it, don't you?'

She nodded like a child being coaxed out of a sulk.

'But how? Where?'

'We'll leave it in the crib.'

We rose early on Christmas Eve. While Rosa fed the child I gathered up what few belongings we needed to take with us and put them in a suitcase. I found a large plastic carrier bag to put the baby in. Then I had to leave and go to work. The day passed in a frenzy around me, while inside there was a stilled waiting. As usual, Penbridges gave each of us a small, wicker hamper packed with pieces of turkey, a bottle of wine, a pudding, and little jars of preserves, which I put to one side. This gesture, like all the others of the day, seemed at once endearing, and yet chilling, because this was a world I no longer inhabited. At five the store closed.

We rushed to our lockers, changed out of our uniforms and then filed past the clock, which snapped our cards for a moment in its lips, registering our departure with a wheezing whir.

Rosa was sitting outside on the street, perched on the suitcase, the plastic bag sitting primly on her lap. I was suddenly very nervous. I took the bag from her and made my way back against the swell of the crowd. The store was in darkness but one of the managers was stretching up to shoot the last bolt on the door. I tapped on the glass. He peered out at me.

'What is it?' he cried.

'I've forgotten my hamper.'

He opened the door. I smiled at him, hoping that he would not look down into the bag. I could feel the baby stirring.

'You girls are all the same.' He sighed. 'Go on, then.'

Although the store was dark I knew its alleyways by heart. In the faint glow of light from the street I could make out the outline of the escalator. I climbed up its frozen steps to the first floor. There was no one about. I made straight for the crib, pushing aside the pew so I could get closer. I lifted the shiny plastic baby out, and from the bag gathered up Rosa's child and placed it in the hollowed-out manger. It was sleeping and barely stirred as I settled it. Rosa was right – in the darkness no one would know the difference. The pale faces of Joseph and Mary looked down lovingly at the dark creature. I put the doll in the bag. I found its glassy eyes and puckered, rosebud smile unsettling, so I covered it up. As I made my way down to the locker-room by a back stairway I thought for a moment about the child who would wake sometime in the night and wail, its cries echoing eerily around the empty store, which by then would be turning to coldness as the generators wound themselves down. I knew the pattern of the security men well. They would sit in their little box at the back entrance for the festive season, or go to a nearby pub and get quietly drunk.

They would not hear the child, or if they did, would imagine it was some trick of the old building releasing the daytime cries of hundreds of children slowly into the night. When they dismantled the crib in the new year they would find a creature as dead and as frozen as the one originally placed there. And Rosa and I would be far away. From the deserted locker-room, its metal cabinets closed firmly against me, I collected the hamper and put it in the bag. I passed, unseen, by the staff entrance into a blind side-alley.

Rosa without her burden was almost gay. The Christmas lights strung across the scrawny neck of the street blinked dazedly. Hoarse-voiced hawkers thrust great bunches of balloons at us and frantic, whirring toys, furry creatures with metal hearts embedded deep within them, set off by the cold click of a key. We bought provisions – freshly baked bread, bottles of stout, eggs, a side of ham – because Father would have nothing in the house. From a stall I bought a pair of gold earrings for Rosa. She put them on immediately, catching her thin lobes between her fingers as if each were a delicate scrap of gauze. We took the train home, crushed up against one another, rocking gently through the dark countryside, amid packages and boxes and bright peals of laughter.

For once, Father seemed pleased to see us. We swept through the house, cleaning and polishing. Rosa was energetic at first, scrubbing away at encrusted stains on the stove, but later she crumpled and I had to help her to the sagging double bed we shared in the back room. For the first time in years Father lit the Christmas candle and left it burning in the dark hollow of the window while we went to midnight mass together. The village church was crowded. I was back once more in familiar territory, among women with soft, sloping shoulders cowled in downy coats. From the back it seemed they wore scarves of children's arms, while other small hands clawed excitedly at the crooks of their elbows. Behind us there was the scuffing of men and boys gathered at the back of the church, and as always, that odour of candle grease which as a child I thought was the smell of hair singeing in hell.

On Christmas morning Rosa and I moved the kitchen table into the arms of the bay window and threw a white cloth over it. The room was filled with bubbling smells as the ham and pudding spluttered on the stove. Father sat in his usual place by the fire, smiling moistly at us, as if sensing that it would be our last time together. He never asked about the child, although when we sat down to eat there were stains on Rosa's blouse – her milk was coming in and her swollen breasts were sore and tender. After dinner he grew garrulous on the stout we had brought, and as we cleared up, he began to sing in a voice entangled in phlegm:

There was an old woman and she lived in the woods
Weile, weile, wáile,
There was an old woman and she lived in the woods
Down by the river Sáile.

She had a baby three months old
Weile, weile, wáile,
She had a baby three months old
Down by the river Sáile.

She had a penknife long and sharp
Weile, weile, wáile,
She had a penknife long and sharp
Down by the river Sáile.

She stuck the penknife in the baby's heart
Weile, weile, wáile,
She stuck the penknife in the baby's heart
Down by the river Sáile . . .

From the scullery we joined in on the chorus, eyeing one another as we carried him through verse after verse. It made me wonder, as our voices rose and fell in ragged unison, if we don't all have murder in our hearts.

SEAN O'FAOLAIN

Before the Daystar

When you come out into the Place Pigalle from its dark side-streets your first impression is of its brightness, then crowds, then noise, and then you become one more aimless wanderer around the jammed pavements. Tonight there was a sharp sense of liveliness, even gaiety, almost like the end of a feast-day, although the streets were cold and damp and a cobweb of pink mist hung suspended over the roofs. It was Christmas Eve, about ten minutes short of midnight.

In a corner of the overcrowded terrace of *Le Rève* five young people, three young men and two young women, sat crushed about a small table behind the fogged glass partitions, talking loudly to make themselves heard above the gabble. The youth who was doing most of the talking looked like a light-weight boxer. He wore a black polonecked sweater; his blue-black hair, harsh as metal, peaked over his forehead like a wound-up watch-spring; his smile was a lighthouse flash. The others interrupted him only to spur him on. Their Scherazade? Their pet liar? Indulged. Bantered. Approved.

In a pause in his flow of talk the fair-mousy, pretty girl at his side tilted her scarlet tarboosh so as to tickle his cheek with its blue, silk tassel, and said, 'Happy now, Andy? This is better than Dublin, isn't it? Or isn't it?'

He gave her his white grin, gripped her frail arm and squeezed it.

'As happy, Jenny, as a lamb with two mothers.'

He turned swiftly to the fat youth at his other side. 'Jaysus, Fatso, I wonder what'd we be all doing this minit if we were back in Dublin?'

Fatso raised a finger for silence, groped inside his mustard-and-cress overcoat and slowly, very slowly, drew a vast, silver half-hunter from the well of his fob-pocket. He clicked it open with the air of an ancient out of an ancient world, considered its convex face, smooth, shiny and milk-white as his own; and pronounced in a slow Abbey Theatre brogue.

'I would be afther thinking, dearly beloved, that at this minit we would all be up in the Lamb Doyle's, or in The Goat, or The Cross Guns, or The Purty Kitchen where George the Fourth had his first glass of Guinness, being thrun out on our ears for the fourth time in succession. Althernatively, Andy, you would be snoring in your little white cot in your little white home in Templeogue.'

'Would I now? Well, then, let me tell you, Mister Laurence-O-bloody-well-Toole, I'd be doing no such a thing. I'd be being hauled off by my ma by the short hairs to Midnight Mass. That is, after the usual couple of preliminary breast-wallopings with the Dominican fathers up in Blackhorse Lane.'

He paused to turn to Biddy.

'Our privileged heathen,' he mocked.

Champagne-blonde, older than Jenny, not pretty, her splendid pigeon's bust straining her white sweater.

'Yes?' she queried, in an English voice so tiny that the first time they met her they had asked her if she had the pip.

'I mean Confession,' he explained, politely flicking two imaginary crumbs, one-two, from her bosoms. 'The annual clear-out. Old Father Berengarius. A mile of hardy sinners queuing up before me. The ould chapel as cold as a vault, and the wind under the slates moaning like a hundred banshees. He's as deaf as a post. Very convenient for yours truly. Doesn't hear a blooming word you say. Did I ever tell ye the night he disgraced me ma?'

He received their quizzical attention.

'There she was, late on Saturday night, inside in the confession box, asking him, if you please, was it a sin for her to believe in spirits and ghosts, and the mile of hardy boys outside all grumbling, and growling and rearing to get in and get out before the pubs closed on them. "Having commerce with ghosts", was what she called it. "What are ye saying to me?" says he, and his hand to his ear. "Is it a sin, Father," says she at the top of her voice, "to have commerce with ghosts?" "Speak up," says he in a roar that you could hear down at O'Connell Bridge. "To have commerce with ghosts, Father," she squawks, and the buckos outside all leaning sideways to hear the pair of them. "You have been having commerce with goats!" he roars at her. "At your age?"'

Once more they gave him the soft accolade of their laughter. Modestly rejecting the honour he turned aside and as suddenly turned back. Crook-necked he gestured to the dark street behind their corner café.

'Will yez look, boys! The foxy-headed whore is back again. Trying to click a GI she is this time. They're brazen tonight. Out in the open. He's twice her height. He'll make pancakes of her.'

They all swayed. The nearest of them to the glass partition was Mackinnon. He peered out under his black Homburg hat, low over the boils on his forehead. She was a small, skinny woman in a sheepskin jacket, a white beret, a white satin bottom as taut as two mushrooms.

'She must be frozen,' said Jenny pityingly.

'Behold the fruits of French logic,' Biddy piped. 'They close the brothels and every woman in Paris gets pneumonia. That foolish man will be streaming at the nose tomorrow morning.'

'I consider it most unseemly,' said Mackinnon. 'On Christmas Eve!'

Andy pointed his index finger at him, pulled the trigger, said, 'Bang, you're dead!' They laughed. They knew their Mac. A tongue of gall. He had never said an original word in his life. He worked at the Irish embassy. He would go far. They called him Mac the Knife.

'Mac!' Andy said, 'I wish you to understand that I am on the side of all rebels, exiles, outcasts and sinners. What Genet called The Saints of the Underworld.'

Biddy calmed his clenched fist with one scarlet-netted palm.

'Easy, Andy! And it was not Genet. Pasolini. And I do trust, dear boy, that you are not going to go all romantic on me tonight. I mean, talking about Dublin. And your mamma. And Midnight Mass. And Confession. And Dominican fathers. And, now, French hoahs.'

He was too fascinated by the comedy in the street to heed her. She enlisted Jenny's help.

'Jenny, is our broth of a boy about to get plawstered on us yet once again?'

'Haven't you observed?' Jenny sniffed, 'whenever he takes to the bottle in a big way it always means the one thing? Some new crisis with his precious Deirdre.'

'Deirdre?' she whispered. 'But that little Irish fool doesn't mean a thing to him. Deirdre is merely the girl he sleeps with.'

At this Jenny laughed so bitterly that Biddy peered one-eyed at her.

'I trust, my dear, that you are not getting soft on him? I mean, as one old harridan to another, you must be hitting twenty. And,' she whispered out of the side of her mouth, 'he is only a poo-o-oodle!'

Jenny considered him seriously. In Paris less than six months, as Dubliny as the first day they met him, light-headed, light-hearted, feckless, a liar, much too fond of his liquor. Nobody was ever going to travel very far on his roundabout. Certainly not Deirdre. As if he felt her looking at him he grinned at her and turned back to the street. She said loftily to Biddy, 'I assure you!'

'There is no need to protest, dawrling. We're all gone about Andy. That irresistible Irish charm. He's even gone about himself. It's his disease.'

Under the table Jenny felt his hand creeping slowly over her knee.

'Andy, why didn't you bring Deirdre tonight?'

His hand withdrew. He sighed, 'Poor little Deirdre.' He burst into a sudden passion. 'Jenny! Do you know what I am? I'm a sink!'

'Tell us, Andy,' she said sympathetically, 'why are you a sink?'

'No! You tell me! Examine me! Have no mercy on me! Tell me what's wrong with me.'

Mac the Knife tapped his arm. His speckled forehead became suffused with venom. He assumed a stage-Cockney's wheeze.

'I'll tell you, chum, wot's wrong with you. You're 'omesick for dear, old, dirty Dublin. Your wrists long for the chains. Your back aches for the lash. Cheer up, chum, this time next year you'll be back there for keeps, with no Pigalle, and no cafés, and no night-clubs, and you'll have your eye on a good job, and be wearing more holy medals than a Lourdes veteran, and you'll be running off like a good little boy to Midnight Mass, and Aurora Mass, and Third Mass, and Fourth Mass, and . . .'

Andy leaped up. His chair fell. All over the terrace heads turned lazily towards them. A waiter paused in his stride.

'Do you want a sock in the kisser?' he roared.

The two girls dragged him down.

'Andy!' Jenny chided and stroked his arm as if he was a cross dog. 'Aa-a-ndy!'

He retrieved his chair. He sat down glowering. Then he leaned over, seized Mac's hand and shook it warmly, rapidly, hurtingly.

'Mac! My old pal from schoolboys' happy days! As one unconverted and thoroughly corrupted Irish crook to another leave us be honest for one brief moment of our all too long and useless lives. Leave us admit that we've both been emancipated by La Belle France. We've killed Mother Ireland. We're free!' His grin fell dead on the table. His visor sank slowly over his toddy. 'We're emancipated. And disbloodywellillusioned.'

'I knew it,' Biddy piped to the striped awning. 'The Celtic Goat of Pure Romance. I saw it coming. I felt it in my bones. And I warn everybody present that I shall not be able to bear much more of it.'

Andy's head shot up.

'Anyway I gave up all that Holy Joe stuff years ago. I was a converted atheist at the age of seven. I was thrown out of school at fourteen for denying the existence of God. I proved it by logarithms.'

'You don't say so?' Mac jeered.

Andy shot him again on a quick draw, turned to Jenny, put his arm about her narrow waist and confided into her ear for all to hear.

'Jenny, my love, I'll tell you why I'm a sink. This morning Deirdre said to me. "Don't go out from me tonight, love! Don't leave me on Christmas Eve," says she. "Okay," says I, "come along with me." "You'll only get tight again, shéri," shays she. "Don't abandon your own loving, little Deirdre," shays she. "Spend it alone with me," shays she. But I did leave her! And I *am* going to get tight! And to hell with her! God Almighty, does she want to turn me into a monk? Imagine a fellow not having a couple of jars with his pals on a Christmas Eve! The trouble with Deirdre is she's not emancipated. There's one for you, Mac, who'll be back in Dublin in six months. In five years she'll have a squawl of kids around her saying the Rosary every night. Still and all I did ditch her. And there's no getting away from it. I'm a lousy sink!'

She stroked his cheek with one long finger.

'I don't think you're a lousy sink, Andy. I think you're a sweet sink. You just can't hold your liquor, any more than you can hold your conscience.'

He tightened his arm about her waist.

'Jenny! You understand me better than anybody else in the entire, global world. You're the grandest girl in all creation!'

'Better than Deirdre?'

He banged the table and shouted.

'I'm worse than a sink. I'm a flamin', flittherin', filthy, finished-off sink!'

'Jesus help me,' Biddy moaned, and began wearily to powder her nose.

Jenny whispered something into the whorls of his ear, he let his head sink on her shoulder, her blue tassel fell over his eye, he put his arm around her again. Mackinnon twirled a palm of antique boredom at Larry Doyle, who beamed pleadingly at him as if begging indulgence for all young lovers. Suddenly Andy flung up his head with a wild jerk.

'Boys and girls! I have a smashing idea! Why don't we all tumble into a taxi and go off to Midnight Mass in the Irish Church?'

'Here it comes,' said Biddy, brightly snapping her compact. 'Back to our vomit. Cassandra the daughter of Priam, that's me. Often heard, rarely heeded, always right. Never let it be said that I am a spoilsport,' she begged them all, gathering up her handbag and a four-foot-long, peacock-blue umbrella. 'Which is this church you mentioned, Charlie? Church of Ireland? Papish? Celtic synagogue? I'm with you all the way even to the Mosque. Or would it do if I led you to some good, old, solid ten-by-twenty Nonconformist tin chapel somewhere?'

Mackinnon rose, took off his black hat, held it to his chest and spoke with Castilian pride.

'*Mademoiselle, vous oubliez que je suis Catholique.*'

She made a soft noise like a duck getting sick, they all laughed, and while Andy was paying the bill they scrambled out on to the pavement. It was jammed by the crowd outside Le *Jardin d'Eve* looking at lighted photographs of naked women with breasts like udders. Biddy said in annoyance to Jenny. 'I notice they always leave him to pay the bill.'

'The boy is a fool. He loves to play the milord.'

'Tell me, does he always get religion when he starts thinking of Deirdre?'

'You've known him as long as I have. Are you getting soft on him now?'

Biddy shrugged.

'I wouldn't mind having a bash at old Andy.'

'He's not your sort. He is what you said. A poodle. A puppy. He's just a kid. Let him alone.'

The kid rushed out and hooked the pair of them into the crowd. They saw the redheaded whore, her eyes circling slowly about her like a slow waltz, glance at and dismiss Mac and Larry. Andy laughed, 'Business bad tonight.' It occurred miserably to Jenny that her eyeballs would be circling under her green eyelids even in her sleep. Larry called out, 'The Irish Church is miles away, can't we go somewhere else?' The crowd bumped them. The doorman of *Le Jardin d'Eve* barked at them to come and see the most nude women in the whole world. 'Ask him,' Andy suggested, and Larry approached him. While Larry and he were comparing silver half-hunter with gold half-hunter Biddy said he was like Georges Brassens' daddy. Jenny said he was like her own daddy. The barker closed his watch, directed them to the Rue des Martyrs, called after them '*Vite, mes enfants! C'est tard!*' Then, behind them his voice soared, '*Les plus nues du monde . . .*'

They turned from the lights, and the crowds, and the rumbling beat of Pigalle's heart into the narrow street whose prolonged silence gleamed distantly with coloured windows. By the time they were filing into the church the congregation were shuffling erect for the Gospel. Biddy halted inside the door. Mac and Larry stayed with her. Andy probed along the aisle and found two empty places in the front row directly facing a small Christmas manger with the Infant, the Virgin, Saint Joseph, the cow, the ass, the shepherds and the coloured kings huddled about a crib under an amber light and a bald electric star. Whoever had arranged the *crèche* had perched a stuffed robin redbreast on the edge of the cot. Andy nudged her, nodded at it, and winked conspiratorially.

She was back, one frosty morning, four years ago, at home, awakened by a thud on her bedroom window: it was a robin lying stunned on the window-sill. In her nightgown by the open window she had held it, throbbing between her palms, staring at the one big eye staring up at her, and for that one sleepy moment all life was as simple as a captured bird. She opened her palms, the robin flew off into the frosty air, and the morning star gleamed above the hills and the murmuring beach. *In splendoribus sanctorum.* The priest was intoning the psalm. In the brightness of the saints, she remembered from other midnight masses. *Ex utero ante luciferum*

. . . From the womb before the day-star, I begot Thee. Did he remember? She touched the hand beside her and they looked at one another. Thereafter, silently from her white shore her bright moment ebbed. It fell as softly as a leaf from a book, a rose petal. Her window empty, her beach dry, she saw, leaning against a pillar beside them, the woman in the sheepskin coat. When the sanctus tinkled everybody else but she knelt. When everyone raised their heads she was still standing there, staring blankly in front of her. Andy was gone. There was no sign of him down the aisle, nor could she see the other three.

Crossly, she made her way back to the doorway, and out to the street. It was so dark that at first she saw nothing; then she made out the four figures on the opposite side of the street clumped like a bunch of gangsters, smoking cigarettes. She crossed over.

'Why did you come out?'

Biddy slowly smoothened her netted fingers and said sullenly, 'It wasn't my show, dawrling.' Larry Doyle looked uncomfortably at Mac the Knife who made a half-moon with his hangdog mouth, performed a high, dissociating shrug, and looked at Andy who let out a zany guffaw and then said sulkily, angrily, 'We should never have gone!'

'It was you who proposed it!'

'We shouldn't have done it!'

'I thought they were doing it very nicely?'

He appealed to them, boxer-crouched.

'When you don't believe in a thing what is it but tomfoolery?' He stood back, his claws to his chest. 'I don't believe in anything. It's all kid stuff. I felt indecent inside there.' He shot out his left. 'And that bloody redhead in there finished me off. God Almighty, people have to be honest, don't they? They have to come clean, don't they? When I saw that wan in there I felt, Jaysus, what am I but another dirty bloody hypocrite?'

Jenny slapped his face, stepped back in dread, ran a few yards downhill, he after her, turned, a lean hare, ran faster and faster until he caught her, whirling her against a black wall under a street lamp, gasping, her palms spread against him. They panted.

'What's wrong, girleen?'

'What's wrong is that you *are* a hypocrite. First Deirdre. Then that street-walker. Who are you going to blame yourself on next? Me? Biddy? Why don't you go back to Dublin and rot there? It's what you want isn't it?'

She turned to the wall and burst into tears. He waited while she sobbed. When she was quiet she turned and asked him for his handkerchief, wiped her eyes, said, 'May I blow?', and blew.

'Why should I want to go back to Dublin? I'm happy here, with you, and Biddy, and all the gang.'

'Are you?' she challenged. She gave him back his handkerchief. 'I think, Andy,' she said quietly, 'you'd better go back now to Deirdre. You know she'll be waiting up for you all night.'

He made a noise of disgust.

'She's not the answer.'

'And what is?'

He took her arm and led her back to the group. Sacerdotally, Larry blessed them with a sweeping arm, '*Benedicat vos. Pax vobiscum.*' Mackinnon said, with immense bonhomie, 'A Happy Christmas to the happy pair!' Biddy said, coldly, 'And what does one do now?' Larry threw his arms around Jenny, and intoned.

My beloved, drink the cup that cheers
Today of past regrets and future fears,
For, ah, tomorrow we may be
With yesterday's seven thousand years.

Nobody commented. The woman was standing alone on the step of the porch looking across at them. As they looked at her Andy walked over and spoke with her. Then the two walked off slowly, out of sight.

Mac gave a beck of his head to Larry, said to the girls, '*Le Rève*', and the two of them went off, hunched together, nose to nose, back to Pigalle. Jenny whirled and stared downhill towards the pink glow over Paris. For a while, Biddy considered her rigid back. Then she contemplated her long slim legs. Then she regarded her left thumb, wiggling it double-jointedly. Then she looked up at the sky and said, 'Andy once told me he spent an entire night discussing the works of Guy de Maupassant with a hoah in Marseille. He said they were still at it when the sun rose behind the Château d'If. Odd! Even in Marseille the sun does not rise in the west. I shouldn't worry about him if I were you, Jenny. He will be back in *Le Rêve* in half an hour as chaste as the dawn and without as much as a franc in his pocket. He'll tell us that she has a grandmother in Provence, or a child in hospital, or that she reads Pascal every night. The party's over. The night is bitter cold. And I am sick at heart. We'll get a taxi and I'll drop you at your door.'

'I want to walk,' Jenny said sourly.

Biddy's fledgling's voice took on an edge.

'In this cold? To Saint Germain? Do you want to die for him, like Mimi?'

'What is he up to? Always expiating for something or other? What's the point of it? Why doesn't he grow up? If he does give that woman all his money he'll only leave Deirdre penniless for a month, and borrow from us, and then borrow from his mamma to pay us back.'

'Unlike us, he is young and innocent. It is what makes him so appealing. In his bothered way he's different.'

'Or is it just that all Irish men are different? Look at the other two. My God! What are we *doing* with them?'

Biddy hooted.

'Dear child, you obviously have no idea what Englishmen are like. I know! I've put dozens of them through my little white hands. Full to the gullet of guilt, black silences, sudden glooms, damp despairs, floods of tears and then that awful, manny, British laughter and "Let's have another one, old girl". Paris has been absolute bliss after London. Every Frenchman a swine. It's been such a relief. It's his only trouble – he thinks he's a sink and he isn't. It takes centuries to produce a really first-class sink. Still he shows promise. The right woman could do a lot for him. Not Deirdre, a silly little Dublin chit, just as stupid as himself. Let's get a cab. I'll pay for it and drop you right at your door.'

'I still want to walk,' Jenny said stolidly.

'It's savage. My ears are dangling by a thread. A cab, for God's sake!'

'Are you trying to get rid of me?'

Biddy regarded her with admiration, and shrugged.

'Biddy! What do we see in him?'

'Ignorance? Hopelessness? Eagerness? Terror? Charm?'

'But he is such a fraud!'

'And as you said, such a fool!'

'But, you say, innocent?'

'As a rose!' Biddy sighed.

'Let's go back to *Le Rêve* and see if he does come back.'

'He will come back. His type always comes back. One of the lads.'

He came, wildly excited, bustling in, penniless, full to the gullet of lies and boastings – or, if they were not lies, of fantasies, and if they were not boastings, of dreams.

'All our lives,' he pronounced, 'we dream of love, and love eludes us. We have fled, Mac, from the sow that eats its own farrow. And all the time we dream of our childhood and are never free of it. O exiles of Erin, love ye one another. My bloody foot! Two single tickets to Dublin, that's the right ticket. But where shall we find her? Every mis-match Irishman a born matchmaker, and good at it. Saving others who cannot save himself. Sitting in a Dublin pool of drink and dreaming of the Arc de Triomphe. I told her I'd follow any woman to the ends of the earth but not to the end of the world. Nobody would take a fellow up on that! Gimme the Queensberry Rules and be God I'll not complain. I want a loving, lovely, innocent wife!'

'With squads of babies?' Jenny asked and felt his hand start to rove over her knee.

'Squads and squads of them!'

'All chawnting the Rosary?' Biddy piped mockingly, and pressed his other hand.

Their mockery could not halt him. The girls looked at one another with big eyes, shook their heads and made wry mouths of self-astonishment. Mac's eyes kept closing and half opening from sleep and drink. 'What are we waiting for?' he asked dully. Larry Doyle looked at his turnip-watch and sighed, 'It's gone two'clock.' The terrace was empty. The pink haze fell as glistening rain on the street. Nobody stirred. Even their talker was silent.

After a while he spoke, looking around at them sullenly.

'I'm going to take a plane to Dublin in the morning. Who'll lend me the money?'

EDDIE STACK

Time Passes

We often threatened to take the Boat on those wintery mornings after Christmas while we waited for the dole office to open. Huddled in deep doorways, sheltering from the spray blown up from the river, we shook our heads in despair. We were sentenced to another year's penance in the wind and rain. Another year in a world of shuttered shops.

There would be no market until the Saturday before Saint Patrick's day and it was common knowledge that some shopkeepers – bored and bothered by the stillness – would take to their beds for weeks at a time, only surfacing for the funerals that always followed the rain. There would be people in town for the funerals. The funerals, the Mass and the dole brought us together to complain and spend the government's money on cold porter. And the more we drank, the more pitiful our situation seemed – grown men being paid by the government to remain on the census sheets and being despised for doing so.

But yet we stayed. For some obscure patriotic reason we lingered on in that place where there was neither hope of work nor lover.

We passed the year threatening to leave for England and retelling tales we heard from the Lads. There was another world on the far side of the water and the Lads were in the thick of it. They were our heroes in those days. Altar boys who went to Camden Town wearing scapulars and came home with blue tattoos. Seven days a week they worked in the midst of rogues and ruffians, ripping up roads and pouring concrete so they could spend Christmas in Ireland.

They arrived the evening before Christmas Eve on a special train that brought them from the Mail Boat, and from early afternoon, that seldom-seen station was the liveliest place in town. Stalls sold hot soup and toffee apples and two women from Barranna hawked naggins of poteen for half the price of shop whiskey. The school choir sang carols and Father White collected money for a new church from a dwindling congregation. For the first time in almost a year, laughter and song drowned the sound of the roaring brown river and months of gloom vanished like the night.

Hours before the train was due, groups of young people walked up and down the windswept platform, cajoling with railway officials and shouting false alarms. The more anxious preferred to wait in the colder waiting room, or sit on icy grey platform benches. Cloaked in scarves and shawls, country women crunched clove sweets because they were too shy to smoke in public. Their husbands sucked pipes and looked up and down the rusty track, conferred with railway officials and reported home.

By four o'clock the gas lanterns were lit and hackney drivers arrived, muffled in coats and scarves. These shrewd men noted what parties were in attendance, what fares to expect, who to solicit and who to avoid. They only left their warm cars when excitement peaked and everyone swarmed to the platform, peering up the line and listening to the harassed rumblings of the approaching Steamer.

The Lads emerged from the dimly lit carriages to a rousing reception of cheers, waves and back slaps. Pink faced and closely shaven they looked angelic. Helpers and hackney drivers took their brown bulging suitcases and Father White's choir sang 'Come All Ye Faithful'. We all joined in. Parents shyly welcomed home their young with tears and we sang louder and marched around the platform. Gloria, Gloria, it was really Christmas.

But there was always someone or other who failed to return, even though they had written to say they were coming. Bewildered relatives put a brave face on grief –

'They'll probably arrive for the New Year,' they said. We nodded in agreement, even though we knew better.

The Lads passed their first night at home and were brought up to date with the year's happenings, the weather, the state of the country, church collections and other burdens the plain people had to bear. Old and new news was exchanged until the travellers showed signs of fatigue. Then they were urged to go to bed with a glass of hot punch and a sprinkle of Knock water.

On Christmas Eve they came to town with their parents and drank moderately in long-ago haunts while the old people did the shopping and attended confessions. There was no end to their money on that day, loans were offered freely and drinks were bought for everyone who wished them well, enquired about the sea crossing or asked –

'How're things Beyond the Pond?'

And things beyond were always good.

By Saint Stephen's day all family dues and duties had been attended to and the Lads rambled to town after breakfast, packing the small bars and attracting hoards of hangers on. It was a day of banging doors, thirsty Paddys criss-crossing town in shoals of blue suits. Bars steamed with sweat, smoke and after-shave lotion. Floors were littered with charred Swan matches, Senior Service cigarette ends and bronze trupenny bits, left for late night sweepers. Pubs hummed every time the Queen's face decorated the counter – no monarch had ever raised so many smiles in Ireland. And later when the Wrenboys descended on the town with flute, fiddle and tambourine, we jumped for joy. We had the best of all worlds then – the Queen's money and plenty music, in our own backyard.

As time passed, old acquaintances were renewed and the Lads trusted us with tales about the parish's forgotten sons and daughters. These secrets were imparted in the strictest confidence and later retold with the same sentiments.

Every second year Rufus Ryan, a man who had emigrated long before I was born, had another wife. Jim Flynn was either in or out of jail. One year we heard in detail why Pat Browne left the priesthood and took up the shovel. And why Mary Scully went on the game after a tempestuous marriage to a Welshman. Hatchet O'Day met her in a boarding house and she cried in his arms and begged him not to tell. But he did, and more.

The Lads began to wither as more time was spent in the pubs than at home. By the fifth day of Christmas, the blue suits were creased and crumpled, white shirts were stout stained and London socks left unchanged. In the mornings, eyes were bloodshot and watery and the Lads resorted to drinking hot whiskey to line their stomachs. They were in topping form by the time faithful friends and professional listeners arrived.

* * *

Their stories and antics brought Kilburn closer to us. We quickly became familiar with the 'Tube' and knew the stops on the Circle Line, the Picadilly and the Jubilee. We heard about their haunts and habits. Wild sprees in Camden Town and dicey nights in the Galtymore. Saturday sessions in the White Hart, Quirke Road Church for Sunday's Irish papers.

Each year we discovered anew that there was little comparison between life at home and in London. The Lads pointed out that we had few comforts. No Soho. Or no Chinese caffs where waiters bowed and took your coat. And bowed again when they served you unidentifiable piles of food, at four shillings for two. We often had to sympathise with them for bothering to return home at all, and they always looked us in the eye and said –

'If it weren't for the aul lad and d'aul lady, I don't think I'd bother.'

And yet they spent little of their holiday at home. They preferred instead to entertain us with stories about subbies from Roscommon, granite hard gangers from Connemara and cute foremen from Cork. All tough men who were respected for their crookedness and cruelty to others.

As the days trickled away our heroes became slovenly, sometimes unruly, often drunk. The sessions were lengthy and sometimes in the evenings, a brother or sister might be dispatched to town in an effort to coax them home for dinner. But they preferred to linger on in the smoke-filled bars and chew dry turkey sandwiches at the counter, turning around between mouthfuls to quip –

'You'll never go back, Scobie.'

They regularly fell asleep beside pub fires, waking unexpectedly to startle us with songs from London juke boxes. Some got awkward when they were refused more drink, publicans were insulted, glasses were broken.

The last day or two of their holiday was spent at home with their families and on the Sixth of January they left again for London. Lonesome men with empty pockets and brave faces, seen off from the station by weeping women and stone eyed old men. There were no hackney cars, no helpers, no stalls, no hymns. The green train rolled into the rain and stole Christmas with it.

Ivy and holly were taken from the walls, the Crib and decorations were stored away for another year and there was a hush in the countryside. We heard the wind and the river again and felt the grey drabness of January that paved the days for Lent. It was a lonely period when even clocks refused to pass the time and their hands lingered between hours for hours on end, or so it seemed. Again we threatened to take the Boat, lonely for company and the spirit that had been whisked away from us. Weeks passed before we got into step with the year and then Christmas became a legend, one to be compared with previous ones.

But time passes, and when Christmas came around again the Lads dutifully returned home. They came every year until the government closed down the railway line, shuttered the station and sold the track to small farmers. Dublin turned its back on us and London slipped further and further away. Then the journey home became full of obstacles and hazards.

After a few Christmases the Lads gave up the ghost. When they did come home it was for family funerals and then they drank too much and cried too much. Angry tears for stolen years. In drink-stained whispers they promised to come home the following Christmas, for old time's sake.

But we rarely saw them again. There was nothing left to return to and the Lads moved on. Life had set its course and school friends drifted away without warning. Time tricked us and it became too late to change, too late to take the Boat, too late to wake up.

We are still on the census sheets and still drinking pints of cold porter for the government, when we meet for the dole, the Mass and the funerals. But there is little life in the public houses, now colder than the station waiting room. Only postmortems are held here in these ghost-ridden rooms where jackdaws block smokeless chimneys. And yet they are our only refuge. It is here we are forced to shelter before moving through the Winter.

Time passes, but memories linger.

JAMES PLUNKETT

Finegan's Ark

It was while he was pushing his way through the Christmas crowds in Moore Street, Finegan told us, he remembered the Noah's Ark the Granny and the Aunt had bought him in that self-same street well over 40 Christmas Eves before.

It was a sudden and vivid memory, he said – the kind that hits you in some vital part of the machinery and makes everything grind to a stop. Did we ever experience anything of that kind?

Joe left down his glass to say he had. I did the same and said I knew what he meant. Casey avoided comment by picking flakes of cigarette ash out of his whiskey with the help of a pencil. A stout man and a nondescript kind of a man with a muffler whom none of us knew leaned over from their table in the corner and listened carefully.

Apart from the two strangers at the table there were only the four of us in the Snug. Normally we would have been in the bar, but what the Boss called 'The Grand Xmas Draw' was to take place that night and this year the four of us had been selected to draw out the tickets and to ensure that all was conducted in accordance with the requirements of justice and fair play.

It was the custom on Christmas Eve to segregate those so honoured from the riff-raff in the public bar. Why, I don't know – perhaps as a precaution against corruption and malpractice and to lend dignity and a sense of occasion. Anyway, there we all were, waiting for the Boss himself to give us the word that everything was in readiness.

'When I looked around,' Finegan said, continuing with his Epiphany, 'dammit if everything wasn't exactly the same as on that evening 40 years ago.'

Then he went on to describe the scene: the fog under the lamps, the thronging people, the carol singers shaking their collection boxes and the traders with barrows jamming both sides of the street, all bawling out their novelties under a forest of balloons. It was a very affecting description.

'I like carol singers,' the stout man told us. 'When I hear the carol singers I do get a lump in my throat.'

'What class of an Ark was it?' Joe asked.

'A wooden one,' Finegan said, 'with a figure of Noah and a collection of animals to go with it.'

'That's a nice gift for a child,' the stout man approved. 'I believe in gifts that encourage a fitting respect for our holy religion in the child.'

Casey, I noticed, looked across at him sourly, but then Casey was looking sourly at practically everything bar his whiskey that night, so nobody minded.

'I remember asking the shopkeeper would it float,' Finegan continued, 'and he told me it would and he patted me on the head.'

'That was for the benefit of the Granny and the Aunt,' Casey put in.

'I think that was very nice,' Joe said getting soft, 'an Ark that floated.'

But Finegan shook his head and said that that was the ugly part of it – that was what he was coming to. After five minutes in a bathtub the joints had opened and Ark and animals had gone to the bottom.

Noah had floated a bit longer than the rest, he told us. And then he described Noah lying on his back staring up at him with saucer-blue eyes, unable to believe that God had let him down.

Joe was astounded.

'That'd shake your faith in anything,' he said.

'There's terrible rogues and liars loose in the world,' the stout man said. And for the first and last time that night the man in the muffler took his nose out of his hot rum.

'A poor little child,' he said, unable to believe it.

Then the Boss brought more drink to us and said everything would be ready very soon. The pair in the corner had more hot rum and the stout man, remarking the notice of 'The Grand Xmas Draw' on the wall, said he'd like a ticket for that and the Boss sold him one. Casey gave him another sour look and turned to Finegan.

'I didn't know the Granny was a Protestant,' he remarked.

Finegan was astounded.

'The Granny was no bloody Protestant,' he said, putting his glass down to bang the table, 'and I'd like to know who's spreading a rumour like that about me and mine.'

'In the name of God,' Joe said to Casey, scenting a row, 'what made you say a thing like that?'

'It struck me that a Noah's Ark is a very Protestant class of a toy – that's all,' Casey said, very coolly, I thought.

At that moment, by good fortune, the Boss arrived in with more drink, which had a soothing effect on everybody, especially the stout man, who now butted in to mollify all concerned.

'And do you honestly think they'll be better educated children than you were, that the way we educated you was wrong?'

Liam paused.

'Well it's an alternative.'

His father didn't respond, thinking of nationalistic comradely Irish school-teachers long ago. Nothing could convince him that the discipline of the old style of education wasn't better, grounding children in basic skills. Silence somehow interrupted a conversation, darkness deep around them, the water of the floods shining, reflecting stars.

Liam said goodnight. Liam's father grunted. Susan already lay in bed. Liam got in beside her. They heard a bird let out a scream in the sky like a baby and they went to sleep.

Gerard woke them in the morning, strumming a guitar.

Saint Stephen's day; mummers stalked the street, children with blackened faces in a regalia of rags collecting for the wren. Music of a tin whistle came from a pub, the town coming to life. The river shone with sun.

Susan divined a child dressed like old King Cole, a crown on her head and her face blackened. Gerard was intrigued. They walked the town. Mrs Fogarthy had lunch ready. But Liam was worried, deeply worried. His father lay above, immersed in the past.

Liam had his past too, always anxious in adolescence, running away to Dublin, eventually running away to England. The first times home had been odd; he noticed the solitariness of his parents. They'd needed him like they needed an ill-tended dog. Susan and he had married in the local church. There'd been a contagion of aunts and uncles at the wedding. Mrs Fogarthy had prepared a meal. Salad and cake. The river had not been in flood then.

In England he worked hard. Ireland could so easily be forgotten with the imprint of things creative, children's drawings, oak trees in blossom, Tudor cottages where young women in

'Let's all remember it's the Eve of Christmas,' he said, 'and listen to that lovely singing there outside.'

There were tears in his eyes. The sound of a carol drifted in and when I looked around I saw silhouettes against the frosted glass. The smaller figures, the children, held candles that flickered behind cardboard shields. Looked at through the glass, each flame wore a nimbus.

It made Joe remember in his turn going down Moore Street as a child. It was the Granny and the Mammy *he* used to go with he told us – God be good to them, for they were both long since in their clay.

'I remember often enough,' he said, 'standing outside the public-house waiting for them. I knew well enough they were in there coaxing themselves to a couple of hot clarets on the sly, but of course – so as not to give scandal or bad example – they used to pretend to me that they were short taken.'

Casey looked up at heaven. The stout man lowered a man-sized mouthful of the rum and said that it only went to show what a shining thing Irish Catholic motherhood could be, and that Christmas, when all was said and done, was really a time for the children.

He used to sing in the Church choir himself at Midnight Mass, he said, which was the happiest days of his life. Where would a man be without his Irish mother and the comforts of God's Holy Religion. We all agreed with him.

'Listen to that, for instance,' he said, pointing a finger at the ceiling.

We listened. It was shaking under the weight of scores of merrymakers in the upstairs lounge.

'The majority up there,' he said, 'is young blades getting parlatic on the smell of a cork, the holly and ivy drinkers out of our so-called Catholic university. Not to mention the young bits of girls with them, that should be at home helping the mammy to stuff the turkey and wash the kids for early Mass in the morning.'

'Ah, now,' Joe said reasonably, 'suffer the young. Sure we're only young once.'

'I agree with our friend,' Finegan said severely. 'If they were daughters of mine it's sore bottoms they'd all have. That's what they'd suffer from.'

Then the Boss himself came in with another drink and said that all was in readiness for the draw. So Joe raised his glass to everybody and said: 'Well, here's a happy Christmas.'

'A happy Christmas,' we all said.

'With knobs on,' Casey said, and glared again at the stout man.

We trooped up the stairs. A large box full of raffle tickets stood in the centre of the Boss's sitting-room and about it were set out the prizes – turkeys, hams, bottles of whiskey, port and sherry, packets of cigarettes, rich Christmas cakes, boxes of chocolates.

We began the draw, and of course the inevitable happened. The first ticket out was number 445 and we all remembered it belonged to the stout man.

'There's the luck of the draw for you now,' Joe said. 'We're drinking here all the year round and a stranger comes along and has the coolness to win first prize.'

'He has,' Casey said, 'and do you know who that stranger is?'

'A Protestant, no doubt,' Finegan said, his resentment flaring up again.

'Whoever he is,' Joe said peaceably, 'he's a decent poor divil anyway, with a nice, natural upbringing. Did you see the way he cried when he heard the children singing the carols?'

'Let me tell you who he is,' Casey said, glaring at him. 'He's a notorious bloody receiver of stolen articles – a fence. And that skinny little gurrier with him is just out of the gaol after a sentence for burglary.'

Casey works in the Courts, delivering summonses and all that class of thing, so none of us dared to doubt him. The Boss got pale.

'Merciful God,' he said, 'ruined.'

We all understood what he meant. If it got noised abroad that fences and burglars were taking to frequenting his premises in such numbers that they won prizes in his Grand Xmas Draw it would do his business no good in the world. It was a time for swift decisions. Casey looked at the Boss, then at us. Without a word he took ticket number 445 and tore it up.

'Is that agreed, boys?' he asked.

We all nodded. There was no need to ask what he meant.

'Right,' Casey said, 'now, in the name of God, let's start the draw.'

When it was over we went back to the bar and certified that everything had been done in strict accord with honesty and fair play and we announced the results. We returned to the Snug again for more drink, this time on the house. The Boss had one with us and so had Muffler and the stout man.

The carol singers outside began again. The stout man wept copiously, so that the tears splashed into his hot rum. Casey, raising his glass, gave us a toast.

'Here's to Noah,' he said, staring hard at Finegan. I looked into my glass and saw two unbelieving, saucer-blue eyes.

MAEVE BRENNAN

Christmas Eve

The fireplace in the children's bedroom had to be swept out and dusted so that Father Christmas would have a place to put his feet when he came down the chimney. Lily and Margaret Bagot watched their mother, who knelt close in to the grate, brushing the last few flecks of ash out of the corners. Lily was eight and Margaret was six, and the long white nightgowns they wore fell in a rumpled line to their ankles. They wore no dressing gowns although the room was cold – they would be getting into bed in a minute. It was a square room, the back bedroom, with faded garlanded wallpaper in blue and pink and green, and it was lighted by a single bulb that hung from the middle of the ceiling. One large window looked out onto the garden and the adjoining gardens. Mrs Bagot had pulled the blind down all the way to the sill. She wanted the children to have their privacy and, beyond that, she wanted them to be safe. She didn't really know what she meant by safe – respectable, maybe, or successful in some way that she had no vision of. She wanted the world for them, or else she wanted them to have the kind of place that was represented to her by lawyers and doctors and people like that. She wanted them to go on believing in Father Christmas and, more than that, she wanted to go on believing in Father Christmas herself. She would have liked to think there was someone big and kind outside the house who knew about the children, someone who knew their names and their ages, and that Lily might go out into the world and make something of herself, because she was always reading, but that Margaret was very defenceless and unsure of herself. Lily was maybe a bit too sure of herself, but at the same time she was very soft, very nice to people who maybe wouldn't understand that it was her nature and that she wasn't the fool she seemed to be. Father Christmas knew that Lily was clever, always getting good marks at school. No matter where the presents came from, Father Christmas came down the chimney, Mrs Bagot was sure of that. He was probably hovering over Dublin now, seeing how the city had changed since last year. The children were all older, that was the great change. It was always the great change, every day, not just once a year. She placed her dusting brush across the paper in the scuttle and stood up.

'Now Father Christmas will have a place to put his feet,' Lily said.

'He wears big red boots,' Margaret whispered.

'Time to go to bed now,' Mrs Bagot said. 'Come on now, into bed, both of you. Margaret is nearly asleep as it is.' She had left them up long past their usual bedtime and Margaret was drooping. Lily was as wide awake as ever; she'd be awake all night if this kept up. But it was Christmas Eve, and Martin was home early from work. He was downstairs now, reading the paper and waiting to come up and say good night to them. Because Martin was home, the two cats and Bennie, the dog, were all shut up in the kitchen. He hated to see the animals around the house, and the animals seemed to know it – they had all settled themselves very comfortably around the stove the minute she told them to stay. They were all stray animals that had found their way to the house at one time or another, and they had never lost their watchfulness. They knew where their welcome was. Bennie was Mrs Bagot's special pet. He was a rough-haired white terrier with bits of black here and there. Mrs Bagot had rescued him years before from a gang of small boys who were tormenting him, and since then she had seldom been out of his sight. He slept on her bed at night. Martin Bagot didn't know that. Martin had his own room at the back of the house. He generally got home from work very late, after Mrs Bagot and the children and Bennie and the cats were all asleep. He didn't like to have Mrs Bagot wait up for him, she had to get up so early in the morning to get the children off to school. He thought the animals all slept in the little woodshed behind the house.

Daisy, the thin black cat, belonged to Lily, but Rupert was Margaret's. Rupert was a fat orange cat who was so good-natured that he purred even the time his tail was caught in the kitchen door. Martin knew the names of the animals and sometimes he asked the children, 'How is Daisy?' or 'How is Rupert?' but he liked them kept out of the house. He half believed the animals carried disease and that the children would suffer from having them around.

Downstairs in the front sitting room Martin was watching the flames in the grate. He had thrown the evening paper aside. There was nothing in it. He was thinking it was nice to be home at the time other men got home at night. Nice for once, anyway. He wouldn't want to have to get home on time every night the way other men did, walking into a squalling household, with the children trying to do their homework on the same table where their mother was trying to set the tea. But, of course, he was different from other men. He wasn't the least bit domesticated. Nobody could call him a domestic animal. How many other men in Dublin had their own room with their own books in it, and their own routine going in the house – an unbreakable, independent routine that was perfectly justified because it depended on his job and his job depended on it. Delia had her house and the children and he had his own life and yet they were all together. They were a united family all right. Nobody could deny that. Delia was a very good mother. He had nothing to worry about on that score. Ordinary men might want to be lord and master in the house, always throwing their weight around, but not Martin. A bit more money would have come in handy, but you couldn't have everything.

The room was decorated for Christmas. He and the children had worked all afternoon on it, with Delia running up and down from the kitchen to see how they were getting along. They had all had a great time. Even Margaret had come out of herself and made suggestions. There were swags of red and green paper chain across the ceiling and he had put a sprig of holly behind every picture. The mistletoe was over the door going out into the hall. At one point Delia had come hurrying up to say they must save a bit of holly to stick in the Christmas pudding and he had caught her under the mistletoe and given her a kiss. Her skin was very soft. She looked like her old self as she put her hand up against his chest and pretended to push him away. Then the children came running over and wanted to be kissed too. First he kissed them and then Delia kissed them. They were all bundled together for a minute and then the children began screaming, 'Daddy, kiss Mummy again! Daddy, kiss Mummy again!' and Delia said, 'Oh, I have to get back to the kitchen. All this playacting isn't going to get my work done.' Lily said, 'Women's work is never done.' Lily was always coming out with something like that. You never knew what she'd say next. Margaret said, 'I want to kiss little Jesus,' and she went over to the window where the crèche was all set up, with imitation snow around it and on its roof.

The window was quite big, a bow window that bulged out into the street. Delia had filled it with her fern collection. They were mostly maidenhair ferns, some of them very tall, and she had them arranged on small tables of varying heights. Sometimes Martin felt the ferns were a bit overpowering and that they darkened the room, but tonight they made a wonderful background for the crèche, making it seem that the stable and the Holy Family and the shepherds and their animals were all enclosed and protected by a benign forest where they would always be safe and where snow could fall without making them cold. The Three Wise Men stood outside the stable as though they were just arriving. Lily had carefully sprinkled snow on their shoulders. Some of the snow had sifted down onto the carpet, where it lay glittering in the firelight.

On his way home today, Martin had bought two small gold-coloured pencils for the children. Each pencil was in its own box, and the girl in the shop had wrapped the boxes in white tissue paper and tied them with red ribbon. They were out in his coat pocket in the hall now, together with a special present he had bought for Delia in the same shop, and he wanted to get them and put them on the kitchen table so that they wouldn't be forgotten. He knew Delia had the rest of the children's presents hidden in the kitchen. He'd better do it now, while he was thinking about it. He went out into the hall, shutting the door quickly after him to keep the heat in the sitting room, and as he fumbled in his pocket for the pencils he heard Delia talking to the children in the room upstairs. Her voice was low, but it was very calm and definite, as though she was explaining something to them, or even laying down the law about something. He had the pencils now and he stood very still. He couldn't hear what she was saying, only her voice, and once or twice he thought he heard the children whispering to her. It was very peaceful standing there in the hall, very peaceful and comfortable, although the hall was a bit cold after the warmth of the sitting room. But he felt very comfortable, very content. All of a sudden he felt at peace with the world and with the future. It was as though the weight of the world had fallen from his shoulders, and he hadn't known the weight of the world was on his shoulders, or even that he was worried. In a few years he would be making a bit more money, and then things would be easier. He had no desire to know what Delia was saying, or to go up there and join in. That was all between her and the children. He would only upset her if he went up there now – he would wait till she called him. It was dark in the hall except for the faint light filtering through the glass panels in the front door from the street lamp outside. He listened to Delia's voice, so quiet and authoritative, and he had the feeling he was spying on them. Well, what if he was. He didn't often have the chance to watch them like this, in the gloaming, as it were. How big this little house was, that it could contain them all separately. He might have been a thousand miles away, for all they knew of him. They thought he was in there in the room reading the evening paper, when in fact he was a thousand miles above them, watching them and watching over them. Where would they all be if it wasn't for him? Ah, but they held him to earth. He had to laugh when he thought of the might-have-been. He might have travelled. There was very little chance now that he would see the capitals of the world. He never knew for sure whether Delia and the children were his anchor or his burden and at the moment he didn't much care. He had seldom felt as much at peace with himself as he did now. It would be nice to fall asleep like this, happy like this, and then wake up in the morning to find that the world was easy. He had often thought the house cramped, and imagined it held him down, but tonight he knew that he could stretch his arms up through this hall ceiling and on up through the roof and do no damage and that no one would reproach him. There was plenty of room. He was as free as any man, or at least as free as anybody could be in this day and age. Now he would run down to the kitchen with the pencils. Delia would be calling him any minute. But the light was switched on on the landing above, and Delia appeared at the head of the stairs and saw him.

'Oh, Martin, I was just coming down to get you,' she said.

'I was just coming up,' he said, and he started up the stairs, two steps at a time.

The closer it came to their bedtime the more excited the children were, although they stayed very quiet. Delia was afraid they wouldn't sleep, or that if they did sleep they'd wake up in time to find herself and Martin creeping into their room with their presents. She stood by their bed, talking to them to calm them down, and she found that the sleepier they became the more apprehensive she herself was. She was getting what she called 'nervous' and she couldn't understand it, because she had been looking forward to Christmas. She didn't know what was the matter with her. She was as fearful tonight as she used to be long ago at home when she lay in bed listening to the wind blowing around and around the house. The fear was the same in this house, exactly the same, except that this house was attached on both sides to other houses and so the wind couldn't blow around it but only across it. But the fear was the same. She hated the wind. In the daytime she was able to keep busy, but at night as she lay alone in the dark her mind went back, and instead of going back into dreaming, like daydreaming, it went back into conjecture and from there into confusion. Instead of rebuilding the past to her own design and making things happen as they should have happened, she was blown by the noise of the wind against bitter obstacles that she was able to avoid when the weather was steady. Words like 'why' and 'when' and 'how' rose up against the dreaming that rested her, and she was forced back on herself, so that instead of rearranging things she had to face them. The past led to the present – that was the trouble. She couldn't see any connection at all between herself as she used to be and herself as she was now, and she couldn't understand how with a husband and two children in the house she was lonely and afraid. She stood there talking to the children about what a lovely day they were all going to have tomorrow, and she was well aware that she was falling into a morbid frame of mind. And there was no excuse for her. She had nothing to worry about, not tonight anyway. There wasn't even any wind, although it had rained earlier and would probably rain again before morning. There was really nothing to worry about at the moment, except, of course, how to get Bennie up out of the kitchen and into her room without Martin knowing about it. It would be terrible, awful, if Martin found out that Bennie slept every night on her bed, but she couldn't leave him out in the shed in the cold. The cats always slept on the children's bed, but they'd be all right in the shed for the one night. She had a basket out there for them. They could curl up together. But Bennie couldn't go out there – she'd miss him too much. She wished she could talk to Martin and explain to him that Bennie was important, but she knew there was no use hoping for that. It was time now to go down and call him to come up and say good night to Lily and Margaret, but when she walked out on the landing she saw him standing in the hall below.

The hall was quite narrow, and was covered with linoleum, and it served its purpose very well, both as an entrance to the house and as a vantage point from which the house could be viewed and seen for what it was – a small, plain, family place that had a compartmented look now in winter because of all the doors being closed to keep whatever heat there was inside the rooms. In the hall there was a rack with hooks on it for coats, and there was an umbrella stand, and a chair nobody ever sat on. Nobody ever sat on the chair and nobody ever stood long in the hall. It was a passageway – not to fame and not to fortune but only to the common practices of family life, those practices, habits, and ordinary customs that are the only true realities most of us ever know, and that in some of us form a memory strong enough to give us something to hold on to to the end of our days. It is a matter of love, and whether the love finds daily, hourly expression in warm embraces and in the instinctive kind of attentiveness animals give to their young or whether it is largely unexpressed, as it was among the Bagots, does not really matter very much in the very long run. It is the solid existence of love that gives life and strength to memory, and if, in some cases, childhood memories lack the soft and tender colours given by demonstrativeness, the child grown old and in the dark knows only that what is under his hand is a rock that will never give way.

In the big bed in the back room upstairs, Lily Bagot lay sleeping beside her sister, and if they dreamed nobody knew about it, because they never remembered their dreams in the morning. On the morning of Christmas Day they woke very early, much earlier than usual, and it was as though the parcels piled beside their bed sent out a magic breath to bring them out of their sleep while the world was still dark. They moved very slowly at first, putting their hands down beside the bed and down at the end of the bed to feel what was there, to feel what had been left for them. They went over each parcel with their hands, getting the outline and trying to make out from the shape what was inside. Then they couldn't wait any longer, and Lily got out of bed and put on the light so that they could see what they had been given.

BERNARD MacLAVERTY

Remote

Around about the end of each month she would write a letter, but because it was December she used an old Christmas card, which she found at the bottom of the biscuit tin among her pension books. She stood dressed in her outdoor clothes on tiptoe at the bedroom window waiting for the bird-watcher's Land Rover to come over the top of the hill two miles away. When she saw it she dashed, slamming the door after her and running in her stiff-legged fashion down the lane on to the road. Her aim was to be walking, breathing normally, when the Land Rover would indicate and stop in the middle of the one-track road.

'Can I give you a lift?'

'Aye.'

She walked round the front of the shuddering engine and climbed up to sit on the split seat. Mushroom-coloured foam bulged from its crack. More often than not she had to kick things aside to make room for her feet. It was not the lift she would have chosen but it was all there was. He shoved the wobbling stick through the gears and she had to shout – each month the same thing.

'Where are you for?'

'The far side.'

'I'm always lucky just to catch you.'

He was dressed like one of those hitch-hikers, green khaki jacket, cord trousers and laced-up mountain boots. His hair was long and unwashed and his beard divided into points like the teats of a goat.

'Are you going as far as the town this time?'

'Yes.'

'Will you drop me off?'

'Sure. Christmas shopping?'

'Aye, that'll be right.'

The road spun past, humping and squirming over peat bogs, the single track bulging at passing places – points which were marked by tall black and white posts to make them stand out against the landscape. Occasionally in the bog there were incisions, a black-brown colour, herring-boned with scars where peat had been cut.

'How's the birds doing?' she shouted.

'Fine. I've never had so many as this year.'

His accent was English and it surprised her that he had blackheads dotting his cheekbones and dirty hands.

'Twenty-two nesting pairs – so far.'

'That's nice.'

'Compared with sixteen last year.'

'What are they?'

He said what they were but she couldn't hear him properly. They joined the main road and were silent for a while. Then rounding a corner the bird-man suddenly applied the brakes. Two cars, facing in opposite directions, sat in the middle of the road, their drivers having a conversation. The bird-man muttered and steered round them, the Land Rover tilting as it mounted the verge.

'I'd like to see them try that in Birmingham.'

'Is that where you're from?'

He nodded.

'Why did you come to the island?'

'The birds.'

'Aye, I suppose there's not too many down there.'

He smiled and pointed to an open packet of Polo mints on the dashboard. She lifted them and saw that the top sweet was soiled, the relief letters almost black. She prised it out and gave it to him. The white one beneath she put in her mouth.

'Thanks,' she said.

'You born on the island?'

'City born and bred.' She snorted. 'I was lured here by a man forty-two years ago.'

'I never see him around.'

'I'm not surprised. He's dead this long time.' She cracked the ring of the mint between her teeth.

'I'm sorry.'

She chased the two crescents of mint around with her tongue.

'What did he do?'

'He drowned himself. In the loch.'

'I'm sorry, I didn't mean that.'

'On Christmas Day. He was mad in the skull – away with the fairies.'

There was a long pause in which he said again that he was sorry. Then he said, 'What I meant was – what did he do for a living?'

'What does it matter now?'

The bird-man shook his head and concentrated on the road ahead.

'He was a shepherd,' she said. Then a little later, 'He was

the driver. There should always be one in the house who can drive.'

He let her off at the centre of the village and she had to walk the steep hill to the Post Office. She breathed through her mouth and took a rest halfway up, holding on to a small railing. Distances grew with age.

Inside she passed over her pension book, got her money and bought a first-class stamp. She waited until she was outside before she took the letter from her bag. She licked the stamp, stuck it on the envelope and dropped it in the letter box. Walking down the hill was easier.

She went to the Co-op to buy sugar and tea and porridge. The shop was strung with skimpy tinselled decorations and the music they were playing was Christmas hits – 'Rudolf' and 'I saw Mammy Kissing Santa Claus'. She only had a brief word with Elizabeth at the check-out because of the queue behind her. In the butcher's she bought herself a pork chop and some bacon. His bacon lasted longer than the packet stuff.

When she had her shopping finished she wondered what to do to pass the time. She could visit young Mary but if she did that she would have to talk. Not having enough things to say she felt awkward listening to the tick of the clock and the distant cries of sea birds. Chat was a thing you got out of the habit of when you were on your own all the time and, besides, Mary was shy. Instead she decided to buy a cup of tea in the café. And treat herself to an almond bun. She sat near the window where she could look out for the post van.

The café was warm and it, too, was decorated. Each time the door opened the hanging fronds of tinsel fluttered. On a tape somewhere carols were playing. Two children, sitting with their mother, were playing with a new toy car on the table-top. The cellophane wrapping had been discarded on the floor. They both imitated engine noises although only one of them was pushing it round the plates. The other sat waiting impatiently for his turn.

She looked away from them and stared into her tea. When they dredged him up on Boxing Day he had two car batteries tied to his wrists. He was nothing if not thorough. One of them had been taken from his own van parked by the loch shore and the thing had to be towed to the garage. If he had been a drinking man he could have been out getting drunk or fallen into bad company. But there was only the black depression. All that day the radio had been on to get rid of the dread.

When 'Silent Night' came on the tape and the children started to squabble over whose turn it was she did not wait to finish her tea but walked slowly to the edge of the village with her bag of shopping, now and again pausing to look over her shoulder. The scarlet of the post van caught her eye and she stood on the verge with her arm out. When she saw it was Stuart driving she smiled. He stopped the van and she ducked down to look in the window.

'Anything for me today?'

He leaned across to the basket of mail which occupied the passenger seat position and began to rummage through the bundles of letters and cards held together with elastic bands.

'This job would be all right if it wasn't for bloody Christmas.' He paused at her single letter. 'Aye, there's just one.'

'Oh good. You might as well run me up, seeing as you're going that way.'

He sighed and looked over his shoulder at a row of houses.

'Wait for me round the corner.'

She nodded and walked on ahead while he made some deliveries. The lay-by was out of sight of the houses and she set her bag down to wait. Stuart seemed to take a long time. She looked down at the loch in the growing dark. The geese were returning for the night, filling the air with their squawking. They sounded like a dance-hall full of people laughing and enjoying themselves, heard from a distance on the night wind.

DESMOND HOGAN

The Mourning Thief

Coming through the black night he wondered what lay before him: a father lying dying; Christmas, midnight ceremonies in a church which stood up like a gravestone; floods about his home.

With him were his wife and his friend Gerard. They needn't have come by boat but something purgatorial demanded it of Liam, the gulls that shot over like stars, the roxy music in the juke box, the occasional Irish ballad rising in cherished defiance of the sea.

The night was soft, breezes intruded, plucking hair, threads lying loose in many coloured jerseys. Susan fell asleep once while Liam looked at Gerard. It was Gerard's first time in Ireland; Gerard's eyes were chestnut. His dark hair cropped like a monk's on a bottle of English brandy. With his wife sleeping Liam could acknowledge the physical relationship that lay between them. It wasn't that Susan didn't know but despite the truism of promiscuity in the school where they worked there still abided laws like the Old Testament God's, reserving carnality for smiles after dark.

A train to Galway, the Midlands frozen in.

Susan looked out like a Botticelli Venus, a little worried, often just vacuous. She was a music teacher, thus her mind was penetrated by the vibrations of Bach whether in a public lavatory or a Lyon's Café.

The red house at the end of the street; it looked cold, pushed away from the other houses. A river in flood lay behind. A woman, his mother, greeted him. He an only child, she soon to be widow. But something disturbed Liam with excitement. Christmas candles still burned in this town.

His father lay in bed, still magically alive, white hair smeared on him like a dummy, that hard face that never forgave an enemy in the police force still on him. He was delighted to see Liam. At eighty-three he was a most ancient father, marrying late, begetting late, his wife fifteen years younger.

A train brushed the distance outside. Adolescence returned with a sudden start: the gold flurry of snow as the train in which he was travelling sped towards Dublin, the films about Russian winters. Irish winters became Russian winters in turn, and half Liam's memories of adolescence were of the fantasised presence of Russia. Ikons, candles, streets agleam with snow.

'Still painting?'

'Still painting.' As though he could ever give it up. His father smiled as though he were about to grin. 'Well we never made a policeman out of you.'

At ten, the day before he was to be inaugurated as a boy scout, Liam handed in his uniform. He always hated the colours of the Irish flag, mixing like the yolk in a bad egg.

It hadn't disappointed his father that he hadn't turned into a military man, but his father preferred to hold on to a shred of prejudice against Liam's chosen profession, leaving momentarily aside one of his most cherished memories, visiting the National Gallery in Dublin once with his son, encountering the curator by accident, and having the curator show them around, an old man who'd since died, leaving behind a batch of poems and a highly publicised relationship with an international writer. But the sorest point, the point now neither would mention, was arguments about violence. At seventeen Liam walked the local hurling pitch with petitions against the war in Vietnam.

Liam's father's fame, apart from being a police inspector of note, was fighting in the GPO in 1916 and subsequently being arrested on the republican side in the civil war. Liam was against violence, pure and simple. Nothing could convince him that 1916 was right. Nothing could convince him it was different from now, old women, young children, being blown to bits in Belfast.

Statues abounded in this house; in every nook and cranny was a statue, a statue of Mary, a statue of Joseph, an emblem perhaps of some saint Mrs Fogarthy had sweetly long forgotten. This was the first thing Gerard noticed and Susan, who had seen this menagerie before, was still surprised. 'It's like a holy statue farm.'

Gerard said it was like a holy statue museum. They were sitting by the fire, two days before Christmas. Mrs Fogarthy had gone to bed.

'It is a museum,' Liam said, 'all kinds of memories, curious sensations here, ghosts. The ghosts of Irish Republicans, of policemen, military men, priests, the ghosts of Ireland.'

'Why ghosts?' Gerard asked.

'Because Ireland is dying,' Liam said.

Just then they heard his father cough.

Mr Fogarthy was slowly dying, cancer welling up in him. He was dying painfully and yet peacefully because he had a dedicated wife to look after him, and a river in flood around, somehow calling Christ to mind, calling penance to mind, instilling a sense of winter in him that went back a long time, a river in flood around a limestone town.

Liam offered to cook the Christmas dinner but his mother scoffed him. He was a good cook Susan vouched. Once Liam had cooked and his father had said he wouldn't give it to the dogs.

They walked, Liam, Susan, Gerard, in a town where women were hugged into coats like brown paper accidentally blown about them. They walked in the grounds of Liam's former school, once a Georgian estate, now beautiful, elegant still in the east Galway winter solstice.

There were tinkers to be seen in the town and English hippies behaving like tinkers. Many turkeys were displayed, fatter than ever, festooned by holly. Altogether one would notice prosperity everywhere, cars, shining clothes, modern fronts replacing the antique ones Liam recalled and pieced together from childhood.

But he would not forfeit England for this dull patch of Ireland, southern England where he'd lived since he was twenty-two; Sussex, the trees plump as ripe pears, the rolling verdure, the odd delight of an Elizabethan cottage.

He taught with Susan, with Gerard, in a free school. He taught children to paint. Susan taught them to play musical instruments. Gerard looked after younger children though he himself played a musical instrument, a cello.

Once Liam and Susan had journeyed to London to hear him play at St Martin-in-the-Fields, entertaining ladies who wore poppies on their lapels, as his recital coincided with Remembrance Sunday and paper poppies generated an explosion of remembrance.

Susan went to bed early now, complaining of fatigue, and Gerard and Liam were left with one another. Though both were obviously male they were lovers, lovers in a tentative kind of way, occasionally sleeping with one another. It was still an experiment, but for Liam held a matrix of adolescent fantasy. Though he married at twenty-two, his sexual fantasy from adolescence was always homosexual. Susan could not complain. In fact it rather charmed her. She'd had more lovers since they'd married than fingers could count; Liam would always accost her with questions about their physicality, were they more satisfying than him? But he knew he could count on her; tenderness between them had lasted six years now.

She was English, very much English. Gerard was English. Liam was left with this odd quarrel of Irishness. Memories of adolescence at boarding school, waking from horrific dreams nightly when he went to the window to throw himself out but couldn't because the window frames were jammed. His father had placed him at boarding school, to toughen him like meat. Liam had not been toughened, chastened, ran away once or twice. At eighteen he left altogether, went to England, worked on a building site, put himself through college. He'd ended up in Sussex, losing a major part of his Irishness but retaining this: a knowledge when the weather was going to change, a premonition of all kinds of disasters and, ironically, an acceptance of the worst disasters of all, death, estrangement.

Now that his father was near death old teachers, soldiers, policemen called, downing sherries, laughing rhetorically, sitting beside the bed covered by a quilt that looked like twenty inflated balloons. Sometimes Liam, Susan, Gerard sat with these people, exchanging remarks about the weather, the fringe of politics or the world economic state generally.

Mrs Fogarthy swept up a lot. She dusted and danced around with a cloth as though she'd been doing this all her life, fretting and fiddling with the house.

Cars went by. Geese went by, clanking terribly. Rain came and church bells sounded from a disparate steeple.

Liam's father reminisced about 1916, recalling little incidents, fights with British soldiers, comrades dying in his arms, ladies fainting from hunger, escape to Mayo, later imprisonment in the

Curragh during the civil war. Liam said: 'Do you ever connect it with now, men, women, children being blown up, the La Mon hotel bombing, Bessbrook killings, Birmingham, Bloody Friday? Do you ever think that the legends and the brilliance built from your revolution created this, death justified for death's sake, the stories in the classroom, the priests' stories, this language, this celebration of blood?'

Although Liam's father fought himself once he belonged to those who deplored the present violence, seeing no connection. Liam saw the connection but disavowed both.

'Hooligans. Murderers,' Liam's father said.

Liam said, 'You were once a hooligan then.'

'We fought to set a majority free.'

'And created the spirit of violence in the new state. We were weaned on the violence, me and others of my age. Not actual violence but always with a reference to violence. Violence was right we were told in class. How can one blame those now who go out and plant bombs to kill old women when they were once told this was right?'

The dying man became angry. He didn't look at Liam, looked beyond him to the street.

'The men who fought in 1916 were heroes. Those who lay bombs in cafés are scum.'

Betrayed he was silent then, silent because his son accused him on his deathbed of unjustifiably resorting to bloodshed once. Now guns went off daily in the far off North. Where was the line between right and wrong? Who could say? An old man on his death bed prayed that the guns he'd fired in 1916 had been for a right cause and, in the words of his leader Patrick Pearse, had not caused undue bloodshed.

On Christmas Eve the three young people and Mrs Fogarthy went to midnight mass in the local church. In fact it wasn't to the main church but a smaller one, situated on the outskirts of the town, protruding like a headstone. A bald middle-aged priest greeted a packed congregation. The cemetery lay nearby but one was unaware of it. Christmas candles and Christmas trees glowed in bungalows.

'Come all ye faithful' a choir of matchstick boys sang. Their dress was scarlet, scarlet of joy.

Afterwards Mrs Fogarthy penetrated the crib with a whisper of prayer.

Christmas morning, clean, spare, Liam was aware of estrangement from his father, that his father was ruminating on his words about violence, wondering were he and his ilk, the teachers, police, clergy of Ireland responsible for what was happening now, in the first place by nurturing the cult of violence, contributing to the actuality of it as expressed by young men in Belfast and London.

Sitting up on Christmas morning Mr Fogarthy stared ahead. There was a curiosity about his forehead. Was he guilty? Were those in high places guilty as his son said?

Christmas dinner; Gerard joked, Susan smiled, Mrs Fogarthy had a sheaf of joy. Liam tidied and somehow sherry elicited a chuckle and a song from Mrs Fogarthy. 'I have seen the lark soar high at morn.'

The song rose to the bedroom where her husband who'd had dinner in bed heard it.

The street outside was bare.

Gerard fetched a guitar and brought all to completion, Christmas, birth, festive eating, by a rendition of Bach's 'Jesu, Joy of Man's Desiring'.

Liam brought tea to his father. His father looked at him.

''Twas lovely music,' his father said with a sudden brogue. 'There was a Miss Hanratty who lived here before you were born who studied music in Heidelberg and could play Schumann in such a way as to bring tears to the cat's eyes. Poor soul, she died young, a member of the ladies' confraternity. Schumann was her favourite and Mendelssohn came after that. She played at our wedding, your mother's and mine. She played Mozart and afterwards in the hotel sang a song, what was it? O yes, "The Star of the County Down".

'Such a sweetness she had in her voice too. But she was a bit of a loner and a bit lost here. Never too well really, she died maybe when you were a young lad.'

Reminiscences, names from the past, Catholic names, Protestant names, the names of boys in the rugby club, in the golf club, Protestant girls he'd danced with, nights at the October fair. They came easily now, a simple jargon.

Sometimes though the old man visibly stopped to consider his child's rebuke.

Liam gauged the sadness, wished he hadn't said anything, wanted to simplify it but knew it possessed all the simplicity it could have, a man on his deathbed in dreadful doubt.

Christmas night they visited the convent crib, Liam, Susan, Gerard, Mrs Fogarthy, a place glowing with a red lamp. Outside trees stood in silence, a mist thinking of enveloping them. The town lay in silence. At odd intervals one heard the gurgle of television but otherwise it could have been childhood, the fair Green, space, emptiness, the rhythm, the dance of one's childhood dreams.

Liam spoke to his father that evening. 'Where I work we try to educate children differently from other places, teach them to develop and grow from within, try to direct them from the most natural point within them. There are many such schools now but ours, ours I think is special, run as a co-operative, we try to take children from all class backgrounds and begin at the beginning to redefine education.'

pinafores served tea and cakes, home-made and juiced with icing.

He'd had no children. But Gerard now was both a twin, a child, a lover to him. There were all kinds of possibilities. Experiment was only beginning. Yet Ireland, Christmas, returned him to something, least of all the presence of death, more a proximity to the prom, empty laburnum pods and hawthorn trees naked and crouched with winter. Here he was at home with thoughts, thoughts of himself, of adolescence. Here he made his own being like a doll on a miniature globe. He knew whence he came and if he wasn't sure where he was going at least he wasn't distraught about it.

They walked with his mother that afternoon. Later an aunt came, preened for Christmas and the imminence of death. She enjoyed the tea, the knowledgeable silences, looked at Susan as though she was not from England but a far off country, an Eastern country hidden in the mountains. Liam's father spoke to her not of 1916 but of policemen they'd known, irascible characters, forgetting that he had been the most irascible of all, a domineering man with a wizened face ordering his inferiors around.

He'd brought law, he'd brought order to the town. But he'd failed to bring trust. Maybe that's why his son had left. Maybe that's why he was pondering the fate of the Irish revolution now, men with high foreheads who'd shaped the fate of the Irish Republic. His thoughts brought him to killings now being done in the name of Ireland. There his thoughts floundered.

From where arose this language of violence for the sake and convenience of violence?

Liam strode by the prom alone that evening, locked in a donkey jacket. There were rings of light around distant electric poles. He knew his father to be sitting up in bed; the policemen he'd been talking about earlier gone from his mind and his thoughts on 1916, on guns, and blazes, and rumination in prison cells long ago. And long after that thoughts on the glorification of acts of violence, the minds of children caressed with the deeds of violence. He'd be thinking of his son who fled and left the country.

His son now was thinking of the times he'd run away to Dublin, to the neon lights slitting the night, of the time he went to the river to throw himself in and didn't, of his final flight from Ireland. He wanted to say something, urge a statement to birth that would unite father and son but couldn't think of anything to say. He stopped by a tree and looked to the river. An odd car went by towards Dublin.

Why this need to run? Even as he was thinking that a saying of his father returned, 'Idleness is the thief of time.' That statement had been flayed upon him as a child, but with time, as he lived in England among fields of oak trees, that statement had changed; time itself had become the culprit, the thief. And the image of time as a thief was for ever embroiled in a particular ikon of his father's, that of a pacifist who ran through Dublin helping the wounded in 1916, was arrested, shot dead with a deaf and dumb youth. And that man, more than anybody, was Liam's hero, an Irish pacifist, a pacifist born of his father's revolution, a pacifist born of his father's state.

He returned home quickly, drew the door on his father. He sat down.

'Remember, Daddy, the story you told me about the pacifist shot dead in 1916 with a deaf and dumb youth, the man whose wife was a feminist.'

'Yes.'

'Well, I was just thinking that he's the sort of man we need now, one who comes from a revolution but understands it in a different way, a creative way, who understands that change isn't born from violence but intense and self-sacrificing acts.' His father understood what he was saying, that there was a remnant of 1916 that was relevant and urgent now, that there had been at least one man among the men of 1916 who could speak to the present generation and show them that guns were not diamonds, that blood was precious, that birth most poignantly issues from restraint.

Liam went to bed. In the middle of the night he woke muttering to himself 'May God have mercy on your soul', although his father was not yet dead, but he wasn't asking God to have mercy on his father's soul but on the soul of Ireland, the many souls born out of his father's statelet, the women never pregnant, the cruel and violent priests, the young exiles, the old exiles, those who could never come back.

He got up, walked down the stairs, opened the door on his father's room. Inside his father lay. He wanted to see this with his own eyes, hope even in the persuasion of death.

He returned to bed.

His wife turned away from him but curiously that did not hurt him because he was thinking of the water rising, the moon on the water and as he thought of these things geese clanked over, throwing their reflections onto the water grazed with moon which rimmed this town, the church towers, the slate roofs, those that slept now, those who didn't remember.

ROBERT DUFFY

Homeland

A minor argument happened as they packed Christmas biscuits into the car. Tom wanted to spend minimum time with his in-laws in Loughrea. Helen wanted to spend longer. Martin was home from Japan, that's why, and Tom wanted to meet his best pal as much as possible. Loughrea is too far away. Stay close. Athy's just up the road. Tom you can't be greedy either. Martin would be around for a fortnight. Helen wanted a week with her mother.

'My office party is on Wednesday night. You will not be welcome to that *too* early anyhow. Go on to Martin and meet me at ten o'clock or therabouts.'

A sensible idea. She's always right. Love her. Two hours chinwag with Martin before we head west should be grand. Besides, it is a chance to arrange another long chat.

Helen went to her party. Tom rang Martin and was invited to tea. The roads were icy, the trip worthwhile. A good friend, welcome back. The chat was muted. His mother wondered how he did his washing in Japan. He told her. How did he dry his clothes? He told her. Ho-hum profundities, Tom thought. Our year in the flat was great gas. He reached for a photo album with a Japanese scrawl down the spine. Martin pulled his chair closer. China.

'Yer man there, he's a Frenchman. The Irish and English went home. We went to China. Those kids, there, rushed up. "Photo me, mister?" I did and the mother gave me the address and I sent an enlargement. I hope they aren't arrested.'

Martin's mother was politely excluded. She had seen the photos and had heard the commentary. The lads were left alone. The Chinese pictures were ordinary masterpieces: people standing on a train platform, riding black bicycles, or using box-cameras.

'God, Martin. I'd have about fifty at the Great Wall and shag all elsewhere. It takes you to take everything.'

'You won't get a true idea of anything unless you watch the normal carry-on. No point in being like the sort of Yank who gawks around Galway Cathedral and misses the crack of a fair-day. Keep down to earth man! You're a fierce dreamer anyway.'

A fierce dreamer. Tom thought about that on his way back to Carlow. His reluctance about Loughrea was in order to flood his brain with oriental anecdotes as related by his best friend. Loughrea. Yes. A week. Yes. Watch your own habitat, Tom. People here are no better, no worse than anywhere. Stop jumping into space you fool. You are. Here. Now go on and pick up the missus.

Helen's party consisted of the entire workforce cramming into a pub. Forty of them. Four office girls, three management and all the boys from the yard. Young ones, old ones, capped ones, open shirt ones, all a wee bit merry. The boss was buying the drink. A noble family splintering gesture. Stop that. Not true. It's Christmas. An expected, appreciated treat. Look. Could Tom's camera catch this? Martin's could.

Tom bought his own pint of Guinness, smiled and watched what was happening. They used to be gurriers that worked with Helen.

People Tom, people. Old talking to young in a mixumgatherum of noise and spillages. Pat is a bit gone. He wouldn't be leaning over Kathleen like that back at the yard. Probably fancies Helen too. I wonder how jarred he is. No there he goes. Pat sat down beside a grinning Ned Reilly. Those eyes. Bet he was a wild boyo thirty years ago. Maybe he still is. Must ask Helen.

'What are you having, Tom? Guinness?'

'Ah Mr Doyle. Thanks all the same. But I'm not . . . Anyway I'm driving tonight.'

'Go on. You haven't had much. Go on. It's Christmas.'

'A *glass* of Guinness so. Thanks.'

Mr Doyle is dead decent. No need for that. Still, the wifeín is not finished. Love you Helen.

'I love you,' Tom whispered loudly in her ear.

'Love you too,' but her eyes were more eloquent.

They drove to Loughrea after the pub closed. Sober driver, sleepy wife, glassy roads. They reached Helen's home at three o'clock. A pouted, worried mother pulled the curtains as she heard another car enter the avenue. Eyebrow movement. Tom could see that. What a wonderful woman. Worried sick probably. Nothing surer. Great composure. She had not phoned Tom's parents. She had strained alone to wait. A fruitless phone call would have upset a second household. Eyebrow movement. A smile. You are a wonderful woman, Mrs Horgan. God, what can I call her? Mammy? Mrs Horgan? Imelda?

Helen kissed her. Tom did not. He kissed his wife frequently. Nobody else. They were too tired for a pot of tea, especially Tom after his hundred miles of skating.

The pair of them surfaced for a late lunch. They stayed in the house until seven o'clock. Fine, no lazy conscience, but Tom had an unusual craving to mix with people. He looked forward to the evening's visit to Helen's cousins. Wild chaps all. Auntie Mary?

Mrs O'Mahoney? Mr O'Mahoney? He mumbled over it. One, two, three . . . twelve people in this room. Noise. Look at them. Think of Leonardo. Look at Joe's face, that profile. God he is a pup, but look. Group them. Form without symmetry. Imagine Grace a little pushed to the left. Like a Raphael gathering or like that opening frame of Bertolucci's '1900'. Blast Grace! Leave that telly alone.

'Here is your Christmas present, Imelda.' Mrs O'Mahoney entered the room with a Yorkshire terrier pup in a basket. The children collectively scrambled towards her. Their interest in that dog was total, focussed. Shouts and jumps and outstretched arms. Mother ruled. The creature was passed to its new owner. Helen smiled. Tom smiled. They looked at Mrs Horgan. He placed his hand on her leg and she placed her hand on his hand. Martin? Minced pies and the price of bread in Tokyo I suppose. Ara, I'll see him next week.

Next day, Christmas Eve, Tom and Helen went shopping. They had their presents already but extra drink and a play-ball for Mimi the dog were needed. They walked through the glass and plastic front of Murtagh's and were confronted by an awesome gathering of stock. It was probably a grand place once, Tom thought. That sign is stuck over an older one. That's obvious. The drinks counter at the back was satisfactory, the pets shelf ridiculous. All sorts of knick-knacks in carded bags with pictures of dogs or cats on them. Artificial dog chews, twelve varieties of dog food, umpteen more of cat food, leads, bells, beds, squeakies and yes, balls. Too dear. God be with the days when Irishmen died from lack of spuds. They strolled about the shop and found a similar unpacked ball for a third of the price.

Helen wanted girlie things. Tom waited at the other side of the register. That man with glasses; that poor woman's veins; Rosary beads – next to the food mixers no less; Helen: I love her. Hey! That woman is bursting the queue. A woman with a worn grey tweed coat and a scarf with the Eiffel Tower upside-down made her way to pay for a crib. Holy thou. I suppose she never had to queue in the old days when there was a counter. Still . . . Not to worry. She's happy. We's happy and Helen is stuck. Now what?

'How much is this beret? It's not on it.' The assistant took the article, confirmed it was not marked and strolled away to find a price. Helen was third in line. The girl was missing for a long long two minutes. Helen was impatient. She looked at Tom and raised her eyebrows. He winked. She smiled. The lady without the beret stood expressionless with a conspicuous shiny nose. 'Three ninety nine,' the assistant said. 'No I won't take it,' said the woman with the conspicuous shiny nose. Tom raised his hand and giggled underneath it. Helen grimaced. People. Thank God we are all different. What are the Japanese doing? Who cares? Let them care. We are here now. 'Come on, Helen. Don't worry about it. We are in no hurry anyhow.'

Midnight Mass. No rowdy drunks. No nuns, schoolchildren or soldiers bringing up the gifts. It was just a mass at nightime. In the second-from-front crowded seat, Tom prayed and looked for God in the priest. That was easy. The sermon was all about God. Spot the God, Tom thought sarcastically. He had heard the story about the blind man, the poor man and the lonely man knocking on a door at Christmas and how the man inside was expecting God. And later He spoke and said that He had called three times already. Tom was pleased about the pound he had put in a Concern box earlier that day and about the two pounds he had placed in a Simon box in Dublin a few days earlier. Good at that – giving money – he thought. You could do more. Ara stop. I do. Remember those kids on that wet morning and me not going near the school? He let his hand touch Helen. Others might have seen the fidgety movement but she knew that he had Touched her.

Tom intended to catch Mass on Christmas morning and was

annoyed when he failed to do so. The Horgans rarely attended for the second time. He arrived downstairs with Helen to find only a small cluster of packages beneath the tree. The other members of the family had plucked away their own presents. An anti-climax, no joy of sharing, just 'What did we get?' Pity. It's better in my house, Tom thought. The smile on his brother's face last year was just as rewarding as the gift he had received in return. None of that here. What was Monica's, or Peter's, or Mary's, or Mrs Horgan's reaction like? Don't brood on it, Tom. He tried to watch the 'Sound of Music' instead. It was enjoyable in spite of the incessant beeping of little Mary's computer game. Beep, beep, beep, beep, beep, beeeep, 'O damn.' 'Maria makes me . . . laugh! Titter titter,' said the nuns on T.V.

'Mary! Are you coming to the cemetery?' Mrs Horgan asked. She wanted to place a rose on her husband's grave to mark her sixth Christmas without him. There was no need, absolutely no need, for Tom to accompany them, she said. He thought otherwise. He had become part of the family the previous August and wanted to share in the pilgrimage. The film would have been a petty, decrepit reason for staying in the house.

Was he like their Uncle Mark, Tom thought as the family stood silently at the grave. Fatter, I know. I've seen photographs. Looks the same witty sort though. Guffawing just like Mark, I can imagine it. Helen, you are gorgeous. I would love to have known him. I know I call her Mrs Horgan but I can imagine calling him Bob. Forty-four. God he was young. Rough. Mrs Horgan's fantastic. I must call her something else.

During the mile back to the house, little Mary played with her computer game.

Soon they were ready to eat. The table had been set earlier. A huge white tablecloth; crackers criss-crossed, ready to snap; a log and holly and candle centrepiece. Mrs Horgan sat at the head of the table. Mary sat at the other end. Tom and Helen were together and Monica and Peter sat opposite them. The meal turned out to be as good as his Mammy's. Tom wondered how Helen would manage whenever they had to prepare their own. Afterwards he rang home.

'No point in ringing Martin, I suppose,' he said to Helen after finishing with his own parents.

'Not at all,' she said. 'He's just guzzling food like us. Besides, it's a family affair.'

'Don't worry about it. I was just thinking out loud anyhow.'

'Here! Maybe that will keep you quiet.' She passed him Mary's computer game.

'Swine!' he said.

'Swine!' she said.

They winked and smiled at each other and went into the living room.

Compulsive. A little helicopter blinked across a screen. Little people appeared on top of buildings. Beep, beep, beep, pick up a man. Beep, beep, beep, put him down safely. Extra beep and the helicopter crashes. Too slow and a building collapses. Tom scored 350 – ten points for every man rescued. Mary wanted the game. The record was 470. 'Go 'way!' said Tom greedily as he started a new game. Two hours later the record was 1,330. Tom held it. Peter reached 970. Mary had to wait her turn. Without the new dog, she would have gone mad. She was pulling and poking and shoving her. 'Just like you do to me,' whispered Helen. 'Go 'way!' said Tom as he beeped another man to safety.

After a few more minutes he left it aside. No point in banjaxing Christmas with that cursed yoke. I remember John and me getting forts and soldiers from Santy, and Daddy assembling the forts and me wondering how he found it so easy and we found it so hard and Santy had only left them the night before. And John put his fort on one side of the room and I put mine on the other side and he put his soldiers in his fort and I put mine in mine. 'Da-a-ie,' he said, shooting one of my lads with his cap-gun. 'Da-a-ie,' I said, getting one of his. 'Course big brother always won because he had one or two soldiers more than me. Sulk, sulk. Deprived childhood. Don't worry about it. Happy days: honest-to-God toys. Beep, beep. Mary's Christmas. Wait until she is remembering 'fadó . . . fadó'.

The Yorkshire terrier was the centre of attention again. When Mary introduced a mirror, it was a howl. 'Yip! Yip!' Mimi said as she stalked closer and closer. Skipturn runaway. And crawl up again. Great fun. Nobody was interested in the film about the boxer and the racehorses in sunny faraway Florida. Dog and computer and tea and gooey Christmas cake were passed around. It was well into St Stephen's morning by the time everybody got to bed.

'The O'Mahoneys, O'Mahoneys, Mammy, Mammy, the O'Mahoneys.' Mary was much louder than the doorbell as the cousins arrived. They were expected, but only Mary was up to greet them. Tom followed down shortly. He was curious to see what they would get up to. He also wanted to know what Santy had brought to that house. Computer games. More of them. He tried them all. Loud, whirry, complicated, lit-up. He couldn't get the hang of them. Mary's was best. 'Give me this! Auntie 'melda! Mammy! Mimi! No me! I have it! Watch! Look! Ah no, stop! Go 'way! I'll hit ya! I'll hit ya!' They settled down to a tolerable hum after half an hour or so. There was no point in watching television unless the children wanted to.

'Helen?'

'Yeah?'

'Go for walk?'

They said they would be back shortly. It did not matter. There was no set pattern for tea. They left sleepy grown-ups and noisy children and headed towards town. Tom tried to put his arm around Helen. She wouldn't have it, not in her home town. Old ones looking out at them. They held hands.

'Horrible yucky day,' said Helen.

'Reduced to that, are we? Talking about the weather now?'

'No but it's not Christmassy. It could pour any minute and there's no snow. It's just . . . I don't know.'

'The Japs would love it. They are either roasted or frozen. We've got curly clouds and a week off and open spaces. Fierce lucky we are. You loves me. I loves you.'

'I suppose,' said Helen, mimicking a previous girlfriend of Tom's.

He grasped her. She pushed him away mockingly. They continued walking, holding hands. Heavy rain fell suddenly and they sheltered under the canopy of a drapery shop. They shared the deserted street with a spiny stray dog. He ran down a passageway on the far side. The clamour of raindrops eased. They ran to another shelter and had to wait again. The challenge of racing the rain was enjoyable. By the time Helen was putting her key in the hall-door, they were damp, but not soaked through. Once inside, the children were audible but out of sight. Tom could hold her now. They shared a long slow kiss. The noise of two children grew louder and louder. Tom and Helen parted just in time. The children disappeared again. Tom gave Helen a sideways nod and both of them went upstairs. As it happened, there was a bolt on the bedroom door. They used it. A pillow stuffed between the bedhead and the wall stopped the bed from creaking.

'Helen, you're lovely.'

'I know,' she giggled. 'You're not so bad yourself.'

'Swine! I love you.'

'Squeeze me.'

He did.

'Oyourhandsarecold!' Helen said, twitching a little.

'That better?'

It was. And moments later . . .

'Sorry,' said Tom.

'Sorry? Why?'

'I don't know. 'Cause I'm happy I suppose.'

'No reason why you should be sorry.'

'But I thought I wouldn't be, with Martin home and a drove of noisy cousins here. I was grumpy last week.'

'Yeah! You're grumpy, I'm Happy and all the other dwarfs are downstairs. Don't be silly. Squeeze me again.'

He did, and buried his smiling face in that nook between her head and left shoulder.

Afterwards he looked at her smile. 'A nice smile' was all that he could think – the same smile he had noticed four years earlier.

Four more days were spent at the Horgan home, four sleepy days with greycottoned skies. Tom loved them. They went for more walks together; they drove out to O'Mahoneys again; they ate the biscuits which had come from Carlow; and Christmas cake; and sweets. Tom never made up his mind what to call Mrs Horgan. They had to leave in order to visit Tom's parents and to say hello to Martin who was home from Japan.

'Goodbye Mammy,' said Helen.

'Goodbye now,' said Tom. 'Thanks a million.'

Mrs Horgan watched and waved until the car turned out of sight on its way back to Carlow.

WILLIAM TREVOR

Another Christmas

You always looked back, she thought. You looked back at other years, other Christmas cards arriving, the children younger. There was the year Patrick had cried, disliking the holly she was decorating the living-room with. There was the year Bridget had got a speck of coke in her eye on Christmas Eve and had to be taken to the hospital at Hammersmith in the middle of the night. There was the first year of their marriage, when she and Dermot were still in Waterford. And ever since they'd come to London there was the presence on Christmas Day of their landlord, Mr Joyce, a man whom they had watched becoming elderly.

She was middle-aged now, with touches of grey in her fluffy jet-black hair, a woman known for her cheerfulness, running a bit to fat. Her husband was the opposite: thin and seeming ascetic, with more than a hint of the priest in him, a good man. 'Will we get married, Norah?' he'd said one night in the Tara Ballroom in Waterford, November 6th, 1953. The proposal had astonished her: it was his brother Ned, bulky and fresh-faced, a different kettle of fish altogether, whom she'd been expecting to make it.

Patiently he held a chair for her while she strung paper-chains across the room, from one picture-rail to another. He warned her to be careful about attaching anything to the electric light. He still held the chair while she put sprigs of holly behind the pictures. He was cautious by nature and alarmed by little things, particularly anxious in case she fell off chairs. He'd never mount a chair himself, to put up decorations or anything else: he'd be useless at it in his opinion and it was his opinion that mattered. He'd never been able to do a thing about the house but it didn't matter because since the boys had grown up they'd attended to whatever she couldn't manage herself. You wouldn't dream of remarking on it: he was the way he was, considerate and thoughtful in what he did do, teetotal, clever, full of fondness for herself and for the family they'd reared, full of respect for her also.

'Isn't it remarkable how quick it comes round, Norah?' he said while he held the chair. 'Isn't it no time since last year?'

'No time at all.'

'Though a lot happened in the year, Norah.'

'An awful lot happened.'

Two of the pictures she decorated were scenes of Waterford: the quays and a man driving sheep past the Bank of Ireland. Her mother had given them to her, taking them down from the hall of the farm-house.

There was a picture of the Virgin and Child, and other, smaller pictures. She placed her last sprig of holly, a piece with berries on it, above the Virgin's halo.

'I'll make a cup of tea,' she said, descending from the chair and smiling at him.

'A cup of tea'd be great, Norah.'

The living-room, containing three brown armchairs and a table with upright chairs around it, and a sideboard with a television set on it, was crowded by this furniture and seemed even smaller than it was because of the decorations that had been added. On the mantelpiece, above a built-in gas fire, Christmas cards were arrayed on either side of an ornate green clock.

The house was in a terrace in Fulham. It had always been too small for the family, but now that Patrick and Brendan no longer lived there things were easier. Patrick had married a girl called Pearl six months ago, almost as soon as his period of training with the Midland Bank had ended. Brendan was training in Liverpool, with a firm of computer manufacturers. The three remaining children were still at school, Bridget at the nearby convent, Cathal and Tom at the Sacred Heart Primary. When Patrick and Brendan had moved out the room they'd always shared had become Bridget's. Until then Bridget had slept in her parents' room and she'd have to return there this Christmas because Brendan would be back for three nights. Patrick and Pearl would just come for Christmas Day. They'd be going to Pearl's people, in Croydon, on Boxing Day – St Stephen's Day, as Norah and Dermot always called it, in the Irish manner.

'It'll be great, having them all,' he said. 'A family again, Norah.'

'And Pearl.'

'She's part of us now, Norah.'

'Will you have biscuits with your tea? I have a packet of Nice.'

He said he would, thanking her. He was a meter-reader with North Thames Gas, a position he had held for twenty-one years, ever since he'd emigrated. In Waterford he'd worked as a clerk in the Customs, not earning very much and not much caring for the stuffy, smoke-laden office he shared with half-a-dozen other clerks. He had come to England because Norah had thought it was a good idea, because she'd always wanted to work in a London shop. She'd been given a job in Dickins & Jones, in the household linens department, and he'd been taken on as a meter-reader, cycling from door to door, remembering the different houses and where the meters were situated in each, being agreeable to householders: all of it suited him from the start. He devoted time to thought while he rode about, and in particular to religious matters.

In her small kitchen she made the tea and carried it on a tray into the living-room. She'd been late this year with the decorations. She always liked to get them up a week in advance because they set the mood, making everyone feel right for Christmas. She'd been busy with stuff for a stall Father Malley had asked her to run for his Christmas Sale. A fashion stall he'd called it, but not quite knowing what he meant she'd just asked people for any old clothes they had, jumble really. Because of the time it had taken she hadn't had a minute to see to the decorations until this afternoon, two days before Christmas Eve. But that, as it turned out, had been all for the best. Bridget and Cathal and Tom had gone up to Putney to the pictures, Dermot didn't work on a Monday afternoon: it was convenient that they'd have an hour or two alone together because there was the matter of Mr Joyce to bring up. Not that she wanted to bring it up, but it couldn't be just left there.

'The cup that cheers,' he said, breaking a biscuit in half. Deliberately she put off raising the subject she had in mind. She watched him nibbling the biscuit and then dropping three heaped spoons of sugar into his tea and stirring it. He loved tea. The first time he'd taken her out, to the Savoy Cinema in Waterford, they'd had tea afterwards in the cinema café and they'd talked about the film and about people they knew. He'd come to live in Waterford from the country, from the farm his brother had inherited, quite close to her father's farm. He reckoned he'd settled, he told her that night: Waterford wasn't sensational, but it suited him in a lot of ways. If he hadn't married her he'd still be there, working eight hours a day in the Customs and not caring for it, yet managing to get by because he had his religion to assist him.

'Did we get a card from Father Jack yet?' he enquired, referring to a distant cousin, a priest in Chicago.

'Not yet. But it's always on the late side, Father Jack's. It was February last year.'

She sipped her tea, sitting in one of the other brown armchairs, on the other side of the gas fire. It was pleasant being there alone with him in the decorated room, the green clock ticking on the mantelpiece, the Christmas cards, dusk gathering outside. She smiled and laughed, taking another biscuit while he lit a cigarette. 'Isn't this great?' she said. 'A bit of peace for ourselves?'

Solemnly he nodded.

'Peace comes dropping slow,' he said, and she knew he was quoting from some book or other. Quite often he said things she didn't understand. 'Peace and goodwill,' he added, and she understood that all right.

He tapped the ash from his cigarette into an ashtray which was kept for his use, beside the gas fire. All his movements were slow. He was a slow thinker, even though he was clever. He arrived at a conclusion, having thought long and carefully; he balanced everything in his mind. 'We must think about that, Norah,' he said that day, twenty-two years ago, when she'd suggested that they should move to England. A week later he'd said that if she really wanted to he'd agree.

They talked about Bridget and Cathal and Tom. When they came in from the cinema they'd only just have time to change their clothes before setting out again for the Christmas party at Bridget's convent.

'It's a big day for them. Let them lie in in the morning, Norah.'

'They could lie in for ever,' she said, laughing in case there might seem to be harshness in this recommendation. With Christmas excitement running high, the less she heard from them the better.

'Did you get Cathal the gadgets he wanted?'

'Chemistry stuff. A set in a box.'

'You're great the way you manage, Norah.'

She denied that. She poured more tea for both of them. She said, as casually as she could:

'Mr Joyce won't come. I'm not counting him in for Christmas Day.'

'He hasn't failed us yet, Norah.'

'He won't come this year.' She smiled through the gloom at him. 'I think we'd best warn the children about it.'

'Where would he go if he didn't come here? Where'd he get his dinner?'

'Lyons used to be open in the old days.'

'He'd never do that.'

'The Bulrush Café has a turkey dinner advertised. There's a lot of people go in for that now. If you have a mother doing a job she maybe hasn't the time for the cooking. They go out to a hotel or a café, three or four pounds a head – '

'Mr Joyce wouldn't go to a café. No one could go into a café on their own on Christmas Day.'

'He won't come here, dear.'

It had to be said: it was no good just pretending, laying a place for the old man on an assumption that had no basis to it. Mr Joyce would not come because Mr Joyce, last August, had ceased to visit them. Every Friday night he used to come, for a cup of tea and a chat, to watch the nine o'clock news with them. Every Christmas Day he'd brought carefully chosen presents for the children, and chocolates and nuts and cigarettes. He'd given Patrick and Pearl a radio as a wedding present.

'I think he'll come all right. I think maybe he hasn't been too well. God help him, it's a great age, Norah.'

'He hasn't been ill, Dermot.'

Every Friday Mr Joyce had sat there in the third of the brown armchairs, watching the television, his bald head inclined so that his good ear was closer to the screen. He was tallish, rather bent now, frail and bony, with a modest white moustache. In his time he'd been a builder, which was how he had come to own property in Fulham, a self-made man who'd never married. That evening in August he had been quite as usual. Bridget had kissed him good-night because for as long as she could remember she'd always done that when he came on Friday evenings. He'd asked Cathal how he was getting on with his afternoon paper round.

There had never been any difficulties over the house. They considered that he was fair in his dealings with them; they were his tenants and his friends. When the Irish bombed English people to death in Birmingham and Guildford he did not cease to arrive every Friday evening and on Christmas Day. The bombings were discussed after the News, the Tower of London bomb, the bomb in the bus, and all the others. 'Maniacs,' Mr Joyce said and nobody contradicted him.

'He would never forget the children, Norah. Not at Christmastime.'

His voice addressed her from the shadows. She felt the warmth of the gas fire reflected in her face and knew if she looked in a mirror she'd see that she was quite flushed. Dermot's face never reddened. Even though he was nervy, he never displayed emotion. On all occasions his face retained its paleness, his eyes acquired no glimmer of passion. No wife could have a better husband, yet in the matter of Mr Joyce he was so wrong it almost frightened her.

'Is it tomorrow I call in for the turkey?' he said.

She nodded, hoping he'd ask her if anything was the matter because as a rule she never just nodded in reply to a question. But he didn't say anything. He stubbed his cigarette out. He asked if there was another cup of tea in the pot.

'Dermot, would you take something round to Mr Joyce?'

'A message, is it?'

'I have a tartan tie for him.'

'Wouldn't you give it to him on the day, Norah? Like you always do.' He spoke softly, still insisting. She shook her head.

It was all her fault. If she hadn't said they should go to England, if she hadn't wanted to work in a London shop, they wouldn't be caught in the trap they'd made for themselves. Their children spoke with London accents. Patrick and Brendan worked for English firms and would make their homes in England. Patrick had married an English girl. They were Catholics and they had Irish names, yet home for them was not Waterford.

'Could you make it up with Mr Joyce, Dermot? Could you go round with the tie and say you were sorry?'

'Sorry?'

'You know what I mean.' In spite of herself her voice had acquired a trace of impatience, an edginess that was unusual in it. She did not ever speak to him like that. It was the way she occasionally spoke to the children.

'What would I say I was sorry for, Norah?'

'For what you said that night.' She smiled, calming her agitation. He lit another cigarette, the flame of the match briefly illuminating his face. Nothing had changed in his face. He said:

'I don't think Mr Joyce and I had any disagreement, Norah.'

'I know, Dermot. You didn't mean anything – '

'There was no disagreement, girl.'

There had been no disagreement, but on that evening in August something else had happened. On the nine o'clock news there had been a report of another outrage and afterwards, when Dermot had turned the television off, there'd been the familiar comment on it. He couldn't understand the mentality of people like that, Mr Joyce said yet again, killing just anyone, destroying life for no reason. Dermot had shaken his head over it, she herself had said it was uncivilised. Then Dermot had added that they mustn't of course forget what the Catholics in the North had suffered. The bombs were a crime but it didn't do to forget that the crime would not be there if generations of Catholics in the North had not been treated as animals. There'd been a silence then, a difficult kind of silence which she'd broken herself. All that was in the past, she'd said hastily, in a rush, nothing in the past or the present or anywhere else could justify the killing of innocent people. Even so, Dermot had added, it didn't do to avoid the truth. Mr Joyce had not said anything.

'I'd say there was no need to go round with the tie, Norah. I'd say he'd make the effort on Christmas Day.'

'Of course he won't.' Her voice was raised, with more than impatience in it now. But her anger was controlled. 'Of course he won't come.'

'It's a time for goodwill, Norah. Another Christmas: to remind us.'

He spoke slowly, the words prompted by some interpretation of God's voice in answer to a prayer. She recognised that in his deliberate tone.

'It isn't just another Christmas. It's an awful kind of Christmas. It's a Christmas to be ashamed, and you're making it worse, Dermot.' Her lips were trembling in a way that was uncomfortable. If she tried to calm herself she'd become jittery instead, she might even begin to cry. Mr Joyce had been generous and tactful, she said loudly. It made no difference to Mr Joyce that they were Irish people, that their children went to school with the children of I.R.A. men. Yet his generosity and his tact had been thrown back in his face. Everyone knew that the Catholics in the North had suffered, that generations of injustice had been twisted into the shape of a cause. But you couldn't say it to an old man who had hardly been outside Fulham in his life. You couldn't say it because when you did it sounded like an excuse for murder.

'You have to state the truth, Norah. It's there to be told.'

'I never yet cared for a North of Ireland person, Catholic or Protestant. Let them fight it out and not bother us.'

'You shouldn't say that, Norah.'

'It's more of your truth for you.'

He didn't reply. There was the gleam of his face for a moment as he drew on his cigarette. In all their married life they had never had a quarrel that was in any way serious, yet she felt herself now in the presence of a seriousness that was too much for her. She had told him that whenever a new bombing took place she prayed it might be the work of the Angry Brigade, or any group that wasn't Irish. She'd told him that in shops she'd begun to feel embarrassed because of her Waterford accent. He'd said she must have courage, and she realised now that he had drawn on courage himself when he'd made the remark to Mr Joyce. He would have prayed and considered before making it. He would have seen it in the end as his Catholic duty.

'He thinks you don't condemn people being killed.' She spoke quietly even though she felt a wildness inside her. She felt she should be out on the streets, shouting in her Waterford accent, violently stating that the bombers were more despicable with every breath they drew, that hatred and death were all they deserved. She saw herself on Fulham Broadway, haranguing the passers-by, her greying hair blown in the wind, her voice more passionate than it had ever been before. But none of it was the kind of thing she could do because she was not that kind of woman. She hadn't the courage, any more than she had the courage to urge her anger to explode in their living-room. For all the years of her marriage there had never been the need of such courage before: she was aware of that, but found no consolation in it.

'I think he's maybe seen it by now,' he said. 'How one thing leads to another.'

She felt insulted by the words. She willed herself the strength to shout, to pour out a torrent of fury at him, but the strength did not come. Standing up, she stumbled in the gloom and felt a piece of holly under the sole of her shoe. She turned the light on.

'I'll pray that Mr Joyce will come,' he said.

She looked at him, pale and thin, with his priestly face. For the first time since he had asked her to marry him in the Tara Ballroom she did not love him. He was cleverer than she was, yet he seemed half blind. He was good, yet he seemed hard in his goodness, as though he'd be better without it. Up to the very last moment on Christmas Day there would be the pretence that their landlord might arrive, that God would answer a prayer because His truth had been honoured. She considered it hypocrisy, unable to help herself in that opinion.

He talked but she did not listen. He spoke of keeping faith with their own, of being a Catholic. Crime begot crime, he said, God wanted it to be known that one evil led to another. She continued to look at him while he spoke, pretending to listen but wondering instead if in twelve months' time, when another Christmas came, he would still be cycling from house to house to read gas meters. Or would people have objected, requesting a meter-reader who was not Irish? An objection to a man with an Irish accent was down-to-earth and ordinary. It didn't belong in the same grand category as crime begetting crime or God wanting something to be known, or in the category of truth and conscience. In the present circumstances the objection would be understandable and fair. It seemed even right that it should be made, for it was a man with an Irish accent in whom the worst had been brought out by the troubles that had come, who was guilty of a cruelty no one would have believed him capable of. Their harmless elderly landlord might die in the course of that same year, a friendship he had valued lost, his last Christmas lonely. Grand though it might seem in one way, all of it was petty.

Once, as a girl, she might have cried, but her contented marriage had caused her to lose that habit. She cleared up the tea things, reflecting that the bombers would be pleased if they could note the victory they'd scored in a living-room in Fulham. And on Christmas Day, when a family sat down to a conventional meal, the victory would be greater. There would be crackers and chatter and excitement, the Queen and the Pope would deliver speeches. Dermot would discuss these Christmas messages with Patrick and Brendan, as he'd discussed them in the past with Mr Joyce. He would be as kind as ever. He would console Bridget and Cathal and Tom by saying that Mr Joyce hadn't been up to the journey. And whenever she looked at him she would remember the Christmases of the past. She would feel ashamed of him, and of herself.

D.M. LARGE

The Christmas Spirit

There was an air of bustle about the little white house beside the road, and some of the well-scrubbed furniture stood outside the ever-open door, looking forlorn and awkward in its unaccustomed surroundings, where the muddy yard had been swept clean and bare to receive it. In order to knock, one had to step right over the threshold, and an old woman clambered down with great difficulty from the chair on which she was standing beside the dresser; and she spoke chidingly to the aged sheep-dog that barked hoarsely from the warm chimney corner. In bigger houses the call of spring is the signal for this annual turn-out, greatly deprecated by the man of the house; but in every Irish cottage, beside the high road, or far up on the slope of a wind-swept hill, or deep in the hollow of a lonely glen, there must be 'some sort of a readyin' up' for Christmas, and, if possible, a whitewashing of the firelit kitchen.

In bigger houses, where the house-cleaning is regulated by the cessation of fires, or where, worse still, the cessation of fires is dependent upon the house-cleaning, the spring may be a suitable time for such an upheaval; but in a smoke-stained kitchen, where the kindly welcome of a fire is never absent, what time of the year is more fitting for a general clean-up than the week before Christmas?

William was out 'through the sheep,' the old woman said, and he was well enough only for the cough. 'He do cough an' he do cough,' she said cheerfully, 'an' he gets no remuneration; but isn't he only glad to be as well in hisself as he is?' The stiffness in her own old bones was about the same. 'There did a docthor come up here one time,' she said, 'an' he took great note of me. "Don't vegetate wan minnit," he says, "but come on into th' hospital, an' I'll ayther kill or cure you," says he – he's a rale funny man. So off I went in a car; but, bedad, he nayther killed nor cured me; for I kem back the very one way. I let meself go too far, they said,' and she laughed pleasantly, and pushed forward a chair with that perfect hospitality that takes no heed of such a domestic upheaval, but only wishes to make the stranger welcome. 'If we had everythin' we'd like,' she said, 'we'd be too impident.'

The old dog stretched himself stiffly and whined softly, and the woman of the house nodded her white head in an understanding way. 'William do never ax him to go wid him now,' she said, 'unless he couldn't do adout help; for he's not able to do a whole lot this while back. Isn't Micksy Quinn forever quotin' to William to get a young dog, but he says he'll never make as little as that of poor Rover, as long as he can give him a hand at all; for he could never forget what that lad done the time the buyer came to look at the sheep an' William an' me was in the town. Didn't Rover round them all up an' show them to the man hisself, for he knew him well, comin' about the place?'

The old grey muzzle was lifted a little from the warm flag, and the veiled eyes sought the face of the one Rover loved second best.

With a whirl and a scurry, a small black kitten rushed through the doorway, with short legs stiffened ludicrously, and tiny tail erect, then halted in a fusillade of spits just beside the old dog.

'There's two of them little cats,' the old woman said proudly. 'Sure the mother has them abroad in an ould shed. Th' other fella never axes to come near us, but that one'll bate in twenty times in the day, an' the muck does be somethin' dismal upon his little paws; an', if you went to hunt him, he'd make nothin' of you to your face.'

The little black shape was lifted on to a blue checked apron, where it kneaded contentedly, then curled round to sleep with the air of having done all that before, many, many times.

With a muffled squawk of inquiry, a plump 'cuckoo hen' limped out from beneath the fireside seat, and turned one bright and questioning eye upon the stranger, while holding up a bandaged foot from unnecessary contact with the uneven floor.

'That one's not right,' said the old woman. 'Sure she was reared a pet in the first go off; for she was ever an' always a dhreeny-dhrawny kind of a chicken, an' the mother used to walk her into th' earth. So I brought her in here to see could I make annything out of her, an' she got into a grand hin, but she's all humours. You'd be surprised all the things that wan wouldn't ate, she's so delicate in herself.'

The grey hen watched her as she spoke, and made little homely, clucking sounds.

'An' then, what must she do but walk upon a bit of a bottle, an' that's where the desolation started, an' she roared a caution, an' nothin' would answer her but I must tie up the foot an' let her stay widin. Look at the clever ould puss of her now.'

The grey hen hobbled back to the shelter of the bench, and pecked negligently at the Indian meal porridge that had been placed there for her.

There was a slow step in the little yard, and William came in. One big hand made a cradle for a tiny bird, whose weary head had been poked out between the old man's finger and thumb, and now drooped helplessly.

'He has the lime on him,' William said simply, 'but there's not much. I'm thinkin' I could mebbe put him right. He couldn't fly at all – only hoppin' along before me. I knew well what aileded him'; and the big fingers worked gently at the smeared feathers, while the bird's head drooped lower.

The old dog got up, with a groaning sigh for the dear days when his muscles had been like flexible steel. Crossing to where his master sat, he rested his chin on William's knee and stared with dim eyes at the little frightened bird; then wagged his tail slowly as if to say, 'He will help you if anyone can.' On the checked apron the kitten opened a milky blue eye and stretched out a tiny paw, unsheathing for an instant the claws that already were dangerous to any bird that could not fly. The cuckoo hen limped out again and watched too, and from the shed outside there came the querulously questioning call of a small, hungry calf.

'That lad is aiqual to anny clock,' the old woman said; 'for he'd bawl to the very minit every evenin', an', no matther what I do be at, I must attind to him.'

The stranger rose to go, and to her, the little bare kitchen was a place of great beauty, for the real spirit of Christmas was there.

ROBERT BERNEN

A Christmas Visit

It was the shortest day of the year. The sun had set and even the winter twilight was almost at an end as she turned into the farm lane, leaving the smooth asphalt of the road behind her and feeling through her rubber boots the rough and uneven surface of the dirt lane. She was glad she had remembered to bring her old hazel walking-stick. She had not needed it since she had moved into the town, but it was useful on the uneven lane. Ahead of her the kitchen light shone like a beacon at the end of the lane. A measure of distance in the dim evening light, a goal, it marked the scene of the Christmas visit she was about to pay.

The evening was dry, and she was glad she had decided to walk out into the country to pay a Christmas visit. When she had moved to the town earlier in the year she had said she would visit often, but there had been much to do, fixing up the new house, meeting new people, new town activities. So she had postponed her visits to the country farms, where she had spent so much time before, until this day, the shortest one of the year. Always a gloomy day, with its dim, failing light, its inclement coldness, its early night.

Seeing the weather dry, she had decided to walk out along the road she had so often walked before and visit her friends.

Walking up the dirt lane she realised that her feet were relearning the forgotten art of adjusting to unseen and unexpected stones and potholes. There was an art to letting your feet find and adjust to irregularities without twisting your ankles. She was coming nearer to the light, soon she would enter the crowded kitchen.

Crowded. For she could only remember it that way, as crowded. She had seldom seen it otherwise. A kind of clearing house for the neighbourhood of local farmers and country people who walked in and out without knocking or announcing themselves and sat down almost without looking about the kitchen or seeming to notice the people around them, but in fact making some slight gesture or sound of greeting to all, at times resuming some previous conversation just where it had been left off hours or minutes, or at times, indeed, days before, in cryptic abbreviations of expression that she had often thought of as a neighbourhood dialect, incomprehensible in the town only a few miles away. More general topics were discussed in higher, slower tones, more haltingly and in more universal words, the words remembered from school. But the population of the kitchen itself was constantly changing as its occupants came and went without feeling the necessity for salutations, helloes and goodbyes of any sort, apart perhaps from reference to whatever bit of chore or task or diversion was in their minds.

As she approached the kitchen door she remembered this sensation, forgotten in the town where she had learned always to arrange her visits by agreement beforehand, of lifting the latch and entering unannounced, without so much as a knock, to find a kitchen full of people sitting about, or engrossed in games of cards, or dominoes, looking up briefly at the newcomer to utter a quick greeting, a comment on health and weather – and some, she knew, would be so intent on talk or cards that they would forget to look up. The greeting would come later. She put her hand on the latch and pushed the door inward.

The kitchen was empty. A bright bulb suspended in the centre of the ceiling cast its brilliant light through the room, onto the walls, into the corners, illuminating the sumptuous cleanliness of the linoleum floor, the freshness of the brightly patterned wallpaper, the shining polish of the iron range, the careful neatness and order of everything in the room. The brightness of the light and the very perfect order of the room accentuated all the more the emptiness of the kitchen, the absence of its accustomed crowds, who seemed then even more absent by their failure before her coming to derange anything in the room.

She went over to a straight-backed chair near the iron solid-fuel range and sat down. The heat was pleasant after the cold walk from town. She looked about the room. A bowl of farm eggs stood in a window. The Christmas turkey, already plucked and drawn, hung near the back door. The new calendar was already on the wall, anticipating the coming year. A Christmas tree in the corner had been decorated with tiny lights. Signs of life and people, but without people.

Patiently she sat and waited for the woman of the house to appear, and she considered the strange, to her, experience of sitting alone in a room she had never before seen empty. Prepared for the sitters, the talkers, the players of games, the idle small talk of country life alluding in its shorthand, elliptical way to everyday events, she felt the solitude of the empty kitchen intensely. She did not try to puzzle out the cause of the absence of everyone she had expected to find, but accepted it and patiently sat, with no particular thoughts, waiting for someone to appear.

And as she sat she remembered other times she had been in the kitchen, times past. Maggie had sat in the very chair she was sitting in then, old Maggie who had seemed young even when she had become a great-grandmother, and who sat by the iron range and knitted socks and pullovers, and talked, always about the past, herself a link with a previous century. Sitting and thinking about Maggie she even remembered then specific socks that Maggie had been knitting, or darning, and conversations about knitting and darning, and household practicalities, cooking, children, illnesses, occasions and connected customs and ways of doing that extended back to older generations of conversations with women who were themselves great-grandmothers when Maggie was a girl. She remembered Maggie's childhood illness that Maggie had talked of only once, although Maggie had almost died of it, the slow recovery, the joy at returning to health and life. Maggie spoke of it only that once, even in age. She remembered suddenly, compendiously and as though in chronological order, a fullness of details of Maggie's life that she had previously only heard in random conversational fragments, and she became aware that then, two years after Maggie's death, she was for the first time aware of Maggie's life, Maggie's life as a continuity and sequence of events. Before she had only thought of Maggie as an old woman, great-grandmother, knitter and darner of socks. But the totality, the long journey of life by which she had arrived at the place and the time, become what she was, had never been perceived in its completeness. Now, in the empty kitchen, her memories of Maggie made present to her the woman herself as she had never known her living.

And then her thoughts went to James, Maggie's brother, two years older and stiffer and more bent, always two years ahead of Maggie on the road of life, and who had left it exactly two years sooner. Both had died at ninety-three, but James had died just two years earlier than Maggie, as though showing her the way and the time.

She looked at the walking-stick she held still in her hand and remembered that James had given it to her. It had been his stick, and its length, suitable for James in his bent old age, was just right for her woman's height. Without the lucky feminine occupations of knitting and darning, free from the heavy work of his farm, James had merely sat, in his old age, in his kitchen and remembered farm events, animals and seasons and times. Seldom did he even bother to rise to observe the weather. Information about the world came to him mostly from the chattered comments of the visitors who came and went regularly through the kitchen.

So her thoughts and memories went on through the faces she had seen and known in the neat farm-house kitchen: young men and women, some since married, some since emigrated to foreign countries, some working in distant towns or cities. She could almost hear their voices, high, light, rapid, loud or whispered, contrasting with the slow drone of the old people who were talking of times past as they, the young, talked instead of current things, things present, popular, attractive: friends, clothes, dances, entertainments, fashions, machines, jobs, babies, houses, engrossed and satisfied in a world of their own that intermixed with but never entirely dissolved into the old and ancient world around them. And then the babies, babies and children always in rapid transition from one way of being to another, from helplessness to fierce independent activity, never twice the same on any visit to the kitchen.

Young and old in an ancient world, and between them the middle-aged, the active who had little time for sitting or for talk, steadily busy, foddering cattle, carrying hay, feeding hens, bringing in fuel and stoking the fire, putting on the kettle, taking bread from the oven, adding water to the stew. And all this, she suddenly remembered, by the soft glow of an oil-lamp, that hid details and harmonised the many faces into a unity, a oneness that was, she sensed, only a seen equivalent of the real harmony that existed among themselves. The brilliant electric bulb had not been there. It had only come a year or two ago. For a moment she wondered, absurdly, whether it had anything to do with the emptiness of the kitchen whose immaculately clean walls and corners it so scrupulously inspected and laid bare.

The people of the past who had so crowded her memory were gone. She became aware of herself sitting alone in the farmhouse kitchen. Nor did she have any idea how long she had been there. But now, she was aware, the kitchen was no longer empty as it had been when she came in. Within her, at least, memory had peopled the empty kitchen, the memory of all those she had met and known and talked to there. She saw then that she had not been disappointed in her Christmas visit. Even though she had found no one, still she felt that she had visited with many she had known, and with some she had not hoped to see again. She had come to know them, possibly, even better than she had thought she knew them before. She had had her Christmas visit.

She was ready to leave for home and leaned forward in her chair, grasping the hazel stick. Just at that moment the door of an inner room opened and a man's head looked out. For a moment he stared at her as though in surprise, as though himself seeing an image of the dead, as she had just seen the dead within her own recollections. She looked back at him, and so they remained, for just a few seconds, regarding one another in silence. Then they smiled.

'It's good to have a visit,' the man declared. 'How are you keeping?'

'I've come to pay you a Christmas visit,' she said.

'Come in,' he answered. 'We're all in here.'

She got up and followed him to the door he had only partly emerged through. Beyond it she saw a darkened room with many seats and sitting figures barely visible in the dim light. At the far corner a television screen displayed in liquid, life-like colours the forms and contours of a country landscape. Before her eyes transparent greens and blues blended with subtle and delicate browns and golds into images of beauty and reality, tranquil prospects of a peaceful earth, of the earth's own past time in its loveliest aspect.

'You never saw our new set,' he said.

Vaguely she was aware of heads turning briefly for softly grunted greetings before they turned back to attend to the glowing, colourful scene. A chair was offered, a chair in the best position before the set. She sat down and immediately felt herself part of the silent intentness of the assembled watchers. Spectral, prismic successions of trees, hills, lakes and rivers, then animals, horses, cattle, sheep and dogs, and finally people, all succeeding one another in a living and persuasive colour. It was a vast compendium of country life, as she herself remembered it, reduced to the compellingly intense illusion of a flat sheet of glass.

For a moment she watched. Then she looked about the room in expectation of the conversation and fragments of chatter she had been used to in every room full of country people. Silence. A cough. Someone lit a cigarette. A density of smoke filled the dimly illuminated room, the smoke itself accepting the ever-varying tints of reflected colour from the life-like glass screen. A brief comment on the image from someone she could not see. She did not catch the words. Dense smoke. A cough. Silence. Only the drone of a mechanical voice, explaining the country scene.

She got up to go. As quietly as possible she threaded through the rows of chairs to the door. Quietly she opened the door and went back into the kitchen.

The bright electric bulb suspended from the middle of the

ceiling blinded her after the darkness of the other room. She stood for a moment without moving, waiting for her eyes to readjust to the light. As they did she saw that the kitchen was still empty. For an instant she felt a sensation of surprise. She had forgotten, in those few moments in the darkened room, that the kitchen was empty. All that had remained in her mind had been the sensation of the Christmas visit she had imagined, remembered.

For a moment more she stood still recalling that earlier sensation and the memories of only a few minutes before, but as she tried to recall them the memory itself became more distant and all she could recall was the sensation itself of memories filling her thoughts, the illusory sense of a true visit. She could remember only that something had happened, that in the empty kitchen she had had some experience she could not have expected in the bare, empty room. But she could not remember what it was. The kitchen seemed even emptier than before.

She looked once more at the brightly illuminated walls and corners, the polished iron range, the vacant chairs. Then, pulling her scarf about her throat, she buttoned her coat and went to the door. Opening it she went out onto the lane. Once again she paused to let her eyes readjust, this time to the darkness of the winter night. When she had grown able to perceive her way along the lane before her she started for the town.

Acknowledgements

The editor and publishers are grateful for permission to include the following copyright stories in this anthology:

VINCENT BANVILLE: 'Christmas 1939', reprinted from The Irish Press *New Irish Writing* by permission of the author.

ROBERT BERNEN: 'A Christmas Visit', reprinted from The Irish Press *New Irish Writing* by permission of the author.

CLARE BOYLAN: 'The Spirit of the Tree'. First published in *Country Living*. © Clare Boylan 1993. Reprinted by permission of the author and Rogers, Coleridge & White Ltd.

MAEVE BRENNAN: 'Christmas Eve'. First published in *The New Yorker*. © Maeve Brennon 1972. Reprinted by permission of Russell & Volkening as agents for the author.

LEO CULLEN: 'Clouds over Suez', reprinted from *Clocking Ninety on the Road to Cloughjordan* by permission of The Blackstaff Press.

Acknowledgements

ANNE DEVLIN: 'The Journey to Somewhere Else', reprinted from *The Way-Paver* (Faber and Faber), © Anne Devlin 1986, by permission of Sheil Land Associates Ltd.

ROBERT DUFFY: 'Homeland', reprinted from The Irish Press *New Irish Writing* by permission of the author.

AUBREY FLEGG: 'Timpani', reprinted from The Irish Press *New Irish Writing* by permission of the author.

DESMOND HOGAN: 'The Mourning Thief', reprinted from *Children of Lir*, © Desmond Hogan 1981, by permission of Hamish Hamilton and Rogers, Coleridge & White Ltd.

PATRICK McCABE: 'Apaches', reprinted by permission of the Peters, Fraser & Dunlop Group Ltd.

JOHN McGAHERN: 'Christmas', reprinted from *Nightlines* (Faber and Faber, 1970) by permission of the author.

BERNARD MacLAVERTY: 'Remote', reprinted from *The Great Profundo* (Jonathan Cape, 1987) by permission of Random House UK Ltd.

MICHAEL McLAVERTY: 'Father Christmas', reprinted from *Collected Short Stories* (1978) by permission of Poolbeg Press Ltd.

MARY MORRISSY: 'Rosa', reprinted from *A Lazy Eye* (Jonathan Cape, 1993) © Mary Morrissy 1990, by permission of Greene and Heaton Ltd.

Acknowledgements

VAL MULKERNS: 'Home for Christmas', reprinted from *An Idle Woman* (Poolbeg Press, 1980) by permission of the author.

FRANK O'CONNOR: 'The Adventuress', reprinted from *The Cornet Player Who Betrayed Ireland* (Poolbeg Press) by permission of the Peters, Fraser & Dunlop Group Ltd.

SEAN O'FAOLAIN: 'Before the Daystar', reprinted from *The Heat of the Sun* (Jonathan Cape, 1966) by permission of Rogers, Coleridge & White Ltd.

DAVID PARK: 'Angel', reprinted from *Oranges from Spain* (Jonathan Cape) © David Park 1990, by permission of Sheil Land Associates Ltd.

JAMES PLUNKETT: 'Finegan's Ark', reprinted from *Collected Short Stories* (Poolbeg Press, 1977) by permission of the author.

EDDIE STACK: 'Time Passes', reprinted from *The West* (Bloomsbury, 1990) by permission of Christine Green, Authors' Agent.

L.A.G. STRONG: 'Christmas Eve', reprinted from *Darling Tom* (Methuen, 1952) by permission of the Peters, Fraser & Dunlop Group Ltd.

WILLIAM TREVOR: 'Another Christmas', reprinted from *Lovers of Their Time* (The Bodley Head, 1978) by permission of the author.

While every effort has been made to trace all copyright holders, the publishers would be glad to hear from any who may have been omitted.

Biographical Notes

VINCENT BANVILLE: Born Wexford, 1940, he taught for five years in Nigeria, where his novel *An End to Flight*, which won the 1973 Daily Express Robert Pitman Award, was set. His short stories appeared in *Transatlantic Review* and Faber's *Introduction* 4. A Hennessy Literary Award winner, in recent years he has been fiction reviewer for the *Sunday Press* and has written children's books and detective novels.

ROBERT BERNEN: Born in Manhattan, New York, he studied Latin and Greek at Cornell University, did graduate work at Harvard, and in 1970 settled with his wife in Donegal as a sheep-farmer. While there he wrote two widely praised short-story collections, *Tales from the Blue Stacks* and *More Tales from the Blue Stacks*. In the eighties he returned to settle in the US.

CLARE BOYLAN: Born Dublin, 1948, she turned from journalism to full-time creative writing in the early eighties, since when she has published four novels, two short story collections and a book about cats.

MAEVE BRENNAN: Born Dublin, 1917, she emigrated to the US with her parents in 1934. She worked first for *Harper's Bazaar*, and from the forties wrote many short stories for the *New Yorker* which were later published by Scribner's. She died in 1994.

PATRICK CAMPBELL: Born Dublin, 1913, he spent the war years in the Irish Navy and his first job in journalism was as 'Quidnunc' in the *Irish Times*. He moved to London in 1947 and soon gained a national reputation as a leading humorous writer and TV personality. In 1963 he became the third Baron Glenavy. He died in 1980.

LEO CULLEN: Born Co. Tipperary, 1948. A poet and short story writer, *New Irish Writing* published his first story, 'Clocking Ninety on the Road to Cloughjordan', which became the title story of his highly successful 1994 debut collection.

ANNE DEVLIN: Born Belfast, 1951, she lives in England. A Hennessy Literary Award winner, her plays have won the Samuel Beckett Award for TV Drama and the George Devine Award, and her latest play, *After Easter*, has been produced in England and Ireland. She has also published a collection of short stories, *The Way-Paver*.

ROBERT DUFFY: Born Dublin, 1957. A graduate of University College, Dublin, he now lives with his wife and three children in Co. Carlow, and is a member of the Carlow Writers' Group.

AUBREY FLEGG: Born Dublin, 1938, he is a geologist working with the Geological Survey of Ireland. He is currently concentrating on writing for children.

DESMOND HOGAN: Born Ballinasloe, Co. Galway, 1951. He won the John Llewellyn Rhys Memorial Prize in 1980 and has since written four novels, two collections of short stories and a play.

D.M. LARGE: Born Tullamore, Co. Offaly, 1891. A prolific writer of short stories and novels in the twenties and thirties, her novel, *Cloonagh*, was a best-seller.

PATRICK McCABE: Born Clones, Co. Monaghan, 1955, his first short story, published in *New Irish Writing*, won him a Hennessy Literary Award in 1978. His novel, *Butcher Boy*, was shortlisted for the Booker Prize.

JOHN McGAHERN: Born Dublin, 1934, he is a graduate of University College, Dublin, and in 1962 was the first prose writer to receive the AE Memorial Award. He has written three short story collections and five novels, the most recent of which is the award-winning *Amongst Women*.

BERNARD MacLAVERTY: Born Belfast, 1945, he studied English at Queen's University and then moved to Scotland where he taught for some years. He has written two novels which became successful films, and four collections of short stories. He now lives in Glasgow.

MICHAEL McLAVERTY: Born Carrickmacross, Co. Monaghan, 1907, he was a graduate of Queen's University, Belfast. A teacher of mathematics, his eight novels and many short stories established him as one of Ireland's leading writers. He died in 1992.

MARY MORRISSY: Born Dublin, 1957, where she is on the staff of the *Irish Times*. She won a Hennessy Literary Award in 1984 and has published a collection of short stories.

VAL MULKERNS: Born Dublin, 1925, her novel, *The Summerhouse*, won the Allied Irish Banks Prize for Literature in 1984. She has written three other novels and three collections of short stories.

FRANK O'CONNOR: Born Cork, 1903, he is acknowledged as one of literature's masters of the short story. He also wrote two novels, a biography of Michael Collins, two volumes of autobiography, much criticism including books on Shakespeare and on the short story, translations of Irish poetry, and travel books. He died in 1966.

SEAN O'FAOLAIN: Born Cork, 1900, another acknowledged master of the short story, he was one of Ireland's most distinguished twentieth-century men of letters. Novelist, biographer, autobiographer, playwright, travel writer and critic, he was also the founder-editor of the mould-breaking monthly, *The Bell*. He died in 1991.

DAVID PARK: Born Belfast, 1954, a schoolteacher in Co. Down, he is the author of a collection of short stories and two novels.

JAMES PLUNKETT: Born Dublin, 1920, he has written a collection of short stories and three novels, the first of which, *Strumpet City*, was a best-seller and was dramatised for TV.

EDDIE STACK: Born Ennistymon, Co. Clare, 1951. An engineer by profession, he represented Ireland at the International Young Scientist Convention in 1969. He has lived in the US since 1986 and has published one collection of short stories.

L.A.G. STRONG: Born in England, 1896, his mother was Irish and his father half Irish, and he spent much of his childhood in Ireland. A prolific writer, he produced numerous short stories, children's books, school books, literary criticism, an autobiography and many novels. He died in 1958.

WILLIAM TREVOR: Born Mitchelstown, Co. Cork, 1928, he is one of Ireland's most distinguished living writers. His novels and short stories have gained wide acclaim and won many awards, including the Hawthornden Prize, the Allied Irish Banks Prize, and the Whitbread.